The Human Equations

ALSO BY

Dave Creek

A Glimpse of Splendor and Other Stories

Some Distant Shore

———

The Human Equations

By

Dave Creek

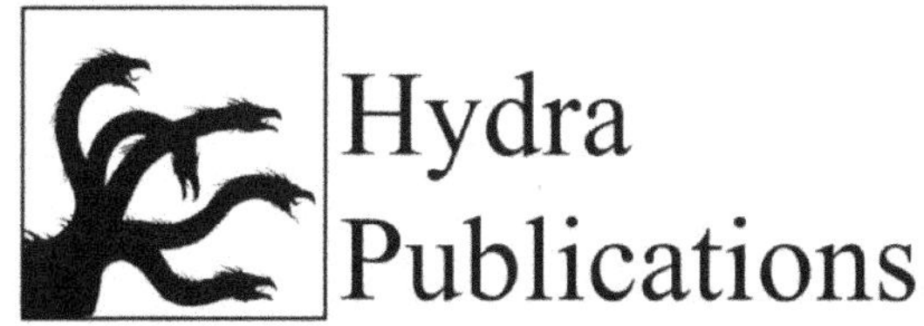

Hydra
Publications

Printed in the United States of America

ISBN: 099608679X
ISBN-13: 978-0-9960867-9-0

Hydra Publications
1310 Meadowridge Trail
Goshen, KY 40026

www.hydrapublications.com

Cover design by R.L. Treadway Atrtink.com

ACKNOWLEDGEMENTS

Zheng He and the Dragon appeared in the January-February 2009 *Analog*. Copyright 2009 by Dave Creek.

The Loophole appeared in the March 1994 *Analog*. Copyright 1994 by Dave Creek.

The Human Equations appeared in the November 2002 *Analog*. Copyright 2002 by Dave Creek.

Unbound appeared in the September 2004 issue of *Analog*. Copyright 2004 by Dave Creek.

The Day That Reveals is original to this volume. Copyright 2014 by Dave Creek.

Infinity's Friend appeared in *Analog*, October 2004. Copyright 2004 by Dave Creek.

On the Welkin Shone the Starres Bright is original to this volume. Copyright 2014 by Dave Creek.

Stealing Adriana appeared in the October 2008 *Analog*. Copyright 2008 by Dave Creek.

Midwife Crisis appeared in the October 2010 *Analog*. Copyright 2010 by Dave Creek.

Art for Splendor's Sake appeared in the December 2011 *Analog*. Copyright 2011 by Dave Creek.

The Unfinished Man appeared in the January/February 2011 *Analog*. Copyright 2011 by Dave Creek.

Kutraya's Skies is original to this volume. Copyright 2014 by Dave Creek.

Dave Creek

TABLE OF CONTENTS

INTRODUCTION
By
Brad R. Torgersen

When a fellow first conceives of sending his stories to *Analog Science Fiction & Fact* magazine, he has to realize the grand history of the publication to which he is applying for acceptance. This is no ordinary science fiction magazine. It is both the oldest and also the most widely-circulated of all the many science fiction magazines which have come (and gone) over the last century. Dozens upon dozens of well-known, successful, and highly-regarded men and women in the field, all got their start in the pages of *Analog*. Indeed, cracking one's way into *Analog* (as well as staying in print through *Analog*) is a bit like being accepted to Oxford, Yale, Harvard, etc. The great, old universities. A pedigree which can take a person far in his or her chosen profession. So that when you see yourself in the table of contents of *Analog* you know you're walking among the best: ladies and gentlemen who are not just good storytellers, they are good scientific storytellers to boot.

Such a man is Dave Creek, who preceded me in *Analog* by a number of years, and whose name I had seen in the table of contents many times, prior to my first acceptance under the editorship of Dr. Stanley Schmidt. In fact, it's impossible to examine the tapestry of *Analog* since the turning of the century without realizing that Dave Creek has been one of the chief contributors. As of the writing of this intro, no fewer than seventeen of Dave's stories have graced the pages of *Analog*. A stupendous achievement considering the fact that to win page space in the magazine, one is going up against (in the most collegial, friendly way possible) some of the greatest writers in contemporary science fiction.

So the book you're about to read is not just a collection of stories. It is a track-work of flags planted proudly in the boundless soil of one of the most venerable on-running publications the field has ever seen. Like Aldrin's or Armstrong's footprints on the moon, Dave Creek's presence in the recent history of *Analog* is unmistakable. He is a fixture. A piece of the landscape. An author without whom, *Analog* in its present incarnation simply wouldn't be *Analog*.

What you will get with Dave is a robust blending of very scientifically-grounded stories, but also very enjoyable explorations of what it might mean to be alien, what it might mean to be human, and how aliens and humans alike might both reflect one another, and change one another. Presuming human and alien ever get the chance to meet.

Consider *"Art for Splendor's Sake,"* re-printed here. It was originally in the December 2011 issue of *Analog*; the first time, in fact, I was privileged to share a table of contents with Dave. The usual pop SF approach to a humans-and-aliens story is to consider the one oppressive, and the other oppressed. Or, as often as not, the one as hunter, with the other as prey. Which can and does make for scintillating storytelling. But Dave's story assumes cooperation in the face of looming calamity. Not so much for the race of men, as much as for the races of the planet Splendor, each of whom occupies a specific niche in not only the geography, but in the overall sociological and religious framework of the world. In examining the playing-out of Splendor's dire predicament, Dave is also examining Earth's history too – humanity's dealings with itself, reflected in the science fictional mirror, as it were.

And this isn't the only example. But I will let you find that out for yourself. Dave's bona fides speak for him. I merely offer my own thoughts on a particular example, which I found intriguing in terms of some of the secondary and tertiary questions it raised in my mind, so that I was thinking about the story-after-the-story. Long past the time I'd read it.

And that, friends, is the mark of a good storyteller.

Someone who can – to borrow Larry Niven's phrase – build playground equipment strong and interesting enough, that we who come to the playground spend time playing on the equipment long after the creator has left the scene. Because where the actual story leaves off, there is still so much more "story" going on. Inside our heads.

I hope you enjoy these tales as much as I and *Analog*'s readers have.

Have fun on the equipment!

A NOTE FROM THE AUTHOR

Most of the stories here in *The Human Equations* continue my fascination with the possibilities of SF to show us places, people, and cultures we've never seen before. Some of those places and cultures may seem utterly alien to us, and some of the "people" may not be shaped like Humans or think anything like them.

Other stories show how the culture of Humanity itself may change — or may cling stubbornly to old traditions while new ones arise all around.

All these stories take place within a shared "future history" — called such even though the first story in this volume, *Zheng He and the Dragon*, takes place centuries ago. Many of these stories feature continuing characters, but my rule is that I have to learn something new about those characters whenever they're in a new story.

We have a long journey to make across these dozen stories — across several centuries and countless light-years — so let's get started.

ZHENG HE AND THE DRAGON

So we start our own voyage six hundred years ago and on the opposite side of the world from where I'm writing.

I first learned of the great Chinese explorer Zheng He when I saw a Discovery Channel special, *Emperor of the Seas*. He led a naval armada consisting of as many as 300 ships and tens of thousands of crewmembers on seven voyages between 1405 and 1433.

His explorations took him across Southeast Asia and even to Africa. One prominent popular historian has suggested Zheng He's craft may even have discovered America seven decades before Columbus, but I'm not convinced of that.

Zheng He wasn't just an explorer, though — he was tasked to make sure other nations understood the extent of Chinese power and to make sure trade routes remained open.

Zheng He's career came to fascinate me, especially since I had a hard time finding much more about him. When the emperor who had ordered the voyages of the "treasure ships" died, his successor cancelled those voyages and ordered all of Zheng He's ships destroyed, along with most of the records of his journeys.

Given such a colorful backdrop along with frequent gaps in the historical record, I decided that perhaps Zheng He could even have made First Contact with an alien race without that fact making it into the history books!

By the way, all the non-SF names and events in this story are real; I don't consider this an alternate history story, and in fact I consider it part of the same fictional background as the rest of the stories in this volume. I worked hard to place Zheng He's "encounter" next to or intertwined with incidents that really happened.

————————

Zheng He's exploits numbered so many! I, Ma Huan, served as his translator during his later voyages and, years after, as the chronicler of his travels in the Western Ocean. By the emperor's command, the admiral headed up the treasure fleet which included as many as 62 nine-masted treasure ships, each as large as a sizable village, and nearly 200 smaller vessels — supply ships, troop transports, water tankers. His crews amounted to nearly 28,000 men.

Through Zheng He's accounts and others' I heard of his earlier voyages — tales of silver and silk, tea and wine, oils and candles offered for trade. Of diplomacy that led to the sacred gilin, once thought a myth, becoming a gift for the emperor. Of pirate ships burning and their commanders executed.

I'd heard or witnessed all the stories, or so I believed.

But it seemed Admiral Zheng kept one story untold. It remained the stuff of rumors during his voyages, and I believe in times to come even those rumors will fade.

Once Zheng He captured a dragon.

*****

Zheng He kept the story of the dragon to himself for many years.

We shared many exploits during his later voyages. I watched as the sultan of Aden bartered pearls, gems, amber, and rose water for our gold, silver, porcelain, and pepper. On a trading and diplomatic mission to Siam, I heard the faint ringing of bells as men strode past, the sound emanating from tiny beads implanted in their scrotums. I stood in witness as Zheng He snubbed the rebel leader Sekanda, so that when he became enraged and attacked us, the admiral possessed a reason to capture him and take him to the emperor for execution.

Finally, he called me to him during his seventh voyage, which would constitute his final one, and said, "I must tell you this most fantastic tale. You may even write it down, though it may never enter your chronicles of my voyages."

Eager to hear any story Zheng He might describe as "most fantastic," given the many wonders he had experienced, I readily agreed.

*****

It happened during the first voyage of the treasure fleet, in the fifth year of Emperor Yongle's rule, which the westerners know as 1407. Zheng He visited the kingdom of Champa to trade porcelains and silks for a rare wood that yielded an expensive and prized incense. His great ships demonstrated the might of Chinese sea power by their mere presence off the countries of Aru and Semudera and Landri, and the Andaman and Nicobar Islands. And in Calicut, which I have referred to in other writings as "the Great Country of the Western Ocean," he established stable prices for our goods.

Then Admiral Zheng's countless ships set sail for home. He could stand at the square stern of his flagship's observation deck and look back at the wakes of his nearly three hundred vessels and consider himself safe in the knowledge that in springtime, the strong winds and rains of the monsoons traveled to the southwest.

So imagine his astonishment one clear afternoon as he heard a gigantic roll of thunder, long and loud. In the instant before he looked skyward, his anger flared — he and his crew had scrupulously offered prayers and incense to the Celestial Consort, Tianfei, to protect the fleet from such sudden storms.

But as Zheng He gazed past the flagship's red bamboo sails, he saw a dragon half the size of his ship leaving a trail of smoke and descending directly into the center of his fleet.

Years later, Zheng He told me he would never forget the smallest detail of the dragon's approach — it must have ceased breathing flame the instant he looked up, he insisted, because its smoke trailed behind in such a way that it gave the illusion of discharging from the beast's dark blue belly. And he wondered why the dragon's wings, also blue, remained spread wide, without flapping even once. He perceived one more detail — the dragon's snout seemed altogether too blunt. He wondered if the dragon had somehow suffered an injury to its face, because Zheng He looked in vain for evidence of its pointed ears or even of its eyes.

But somehow the dragon realized its course bore down upon one of the fleet's water tankers, because at the last instant it swerved in midair, still without a single flap of wing, before splashing into the waters of the Western Ocean. A great plume of water rose into the air, and the ocean churned as Admiral Zheng ordered the fleet to halt — a complex process involving flags and banners, drums and gongs.

Zheng He's flagship circled the area where the dragon had fallen into the sea. Mists lingered in the air, but try as he might, Zheng He failed to sniff out any odor unique to a dragon.

But Zheng He's vision ranked among the best and, leaning over the bow, he quickly spotted movement beneath the ocean. The dragon rising from the ocean's depths?

No — the dragon's wings spanned at least half the length of Admiral Zheng's flagship. Whatever object or creature rose toward the surface, it had no wings, and its span amounted only to about two zhang — about the same as four tall men lying in a straight line.

As it neared the surface, the object revealed itself as a sphere of the same dark blue shade as the dragon. It propelled itself upward with such force that it popped completely out of the water, only to splash down again and bob on the surface.

Those who served under Zheng He learned then why Emperor Yongle had chosen him for such an important command despite his lack of naval experience. Certainly a eunuch had never received such a large responsibility. The emperor's decision came after counsel he received from a court official who spoke well of Zheng He's rough skin and sparkling eyes, who compared his eyebrows to swords and his forehead to a tiger's.

Now the emperor's wisdom displayed itself for all to see as Admiral Zheng's eyes sparkled anew and his forehead wrinkled with determination. "Break out the nets! Bring that dragon's egg aboard," he commanded, and he watched as several of his men gathered giant nets suspended from a wooden frame and tossed it into the ocean. More than one exclaimed his admiration at Zheng He's insight that the sea, having swallowed a dragon, had coughed up one of her eggs. They scooped it up as fishermen would their catch and Zheng He watched as his men strained to lift the egg to the deck.

Within moments, the dripping egg stood on the wooden deck of Zheng He's flagship, its two-zhang height towering over him and his crew. "Excellent," Zheng He told his men, and strode forward to examine the sphere — for this egg truly manifested itself as such, not the expected oval shape. Zheng He ran his fingers across the smooth surface of the blue egg. He told me these many years later that it did not feel proper, having none of the slightly bumpy texture of a hen's egg, for instance, but rather the utter smoothness of one of his flagship's bronze cannons.

As Admiral Zheng's examination of the egg continued, several of his men eased forward, their own curiosity overriding lingering fear.

But then! The dragon's egg began to rumble, a low sound that insinuated itself through the ship's deck. The crewmen who had drawn close exclaimed in fear and many tripped over each other's feet in their desperation to escape.

Zheng He, as befitted his position and courage, stepped back in a more leisurely fashion. He stared impassively at the egg as it began to rock back and forth. He could easily imagine the baby dragon inside, frightened or enraged, determined to crack open his shell and strike out against those around him.

"Archers," Zheng He ordered, and the word passed quickly through the ship and the bowmen arrived within mere heartbeats. They took up position to one side of the egg, bows drawn, awaiting the order to fire should the baby dragon burst forth.

But the egg's rocking motion halted, and its rumblings from within subsided. Even Zheng He later admitted to me what happened next left him without speech for a time.

At first he perceived a vertical line of some sort drawing itself down the side of the egg. Then realization came — not a line, but a seam.

The seam etched itself down nearly half the egg's circumference. Then it created a right angle and traversed the egg horizontally. Another right angle formed, and another, until a square chunk of the egg moved to one side, as if animated on its own. It halted, still somehow attached to the side of the egg.

Then Zheng He caught his first glimpse of the baby dragon, as its blue, lightly-scaled hands grasped the edge of the opening. Crewmen raised a great alarm and scrambled across the flagship's deck in confusion. Zheng He concentrated on the dragon's face as it left the shadows of the egg's interior. Its snout appeared much less pronounced than Zheng He expected, and its eyes stared outward through narrow lids. He did not see the pointed ears he expected, indeed saw no evidence of ears at all. Even the light scales of the dragon's upper body faded out as they approached its face. Zheng He hoped to perceive the dragon's personality and intentions with his examination of its features, but he could not just yet.

Admiral Zheng's men quieted as the dragon stared out at them, but when it raised a foot and began to climb out of the egg, they began to shout again. Several of the archers grew noticeably nervous, and a couple of them drew back their bows even more, clearly ready to loose their arrows.

But Zheng He commanded, "Hold!" The archers eased the tension on their bows. For Zheng He noticed what no one else did:

The dragon wore boots.

*****

Zheng He felt that the dragon seemed weak and listless. It proved difficult for the creature to pull itself out of its egg, and the admiral said the prospect of helping the dragon emerge tempted him. But concern for his safety overcame even him, and he stood and watched as the dragon strained to pull itself up and out of the egg. As more the dragon's body became visible, Zheng He saw that it wore a long tunic of some sort that came down past its knees. The light blue garment contrasted with the dragon's dark blue skin. It featured no belt or pockets or any adornments.

But two vertical slits in back allowed the dragon's wings to move freely — or would have, if the dragon could have mustered enough energy to move them. Instead, they fell limply on either side of the dragon's body. They extended from just above its shoulders to just below its waist, but seemed strangely thin. Zheng He wondered how such feeble-looking wings could lift this creature which, if it ever got to its feet, would stand twice as tall as a man.

A baby dragon would not emerge from its egg fully clothed and dry, Admiral Zheng realized. And the closer he looked at the "egg," the more it resembled something made, not a natural phenomenon.

Yet the large dragon had clearly tumbled from the sky, releasing this one into the ocean. A mystery, Zheng He thought. Perhaps a dangerous one.

The dragon tumbled onto the deck and landed with a heavy, meaty sound. It raised its head to try to take in its surroundings. Many of Zheng He's men remained frightened even of this weakened creature, and told him the archers should fire immediately, that they would find no better moment to destroy the dragon before it took flight and breathed fire and destroyed them all.

"You disappoint me," he told them. "We serve the Emperor, who sits on the Dragon Throne. We know dragons represent goodness and intelligence." He pointed at several crewmembers in turn, and commanded them, "Take the dragon below. Four of the archers will accompany you." To one of his commanders, he said, "Summon doctors. Send them down, as well."

Even the most loyal of men may have taken another look at the dragon and hesitated to obey such an order — except from Zheng He. Even so, a couple of men failed to step forward in a lively manner, only to have their superiors beat them bloody, so they would fear them more than the dragon.

It took considerable effort, but eventually the men managed alternately to carry or drag the dragon down into the hold. They cleared a space among the porcelain and gems and the many gifts for barbarian leaders and placed the dragon among them. They tried to place it sitting up at first, then gave up that goal and allowed the dragon to lie upon its left side, careful not to let it crush those thin wings with its own weight.

Admiral Zheng told the men who had brought the dragon that they had served well and could leave. He positioned the archers in shadowed areas around the hold, so they would not unnecessarily frighten the dragon.

At that moment, the doctors arrived, and upon seeing their patient, stopped abruptly, eyes wide, mouths agape. Zheng He told them, "You represent my wisest medical men. I give you the challenge of your lifetimes — heal this dragon."

The doctors looked at the limp form of the large creature before them, then at one another, and their silence broke apart into half a dozen overlapping conversations, each doctor proposing a course of action to his colleagues, each contradicting all the others.

Finally Zheng He had heard enough: "Silence!" He pointed at one of the doctors immediately before him, an elderly man with grizzled whiskers, but whose eyes remained keen. "Tell me how you would treat the dragon."

"Typically I would conduct an interview," the old doctor said. "I would ask the patient about his sleep habits, what he has eaten, whether he has a stressful life. But I can do none of these things with this patient."

Zheng He indicated the doctor standing next to the old man — a younger fellow with an unlined face and a demeanor suggesting an inordinate curiosity. He said, "I would try to find one of the six pulses in the wrist. But the arrangement of this dragon's wrist must surely differ from yours or mine. How can I find such a pulse?"

The third doctor Zheng He bade speak suggested, "I would examine the tongue, if this creature has a tongue. I would check for the red tongue that would tell me of an inflammation. Or the white tongue which would show that the dragon lacks energy. But a dragon — surely to make such an inspection involves risking the dangers of its fiery breath."

Then the dragon began to stir, and it uttered low moans that began deep within its chest and rumbled outward to rattle boxes and barrels next to it in the hold. Even Zheng He felt suddenly aware of the creature's size as it struggled to rise up on its arms. Once it sat upright, it appeared strangely human in its deportment. It sat with its right knee raised and right hand upon that knee. The left leg stretched out before it and the left hand hung to its side.

Then, for the first time, it looked directly at Admiral Zheng with awareness of its surroundings. Zheng He had always felt himself an excellent judge of men; now he found himself attempting to perceive the nature of this very strange creature, so different from a man yet also at variance from his conception of a dragon.

Zheng He's voice, even after all these years, trembled a bit as he spoke to me of the dragon's discerning gaze. He told me of the intelligence he saw in those eyes, and the gentleness. Others might think the dragon a beast; he rejected that. He realized he stood before a creature that might legitimately consider itself a near-equal to a man.

That realization, he said, represented for him the dragon's most frightening aspect.

*****

At this point in Zheng He's tale, I told him that I did not mind him mocking my trusting nature, but that he did not have to continue his jest. He knows I believe in such things as ghosts and vampires, and I declared myself willing to believe in dragons, as well. But I knew he did not believe in such things.

Admiral Zheng laughed, and insisted upon the truth of every word. "But I did not wish this tale told before I wanted it told."

"What makes this that time?" I asked.

"Let me tell more," Zheng He said. "Then you will realize on your own."

*****

Zheng He decided he should set aside his status as commander-in-chief of the treasure fleet and adopt that of ambassador. As the doctors watched in wonderment, Zheng He spread his arms wide and bade the dragon greetings: he spoke in praise of its wisdom and strength and inquired as to any service he might provide, perhaps a particular herb or a soothing tea. Then he lowered his hands and bowed his head slightly.

The dragon, of course, showed no sign of understanding Zheng He's speech. He chose this time, however, to utter another low moan. The doctors, as one, took several steps backwards; the archers raised their bows a bit higher.

Zheng He raised a hand waist-high to indicate that the bowmen should relax their stance. Zheng He did not know whether the dragon's moans represented an exclamation of pain or an attempt at communication. He must know more. And another thought occurred to him — he had spent this voyage demonstrating Chinese might to the barbarian countries of the Western Ocean. Here sat yet another opportunity to show that might, this time to a supernatural creature!

First, he must make sure the dragon survived. He commanded the doctors: "Fetch fresh water for the dragon! Then, offer it as wide a range of food as you can, whatever your judgment tells you a dragon might find appropriate — pork and fishes, turnips and mushrooms, apples and plums. We must hope the same foods that nourish us provide it with sustenance, as well."

The doctors began to leave, but Zheng He stopped them all with a raised hand. "Then, once you have fed the dragon, you may conduct the interviews and examinations you spoke of."

One protested, "How may we conduct such an interview when the dragon cannot speak to us?"

"Think of him as you would a patient too injured to speak. Also, you mentioned the six pulses and the tongue as providing clues. I trust you possess other ways, as well, to convince a patient's body to give up its secrets. I suggest you employ them."

Admiral Zheng watched for a few moments as the doctors scurried about the hold for provisions appropriate for a dragon. Then he returned his attention to the creature itself, who continued to sit and stare and utter the occasional moan. Zheng He felt for the creature, as he realized it had no way of knowing whether it had found itself among friends or enemies. *It may believe,* he thought, *that I intend to impress it as part of the crew, or that I consider it a mere beast and wish to discover whether its flesh would constitute a delicacy! But a beast doesn't possess the dragon's obvious intelligence. I suspect we could even teach it civilized speech.*

Such a possibility heartens me. After all, it requires a certain intelligence for the creature to understand it must acknowledge my sovereignty over it.

I will demand that most precious treasure of all for the sake of the emperor!

*****

Zheng He watched as two of the doctors, using all their strength, scooted a large barrel of water toward the dragon. It apparently understand the nature of the offering immediately, as its powerful arms easily lifted the container to its mouth. It drank about half the water and placed the barrel next to it. One of the doctors approached the barrel as if to retrieve it and the dragon emitted a loud hissing sound. "I will admit," Zheng He told me all these years later, "that my bowels stirred when I heard that sound, because I believed it certain that flames would engulf the doctor and, perhaps, all of us within seconds."

Yet still the doctor stood, and not even a hint of smoke appeared from the dragon's mouth. All the same, the doctor backed away from the creature.

Of all the foods the doctors offered up, the dragon accepted only various fishes and apples. It did not try to stand for the better part of a day. Zheng He made sure only he and the archers attended as the dragon lifted itself up on two arms, then one, then rose on wobbly legs. "Surely no man has ever stood next to such a formidable creature," Zheng He told me. "Certainly no creature as intimidating, indeed frightening, as the dragon."

Now the dragon looked around, as if searching for something familiar. Then its gaze caught a shaft of light from a porthole just over his head. It turned slowly, took the several steps it required to stand in the light, and slowly spread its thin, translucent wings.

Zheng He saw that the span of the dragon's wings amounted to a distance barely longer than the dragon's height. *How,* he wondered, *can such* small wings support this creature in flight? But, he reasoned, perhaps this baby dragon's wings will grow larger in time.

The dragon stood at such an angle as to receive the light over as much of the area of its wings as possible. The admiral felt his own body grow chilled at the thought that the dragon might accept the warm rays of the sun to power a previously dormant fire-breathing capability.

But after a few minutes, the dragon folded its wings, returned to its previous position, and sat again. It did not breathe fire. It did not appear to provide any threat at all.

Zheng He decided his determination to assert himself over this creature could not flag. He stood straight and tall, spread his arms wide, then clapped his hands against his breast. "Zheng He. Zheng He." Then he reached his arms toward the dragon, bidding it to say its name, if it had one.

Another grunt from the dragon, but this one came out more quietly, more like that of a man wondering how to interpret something than of a creature in pain. The dragon tilted its head much as a curious dog might, then placed its hands on its own chest and said, in a deep but clear voice, "Merabor. Merabor."

Zheng He felt as if his heart would burst from his chest.

*****

In the days afterward, the dragon, Merabor, astonished Zheng He with his healing abilities. The doctors' interviews and examinations proved unnecessary. Perhaps, he reasoned, the dragon had only needed food and water. But another aspect of the creature suggested itself — its apparent need to stand in the sun several times a day. Upon those occasions Merabor seemed renewed, as if the sun provided nourishment food and water could not.

The "egg" also impressed him — after Merabor's exit, it had closed itself up sufficiently that neither Admiral Zheng nor anyone else could perceive that an exit ever existed. He ordered it stored in the hold, but far from the dragon.

Zheng He felt, however, that Merabor's greatest accomplishment remained his swift learning of the rudiments of the Chinese language. Notice, "his," not "its," for the dragon informed Zheng He of its maleness early on. The admiral asked whether Merabor had spoken with people before. The dragon insisted he had not, which the admiral found at best confusing and at worst suspicious. How had it learned civilized speech so quickly?

Admiral Zheng also maintained his fascination with the dragon's clothing. Whoever created it did not appear to have sewn or woven it in any familiar manner. To the unaided eye Merabor's long tunic appeared to encompass a single unbroken piece of cloth. Its sleeves and its neck and wing holes did not even end in hems, nor did the very bottom of the garment; the material simply ended, yet showed no sign of fraying. Zheng He asked Merabor if he may touch the tunic, and the dragon relented easily. The admiral slid his fingers over the tunic, and he gasped as the cloth imparted a minor shock similar to static electricity; the shock did not cease, however, but continued as Zheng He rubbed the cloth between thumb and forefinger. Its texture felt similar to silk, but he could not perceive threads, no matter how fine. Yet the cloth seemed to possess the strength and elasticity of leather without the accustomed thickness.

Zheng He realized his fingers still fondled Merabor's tunic and he released it, wondering at the reluctance he felt as he did so. "It felt as if it holds the spark of life itself!" Zheng He muttered. But the admiral set this idea aside as unworthy of someone of his logical nature.

Zheng He tried to decide what kind of dragon Merabor represented. He knew none that wore clothing, for instance. The admiral stood before Merabor one day as the dragon sat and ate. He'd dismissed the archers day earlier, feeling that he could trust the dragon — also, that if Merabor truly wished to burn them all and destroy his flagship in the process, likely the archers could not prevent it.

Zheng He told Merabor he believed him less logical than the Wood Dragon, nor as competitive as the Fire Dragon — not as diplomatic as the Earth Dragon, nor as ruthless as the Metal Dragon. "I believe you represent a Water Dragon," the admiral said. "You seem less selfish, more inhibited. You appear more able to accept defeat."

Merabor tossed two apples into his mouth as a man might a couple of cherries, and ate them in two gulps. He replied in his deep yet halting voice, "Not...defeated. Not...dragon."

"Not...a dragon?" Zheng He asked.

Merabor placed his hands on his chest as he had when he'd first said his name. "Oldavar. Oldavar. Name of my people."

Zheng He couldn't hide his confusion. "You mean, perhaps, your tribe? Do dragons organize themselves into tribes?"

Merabor tilted his head, dog-like, once more. "No understand." Hands on chest again. "Oldavar. Only Oldavar."

"Ah!" Zheng He said, nodding his understanding. "'Oldavar means 'dragon' in your tongue."

Merabor stopped with another pair of apples midway to his mouth. "No dragon. Oldavar."

Zheng He folded his arms on his chest and frowned. How, he wondered, can a dragon sit there before me and call himself something else? I might as well refer to myself as something other than a man. "A more vexing creature may not exist," he told Merabor. "How might I learn more about you?" He reasoned that for the dragon to acknowledge the emperor's sovereignty over him, he must understand the true nature of his ruler. But to do that, Zheng He must first understand the dragon. The gift, he reasoned, must match the one who receives it.

A moment's thought, and the admiral had his answer: "All things in life express themselves through opposite principles — yin and yang. In order for me to learn more about you, you must learn more about me. Such an opportunity approaches."

Merabor's eyes spoke of an intelligence that sometimes intimidated even Zheng He. The dragon rumbled, "How may I learn more?"

"I have remembered a more vexing creature than you. Someone who may indeed provide you a better understanding of men. You must witness my encounter with the pirate, Chen Zuyi."

*****

Days later, the treasure fleet approached Palembang, in Sumatra, where many Chinese merchants and their families lived. Chen Zuyi had taken control of the city and begun raiding ships in the Strait of Malacca.

This pirate did, indeed, vex Admiral Zheng, and he had grown determined to root out this menace. First, however, he must gather information about the pirate's intentions.

Zheng He wanted Merabor to witness as much as possible of his encounter with Chen and with his own informant, the merchant Shi Jinqing. However, he knew he dared not display the dragon before men who did not serve him as crewmembers. He could order his own men to remain silent about Merabor, knowing that some would speak of him anyway. He could address that problem by punishing severely the men who spoke, while dispatching senior officers to discredit their words.

But the admiral could not effectively silence or discredit those who lived ashore, at least not after the treasure fleet departed.

So Zheng He, under cover of darkness the night before his meeting with each man, instructed trusted members of his crew to clear the path from the hold to an upper deck where the meeting would take place. The admiral escorted Merabor to a small alcove adjacent to the meeting room and secreted him there.

Merabor grumbled about the cramped surroundings, but Zheng He promised him the first meeting, with the pirate himself, Chen Zuyi, would take place in less than an hour, at first light. "You will learn much about how men deal with one another," he told the dragon. "Then you shall learn about how men deal with pirates."

Merabor gave another grumbling response, which Admiral Zheng interpreted as the dragon conceding the point. "I realize you will not understand much of what you hear," the admiral said. "I will explain more afterwards. I will also allow you a lengthy time outside on my observation deck to bask in the sun."

"Then I wait eagerly," Merabor said.

Satisfied with the dragon's response, and with himself, Zheng He started sternward toward his quarters, but a crewman ran up to him, bowed, and pointed excitedly at the ocean's waters just to one side of the treasure ship's wake. The dim rays of the sun shone obliquely on the calm waters, but just enough that Zheng He made out a dark shape beneath the surface — a shape familiar enough that a sense of wonder and awe gripped him.

The shape of the dragon's mother.

And it moved, pacing this very ship.

Zheng He's first instinct told him to rush back to Merabor and demand to know how the dragon mother had survived, and whether she meant his ship harm. But as he admonished the crewman who'd warned him of this possible danger to speak of it to no one else, then dismissed him, a second thought came to him.

He reasoned that Merabor either did not want him to know of his mother's survival, or did not know of it himself. Either way, Zheng He possessed knowledge the dragon did not — and knowledge often represented advantage.

The admiral continued toward his quarters, consciously refusing to glance again at the dark shape.

*****

When Admiral Zheng's flagship docked in the Old Harbor in Palembang, he sent a messenger to Chen Zuyi and his associates, requiring them to submit to his sovereignty.

Zheng He believed the pirate would attempt either an attack or an escape upon this summons. To his surprise, however, Chen Zuyi soon appeared at the Old Harbor to speak with him directly. The pirate came aboard Zheng He's flagship and allowed the admiral's men to direct him to the meeting room. Chen Zuyi bowed deeply, and spoke quietly but confidently: "I have appeared as you requested, Admiral."

"So you have," Zheng He said. He offered the pirate nothing, neither food nor drink nor an offer to sit. "Do you then submit to me?"

Chen Zuyi bowed again. "I have no other choice before such powers as you command."

Zheng He thought of the dragon deep within this very ship. Soon I may have many other powers, he thought. But none to boast of just yet. "Prepare your men," he told Chen Zuyi. "Your days of piracy end here."

The man left, having seemingly acknowledged and accepted Zheng He's sovereignty. If only, he thought, the dragon would accept such so easily. He considered canceling his appointment with his informant, Shi Jinqing, but decided the proper political course meant hearing whatever he might have to say.

First, however, the admiral stepped into the alcove adjacent the meeting room and looked in on Merabor. The dragon still stood silently. Zheng He asked, "Did you gain any insight into people as you listened?"

Merabor's voice rumbled even lower than usual in such close quarters. "You would kill him. The...pirate."

Zheng He displayed his best diplomatic smile. "If he refused to acknowledge my powers and sovereignty, of course I would."

"The pirate...barbarian?"

Admiral Zheng's smile widened into a natural one. "Yes, I consider the pirate a barbarian."

Merabor aimed that piercing gaze at the admiral. "Zheng He...barbarian?"

Admiral Zheng told me, these many years later, that he would have personally beaten a man who said such a thing to him. But the admiral knew he must force down his anger — how could a dragon know what made a man a barbarian? He also admitted that part of him remained concerned regarding the dragon's potential powers, which he feared may lie dormant, awaiting Merabor's full recovery. He told the dragon, tersely, "I do not consider myself a barbarian. You should never utter such words again."

Zheng He expected an apology, but Merabor simply stood mutely once more. He could not help but wonder whether that stance expressed the dragon's own anger or whether he did not have the words allowing him to respond.

The admiral chose to believe the latter, and went back into the larger room to await his informant's arrival.

*****

Shi Jinqing bowed deeply, respectfully, as befitted his status aboard Zheng He's flagship. The admiral, in turn, respected Shi Jinqing's counsel and greeted him warmly. Servants surrounded them both and provided soft pillows for them to sit upon, hot tea to sip, and fresh fruits to eat. Zheng He wasted little time in preliminaries, asking Shi Jinqing, "What do you know of Chen Zuyi's intentions?"

Shi Jinqing took a long sip of tea and said, "The pirate came here to speak with you, did he not?"

"He did."

"And pledged he would submit to you?"

"He did."

"He lies. He intends to attack you here in the strait by bringing his forces quickly from the river channels where they wait. But I know how you may best deploy your great forces to prevent such an attack."

The admiral leaned forward. "Tell me," he commanded.

Shi Jinqing told. And Zheng He remained aware of the dragon listening.

*****

Once his informant departed, Zheng He went to Merabor again. The dragon stretched its wings and asked, "You will kill the pirate now?"

"I intend to," the admiral said. "He lied before. He does not acknowledge my sovereignty."

"You consider it more valuable than his life."

"He must realize my emperor's powers. He steals from my people and laughs at my fleet."

Merabor remained silent for a long moment, leaving Zheng He to wonder what line of thought it pursued. Then Merabor said, "On my world...this does not happen now."

Zheng He blinked in confusion. "Your...world? Only the one exists."

Merabor stretched up to his full height and looked down upon Zheng He. At this moment, the admiral told me, the dragon frightened him, though Merabor made no threatening gesture. Instead, the admiral said, the dragon assumed a superior stance he'd never witnessed previously. Zheng He had considered Merabor dependent upon him since his arrival aboard his treasure ship. He provided him fishes and apples and water, after all, and in a sense represented the dragon's only access to the sun itself, which seemed to revitalize him in a way the admiral still struggled to understand. Zheng He asked, "What other world do you speak of?"

"A light in the sky. So far away you cannot see it."

"We steer our ships by such groupings of stars, such as the Weaving Girl and the Lantern. But surely you cannot live on a point of light."

"Other worlds circle them, just as this one circles your sun."

"Merabor, you speak more confidently than I have heard before. And your vocabulary has grown."

The dragon's wings folded against his back. "You believe me an animal, despite my obvious intelligence. Such a mistake carries dangers."

"I and my crew saved your life. Why would you make such threats?"

"I would never threaten. But I must explain. I violated my orders when I allowed you to rescue me. My society says I must not speak to Humans or even allow them to see me or my ship."

"Ship?" Zheng He asked. "I've seen no ship — only your mother as she crashed into the sea."

"Another mistake. You saw my ship — it contains what you call 'the spark of life,' although one cannot call it truly alive. But it did not give birth to me. I travel in it as you travel aboard this treasure ship. But it grew...ill...unexpectedly and crashed here."

"Enough nonsense. I have dealt with you honestly. Do the same for me. Will you remain and learn more of civilized people? Or do you wish to leave us? If so, will you do so peacefully, or by using your great strength and breath of fire?"

The dragon regarded the admiral through those narrow lids. "I will remain to witness your civilization."

Zheng He still felt uncertain of Merabor's intentions, but kept those thoughts to himself as he had his observation deck at the stern of the ship cleared and escorted the dragon there personally. A commander, Zheng He, knew, must make promises sparingly but must always follow through on them once made.

He watched as Merabor stood with arms widespread and unfolded his wings toward the sun. Those wise, knowing eyes closed and Zheng He felt as if he viewed the earthbound dragon floating free above them all, as if Merabor's freedom of flight might assert itself at any moment.

The dragon's long blue tunic flapped in the breeze as he stood as unmoving as a monument — Zheng He's mouth turned up in a wry smile at that thought, as if Merabor stood there proclaiming his own self-worth simply by maintaining such a stance.

Then the admiral's smile faded. *This dragon does indeed hold such self-worth — such self-importance — within. I recognize that emotion in him because I recognize it within myself.*

Only one of us may entertain such feelings within this fleet, however. Merabor must learn his place.

Zheng He could not help, though, but remain aware of the many eyes aboard other ships that took in the dragon's form and stared in wonderment, even as he himself had stared when he first glimpsed Merabor.

It does not matter, Zheng He thought. *I will tell them what they have seen and what they have not. One day I will command a chronicle of these voyages, and if I wish it to contain tales of a dragon, it will contain them. If not — Merabor will remain a rumor, a legend, the talk of drunken or delusional seamen, perhaps with only his unnatural egg and any knowledge we might gain from it remaining.*

*****

Zheng He positioned his larger ships in the Strait of Malacca to bottle up Chen Zuyi's craft within the river courses from which they would attack. His smaller craft rushed down those courses to engage Chen's ships. Archers aboard those craft, making sure they traveled safely upwind, launched many flaming arrows into Chen's ships, quickly setting them aflame. Still more of Zheng He's craft deployed troops to attack Chen's ships from land.

The battle raged for many hours, well into the night. As the day's last rays faded beyond the horizon, Zheng He ordered his ship positioned broadside to the shoreline. He had the rear observation deck cleared again and brought Merabor there. The admiral stood in silence as ships burned on those inland waterways and explosives rumbled. The smell of gunpowder wafted across the deck. The shouts of victorious men and screams of maimed ones carried across the water to their ears.

Zheng He watched little of this; he focused mostly upon the dragon, wondering what it made of this battle. "Does he think us truly barbarians?" the admiral wondered. *If so, what gives him the right? His people have little to recommend them — Merabor, after all, has allowed me to master him, with barely a protest.*

Finally the dragon turned away from the shoreline and looked down upon Zheng He. "Your skills impress me. Oh, your technical abilities stand far below those of my people, of course. But you and your commanders possess a genius of sorts for organization and tactics."

"'Of sorts,' you say?"

"Look far inland — two of your boats and dozens of your troops coordinate themselves in an attack on one of Chen Zuyi's craft — masterful!"

Zheng He narrowed his gaze, but saw no such drama playing itself out. "In the darkness, my eyes can make out but little beyond the mouths of these rivers."

Merabor's wings fluttered. "That explains much."

Zheng He waved that assertion away with a gesture. "A trifle. Yet in many ways you present me with difficult truths."

"I have another difficult truth for you — have your astronomers perceived an extra star in the sky — one which moves even more quickly than the planets do?"

Zheng He said, "They've told me of no such star."

"Look now in the northern sky." Merabor pointed just about halfway between the horizon and zenith. "Even your eyes should see that star now."

Zheng He placed a hand across his forehead and squinted to help himself focus on that star. "I do see it. And it passes quite quickly."

"As it does several times a night."

"Do your people live there, as well?"

"Imagine another ship, much larger than the one that crashed here, larger even than your ship of the sea. It allows us to travel between the stars. I must return there soon. What you call my 'mother' brought me here. It will take me back."

Blood rushed to Zheng He's face, and for an instant he wondered whether the dragon could perceive that, as well. If he can, the admiral thought, then he hides it well. "How...soon?" the admiral asked.

"I do not know. Before months pass, certainly. Perhaps weeks."

Zheng He decided upon his plan at that moment, especially as it occurred to him that if Merabor could see so well in darkness, perhaps he could see his mother — his "ship," when he and his men could not. Perhaps, he thought, Merabor even speaks with it somehow without us realizing.

But I cannot allow this dragon to leave. He must remain here and return to China with me as the most fabulous prize I or any other admiral might present to the emperor.

For that prize, I will risk my ship, my very life.

*****

Admiral Zheng's forces killed five thousand of the pirates, burned ten of their ships, and captured seven more. Chen himself would travel with them as their prisoner to the imperial capital in Nanjing to face execution.

The pirates dealt with, Zheng He ordered a select group of his men to begin work on a special room for the dragon, in a corner of the hold several bulkheads away. His next thought: This room will house a dragon, not a fool. I must push the men to work quickly, and never allow Merabor to witness their work. As the proverb states, talk does not cook rice.

Zheng He gave considerable thought to his plans for Merabor as he dealt with the aftermath of the battle with Chen Zuyi's forces. Those thoughts inspired action; action transformed itself nearly into obsession.

The dragon would acknowledge his sovereignty.

*****

So the night arrived that Zheng He cleared the observation deck once again and invited Merabor to watch the passage of that swift star in the northern sky. The dragon kept his wings close to his body here on the windy deck — they served no purpose without sunlight, and Zheng He perceived they could easily catch the wind and throw Merabor off-balance.

Admiral Zheng peered to the northeast, and saw Merabor watching the same area of the skies. "You keep watch for the first sign of your star."

"Of course," Merabor said.

"I stood here at dusk," Zheng He said. "I saw dark skies in that direction. It means we will see rain by midnight."

"I must warn you. You will see much more than rain. This ship — all of your marvelous ships — may find themselves engulfed by a storm you cannot comprehend."

Zheng He fought back a smile. "You hope to teach my people meteorology now? If you indeed come from another world, how do you know so much about this world's weather?"

Merabor stared down at the admiral through those narrow lids as he had so many times before. "I still have many surprises to present you."

Zheng He had only known Merabor these short weeks since he had arrived from the skies, but he felt he knew the dragon as well as he did any of his crew. Merabor speaks on many levels this night, the admiral thought. He works to deliver a message to me without saying it outright. This makes him dangerous. I must take that advantage back.

Merabor pointed to the northeastern horizon. "Look! My ship."

Indeed, the moving star rose quickly from the horizon, headed toward northern skies. "You wish to return to your people," Zheng He said to the dragon.

Merabor didn't take his gaze from the swift star. "As a sailor, you must often miss your homeland."

"I consider that I take my homeland with me on this journey. As I will on those that follow. My emperor has commanded me to allow as much of the world as possible to witness the glory of his reign."

"A goal you have fulfilled honorably, as I have seen since my arrival here. Now — do you wish to show me your own surprise?"

Zheng He's face felt warm despite the cool wind that swept across the observation deck. He hoped only a quirk of the dragon's wording made it sound as much like an order as a suggestion. I have decided correctly to act on this night, he thought. "Yes," he told the dragon. "I wish to show it to you now."

*****

Zheng He admitted to me he felt fear as he followed Merabor down into the hold. The dragon always stepped cautiously down the stairs, because his feet easily extended to a length twice that of their width. He also kept his arms and sometimes his wings extended to maintain his balance. Admiral Zheng could not help but watch the muscles of the dragon's great arms as they flexed. He feared what those arms might do if they snatched up a man or hurled a heavy barrel.

Finally Zheng He and the dragon reached the floor of the hold and walked most of the length of the great ship to arrive in a section Merabor had never allowed into before. His private room stood against one bulkhead of the ship, illuminated by a shaft of moonlight that the admiral hoped obscured the fact that darkness claimed most of the rest of the hold.

The room revealed a simple design; smooth, even flimsy-seeming wood with a tall doorway the only entrance. The door, closed for now, towered over Zheng He's head, but he knew Merabor would have to duck slightly to enter. The dragon's fully extended wings might barely touch either side of the room.

"I know these amount to small accommodations," Admiral Zheng said. "But I've not explained their special nature."

That's when three dozen archers stood amid boxes and barrels throughout the hold, each aiming at Merabor.

The admiral's heart hadn't beat as strongly during the battle against Chen Zuyi. He watched as the dragon turned its attention to him. Merabor said, "You cannot call this the gift of a friend."

Zheng He hardened his soul against Merabor's words. "I call it the proper gift for a barbarian."

The dragon said, "You told me I should not utter that word to you. Yet you say it to me?"

"Only a civilized man may decide who deserves the title of barbarian."

Merabor leaned forward and Zheng He fought with every bit of courage and honor he could muster not to take even a single step back. He heard the muted wooden sound of arrow against bow and the soft rustle of clothing as the archers made ready to fire.

Zheng He had convinced himself that this dragon, for whatever reason, did not possess the power to breathe fire. As Merabor stared him down, however, doubt arose within him. He realized the dragon could easily burn him down, however quick his archers' reactions, however sure their aim.

But Merabor did not even open his mouth. Instead, he went to the door of his special room, pulled it open, and walked inside.

That's when several of the archers cast aside their weapons, slammed the door shut, and thrust a broad wooden bar across the doorway, trapping Merabor within.

Zheng He expected to hear a loud protest from the dragon at this point, but he heard none. For whatever reason Merabor does not resist, the admiral thought, I must take advantage of this. He motioned to the archers and they detached the flimsy wood facades from the exterior of Merabor's room, revealing that the dragon stood within a room of thick reinforced timbers.

Merabor told Zheng He, "So now you consider me your prisoner."

"You will arrive in China as the honored guest of our emperor."

"And if I decline this honor?"

"I hope you do not. I respect you, Merabor. I believe once you understand the glory of my emperor's civilization, you will remain of your own free will. But I must insist you give me that opportunity. Several of the archers will keep watch at all times, in case we have underestimated your strength."

Merabor went to the far side of his room and stood with his back against the ship's bulkhead. "We understand one another," he said. "Do what you will."

Zheng He motioned for the archers to lower their weapons for now, thankful for his luck that Merabor did not resist, thankful as well that the dragon's strange egg remained secured in another corner of the hold. He would have his most skilled artisans find a way to crack that egg, and allow his astrologers and doctors to examine its contents soon enough.

Yet as the admiral stared into Merabor's features, he grew concerned. He felt he knew Merabor well enough to read those features — and he perceived only peace and calm reflected there.

So I cannot help but wonder, Zheng He thought, which of us might truly consider himself victorious.

****

Zheng He soon found himself rushing to the observation deck again. Merabor's words had proven themselves correct — he would soon see much more than rain. Approaching clouds made the skies grow darker by the moment, even as ocean waves grew taller and the treasure ship rocked more and more.

The admiral knew typhoons could arise here in the Western Ocean without warning, but when he demanded information from his astrologers and diviners, they told him but little. They insisted that the sky and seas appeared to act independently of one another rather than in concert. They could provide no explanation for the phenomenon.

When pressed for even the smallest detail, they told him only that the seas churned more restlessly than the skies would indicate — that something other than the winds drove the waves to such heights.

Zheng He's mind sped to the image of the dragon's mother — or "ship," as he insisted upon calling it. Its dark presence had concerned him profoundly the only time he'd glimpsed it.

Could it have returned?

As if summoned by the admiral's remembrance of the dragon's mother, a series of waves just ahead and to starboard of the treasure ship began to spin around one another, as if attempting to create a waterspout from the bottom up. The ocean all around began to roil.

Zheng He told the astrologers and diviners to sound the alert throughout the ship. He ordered the great vessel's pilot to steer sharply to port, and its signalers to command the gigantic fleet to do the same — in the darkness, with the other ships unable to see flags and banners, drums and gongs alerted the other ships of the sudden change in course.

As the treasure ship veered, Zheng He rushed to the starboard side of the ship — he had to know whether it would clear the violent upwelling of water successfully.

As the admiral described it to me later, in that moment, the ocean exploded! Its waters lifted up as if a giant hand had swept across the surface of the sea.

Those waters hurled Zheng He against a bulkhead, and awareness fled for several seconds. It returned only reluctantly, with a vague impression of the sea casting the treasure ship from side to side, punctuated by deafening blasts of thunder and blinding bursts of lightning. He felt a sharp pain at the back of his head and reached back with his hand. His hair felt sticky. When he looked at his hand, rain washed blood down his fingers.

As he sat up, Zheng He saw crewmen running to bring down the bamboo sails before the storm could rip them from the masts. He heard them crying out the name of Tianfei, the patron goddess of sailors. Zheng He forced himself to his feet and looked across the windswept ocean. The ships of his fleet, which normally sailed in an orderly pattern, now found themselves cast about at random.

A commotion behind him, and Zheng He saw crewmen staring into the sky in disbelief. His gaze followed theirs, and it took him a moment to admit the reality of what he saw:

Merabor's mother had taken to the skies again, her blue wings that never flapped spanning half the length of his treasure ship as she hovered to its rear.

The very sight of her threatened to cripple Zheng He's reason, and the moment lingered until he made himself turn back toward his crewmen, intending to issue a command. That he had no concept of the nature of that command did not worry him — not Zheng He! His faith in himself told him the words would come.

When he completed the turn, however, he found Merabor towering over him, silhouetted against a series of lightning bolts.

Zheng He admits words left him at this moment, and he cursed his own failure more than he did the dragon or the storm.

Merabor's words rumbled louder than the thunder: "You have much wisdom, Zheng He. But you have found its limits."

Now words released themselves into Zheng He's mouth again: "You dare insult me?"

"Not at all," the dragon said. "You said it properly — 'Only a civilized man may decide who deserves the title of barbarian.' Yet I have seen how you would bring civilization to me." Merabor held his arms up and indicated the storm all around them. "See how I bring it to you, instead!"

Then Merabor's arms reached down, quick as a viper, to grasp Zheng He by the shoulders. The time has arrived, the admiral thought. Finally the flame, or the crushing hands.

Merabor used neither. He lifted Zheng He up before him, the admiral determined not to show fear even with his arms pinned to his sides, his feet dangling. The dragon brought him close to his face and spoke in as quiet a voice as Zheng He had ever heard: "Barbarian."

Then Merabor tossed him to the deck, but Admiral Zheng forced himself to his feet just in time to see Merabor dive off the rear of the observation deck. Zheng He never saw him strike the water — a series of lightning flashes, and Merabor disappeared.

The admiral thought the lightning had incinerated Merabor in midjump. But the dragon's mother took this moment to rise higher into the sky, and Zheng He knew she would never abandon him so easily — somehow she had absorbed her son into herself again.

The admiral stood there as the dragon mother vanished into the low clouds. Those clouds soon dissipated, and within moments Admiral Zheng found his fleet sailing across calm waters beneath blue skies and he heard his crewmen offering up prayers to the Celestial Consort, Tianfei, whose protection had saved them all.

*****

When Zheng He turned from those smooth seas and clear skies and rushed down to the hold, he found the dragon's cage shattered like kindling and the archers lying unconscious. When he went to inspect the dragon's egg, he found it reduced to dust.

Zheng He did not travel on the second voyage of the treasure ships. Instead, he remained in China and traveled to the birthplace of Tianfei, the goddess of seafarers, to repair her temple. After all, the admiral's crewmen believed the violent flashes of light that consumed Merabor represented a "magic lantern" whose illumination banished the storm. Western sailors call such a light "Saint Elmo's fire," and believe only natural forces and not supernatural ones create it.

Zheng He believed neither explanation. "I held a complete lack of faith regarding Tianfei's intervention," he told me. "I also realized my own error in believing a natural form of lightning had struck. My intellect, informed by my emotions, told me that Merabor's mother had generated that lightning — the spark of life, indeed!"

Once again, during his last voyage, Admiral Zheng insisted every word of his tale represented utter truth. But only now could he force himself to tell it.

I asked again the question I'd posed earlier: "What makes this that time?"

"A tale," he said, "should carry a moral. This one does not. I had hoped you would find one within it."

Yet I have not. Zheng He's exploits numbered so many, yet those of silver and silk, tea and wine, diplomacy and burning pirate ships did not consume his thoughts as did this single tale.

The proverb tells us a bird does not sing because it has an answer — it sings because it has a song. What then, constitutes Zheng He's song?

Only this — despite his failure to bring Merabor to the emperor, despite having to hear the unwarranted insult in Merabor's last word to him, a single fact remained, a single accomplishment no other man could claim.

Once Zheng He captured a dragon.

THE LOOPHOLE

In *The Loophole*, I wanted to take the standard space explorer, presumably square-jawed and eager to walk into danger, and test him in a way we don't often see. Alexander Barron desperately wants to travel to the stars — but what if has to consider that his dream might not be possible? What does he do then? Should he give up so easily?

This was my first professionally published story — now-former editor Stanley Schmidt published it in the March 1994 *Analog Science Fact - Science Fiction*. At the time, I assumed that after years of trying and failing to sell anything, that the floodgates were open and I'd immediately sell most anything I wrote.

I didn't sell another story to *Analog* for six years.

After that, the floodgates did open, at least partially, and most of the stories in this volume originally appeared there. Thank you, Stan Schmidt! Stan's mentorship over the succeeding years is why this book is dedicated to him.

By the way, apropos of nothing, I learned years after this story was published that the first professional sale by my favorite SF writer, Arthur C. Clarke, was titled *Loophole*. Doesn't mean a damn thing, but it's a nice bit of synchronicity.

I've seen sentient whale-like creatures floating through the hydrogen and helium of Jupiter's skies, beings without technology whose immense intellects may have turned inward to philosophical discussions that would shame Aristotle or John Locke. I've visited an alien world called the Earth. I've known moments of supreme ecstasy when I felt the universe and I were one, and wept uncontrollably when the universe has shown its true nature and killed without thought, without awareness.

I don't believe I was ever as astonished, though, as when my ex-lover Laney Shackleton tapped me on the shoulder on a beach in the Bahamas.

As I turned and saw those familiar dark features, that short-cropped hair above active brown eyes, so many emotions began to churn within me that I couldn't form a sensible thought. Sheer surprise was dominant; she was the last person I expected to see here. For one thing, she was supposed to be half a world away. Laney was head researcher on a stardrive project at the

Tokyo Space Institute. I'd heard things hadn't been going well for that project. More pain for Laney, to add to what I'd given her two years before when I broke off with her. More guilt for me.

That was the other reason I wouldn't have expected to see her. I couldn't imagine she'd ever want to see me again. Things were pretty bitter between us there at the end.

Here she was, though, which meant she had gone to a lot of trouble to find me. I was taking my first real vacation in many years, and I wanted to be alone, without the press or politicians or hangers-on or curiosity seekers bothering me.

And without thinking about the Arololularians.

That meant Laney had called in a lot of favors just to find me — then gone to the trouble of hopping on the Miami Clipper for the two-hour trip from Tokyo to catch the local shuttle to get to me. Why was she here? Reconciliation? Revenge?

All those thoughts went through my brain in about three-quarters of a second, during which I was standing there in the surf, mouth agape, not looking at all like anyone's image of Alexander Barron, brave planetary explorer and media darling — first man to fly solo through the rings of Saturn, and all that.

Laney didn't speak, either. Instead, she grabbed the back of my neck, drew me down (she's rather short), and planted a long and passionate kiss on me.

"I know," she said. "What the hell am I doing here?"

"My question exactly," I sputtered.

"I take it you've been watching the news nets. The Arololularians."

I'd watched nothing else for days, and had come out to the beach to get away from the barrage of cube images for a while. Leathery-skinned aliens with a name like a bad tongue twister had landed on Earth, and they'd gotten here using a stardrive! It was a technology that had remained out of reach by human scientists, and Laney and others were close to turning their attention to cold sleep as the only option to achieve star flight. Now maybe I had a chance to reach the stars, but my attempts to contact old cronies at NASA and the U.N. had brought no response.

My obsession with the stars had been the whole problem between me and Laney. The physicists had seemed about to break the light barrier for the past two decades, but every new bit of knowledge gained had brought new problems, new technical challenges that were beyond current technology. The more we learned, the less likely a stardrive seemed.

But I wanted the stars. I needed a loophole. I was willing to sacrifice everything. Even Laney. That's how much of a fool I am. She was dedicated to her own work, but she had a more balanced attitude about life.

"Oh, damn," she said, "I'm screwing this up. Yes, they have a stardrive. But nothing that will help you."

"Why not?"

"The team's been picked to make the first trip. Your name came up, but the U.N. council didn't pick you. In fact, they couldn't."

"Come back to my cabin," I said. "You have to tell me all about this."

Soon we sat beneath azure skies on the patio of my rental cabin, with glasses of cold tea before us. I pressed Laney for more information.

Laney told me, "The Arols — That's a lot easier to say, isn't it? Anyway, they're willing to let us learn about stardrive, but they're uncertain of its effects on our physiology until they actually take a few of us. Transitioning into it can have severe physical effects on living tissue. For now, any human who undergoes the stardrive transition on an Arol ship needs to be very young. Preferably under thirty-five, maybe forty tops."

I understood then. "I'm forty-eight."

Laney came to me and embraced me. "And I'm forty-five," she said. "I thought you should hear it from me, Alex. The stars will never be ours. It could take decades for the Arols to figure out how to take any Human, of any age. That dream is dead, at least for us. If you can only let it go, we can at least have each other again. Forever this time."

*****

My first encounter with an inhabited alien world was when I'd returned to Earth three months earlier. It seemed the most wondrous place in the solar system, a world virtually covered with the most precious substance known to humanity — water. I quickly fell in love with the water world, ironically called "Earth."

Virtually an entire globe lay beneath my shuttle as it entered the atmosphere; the terminator was just barely visible at the edge of the planet. Earth was a planet of contrasts as stark as any in the solar system, with browns, blues, and whites swirled together.

The Pacific Ocean was visible in its full cloud-streaked glory and vastness, proclaiming beyond doubt that although human thought and concern gravitated toward the land masses first, the water-world image was more descriptive. Life had begun in those oceans, in an environment less ruled by gravity. Judged on a cosmic scale, its tenure on land would be brief. Now human beings were living in space, a weightless, unbounded environment more akin to their origins.

As we arced eastward, I saw the outline of the North American continent — from Mexico and Baja, past Kansas wheat fields and the ever-growing sprawl that was Chicago, and into much of Canada. Farther north, the polar ice was hidden in cloud cover.

All my life, I would treasure memories of sights, sounds, and smells that brought back a boyish sense of wonder:

The sun, unnaturally bright, blinding me intermittently as I walked through a forest, leaves crackling and rustling beneath my feet, a random kind of sound you never heard on an orbiting habitat.

Emergence into an open field, the landscape frighteningly flat instead of curling up securely around me.

Lying down in Kentucky bluegrass, eyes closed against the uncomfortably empty sky above. The scent of unknown and exotic flora around me told me I rested against a living thing.

I felt an intuitive bond between myself and this planet. I felt a thrill of discovery that was forever denied to anyone who'd never been beyond this planet, who took her wonders for granted.

I desired even more. I wanted to see more worlds, more wonders.

*****

And now it all came crashing down around me. Laney was sitting across from me again, her expression thoughtful. I said, "Isn't there some — "

Laney slammed her glass down onto the table. "Stop it, Alex. You're always looking for the loophole. It's never been there. We never developed a stardrive, and the Arols won't let you go. You're never going to see those alien worlds you still dream about. You've experienced more than most humans ever have in space — be thankful for that, and give up the rest."

"How can I? All my life — "

"All your life you've had a dream. You have to let it go, now. I realize that's difficult. But I've had a dream, too. Of a normal life, of a life with you — an everyday life, with routine and a home and children, not one driven by this irrational dream."

"But if the Arols start to learn more about us — or if we still manage to develop our own stardrive — "

This time Laney put her glass down more gently, but the effect was even more chilling. "I'd hoped you would feel differently. I'm sorry, Alex. I thought the point here was that I love you, and want to be with you. I guess this was a bad idea." She left the patio and started walking down the beach.

*****

Before I knew Laney, I worked with Maarten Ellerson, the brilliant Dutch engineer. He was working on the idea of using hollowed-out asteroids as spacecraft, perhaps even making them into starships eventually. The Dutch, it has been said, are natural ecologists, since half their population lived on land reclaimed from the North Sea. Maintenance of canals and dikes and an understanding of ecological balance were part of their everyday lives.

Tragedy struck, though, on one of the first asteroids Maarten and I studied. We landed a small shuttle on the unnamed rock, looking for structural defects that could split the asteroid apart if acceleration were applied. We bounded lightly over its four-and-a-half billion year old surface. The asteroid's gravity was insubstantial. A good push, and you could find yourself orbiting it or even cast adrift.

Maarten pointed out the blue dot that was Earth in the dark infinity around us. "It's always beautiful to me," he said, "no matter how small it may seem from out here."

"I'm with you," I said. "Let's go ahead and place the drill."

Soon we had the portable drill set in position and stepped back some twenty meters. The device began its work, drilling down just a few meters into the surface of the asteroid. In a moment it would set off the tiniest of explosive charges that would send reverberations through the giant rock. Those reverberations would be recorded by sensors within the drill, revealing the internal structure of the asteroid, without damaging it or endangering us.

The charge didn't go off on schedule, though. Maarten pressed an override control on his spacesuit that was supposed to detonate the charge in case of malfunction, but that didn't work, either.

"I'll check it out," Maarten said.

"Is the charge deactivated?" I asked.

"Yes. I just deactivated it. Confirm." Maarten showed me the readout on his suit that indicated the charge was inert.

"Confirmed inert," I said, and watched as Maarten loped over to the drill and bent over it.

"Here's the problem," he said moments later. "The drill isn't fully extended. These chondrite asteroids are pretty solid. I'll just set it to a higher penetration level and start it up again." Maarten then backed away from the drill, but not far enough, and not in time. An explosive outburst, silent in the vacuum of space, broke the drill — and debris from the explosion shattered Maarten's faceplate and much of the right side of his face. Maarten's body was lifted off its feet, tumbling over and over in the asteroid's micro-gravity, spraying blood. The body had barely settled to the ground by the time I made it over to him.

It was too late, of course. I knew Maarten was dead before his body struck the ground. I realized immediately what had happened — the drill had struck a pocket of ice and vapor beneath the asteroid's surface. Such pockets were often the burned-out nucleus of a comet that had struck the asteroid and buried itself beneath the surface. When the drill hit it, the gases and ice particles would have been released all at once, with a tremendous explosive effect. That explosion also set off the charge within the drill.

I stared down at the mangled features of my friend for a long time, tears flowing freely. This wasn't how things were supposed to happen. It was all supposed to be an adventure. Yet in a single instant, a long life of exploration had ended abruptly.

I buried Maarten under a cairn of rocks. If no one else disturbs him, he'll rest there for all eternity. Since then, my dreams have been tempered with a sense of caution — and of loss. I knew then that however much I might accomplish, I would probably die with some of those dreams unfulfilled.

But not all of them. Soon, with Dutch backing, I captained a mission to Saturn from an asteroidal base. That's when I took my unauthorized flight through the planet's rings. They hated it in Amsterdam, but the rest of the world cheered. I've always regretted that I was so close to that planet without having any idea life existed there, life even more intelligent than that found at Jupiter.

The next year, I arrived at Callisto Base to pilot the first missions into Jupiter's atmosphere, to understand the beings humans had discovered there.

The very first time I met Laney, I thought I might fall in love with her.

She was a biologist, second in command at the base, and commander of the exploratory missions. I first noticed her eyes as we shook hands. They seemed to take me in at a single glance, to understand everything there was to know about me. Thankfully, she seemed to approve of what she saw. "Glad to meet you, Captain Barron. I'm Elaine Shackleton. I've heard a lot about you."

"Please — I'm Alex."

"Great. Then I'm Laney."

"I hope you've only heard the good things about me."

Her smile was wide and radiant, with a hint of mischievousness. "I'll find out if everyone's been telling the truth. You ready for a test run?"

I was taken aback. "Uh — sure. Where?"

"Oh, nowhere in particular. Just a little jaunt."

That "little jaunt" turned out to be a harrowing push-the-envelope flight in a small shuttlecraft just above Callisto's cratered, gray surface, with Laney showing me her favorite geological features — at about six hundred KPH, and seven meters off the deck. Callisto's surface was laced with ridges and cracks — the result of meteor impacts or cracks in its icy crust, which was nearly a hundred kilometers thick. After about fifteen minutes of the tour of the moon, Laney said, "I'm being unfair," and smiled as she punched the buttons that handed control of the craft over to my co-pilot's position. "I've flown over these same features so many times, I know them by heart. Let's see what you can do, now."

As intimidated as this unexpected challenge — and Laney's skill — had made me at first, I liked this woman so much I couldn't be offended. I managed a no-doubt goofy grin and took the controls. "Hold on," I said, then took the shuttle into a steep climb and arced it over toward Callisto's northern hemisphere and its largest surface feature, a circular basin three thousand kilometers across called Valhalla.

Within ten minutes I had tilted the shuttle on its side and was flying it in a circle around the edge of that basin — a much more difficult maneuver than if we were in an atmosphere, in a winged craft. I kept only about ten meters from the basin walls as I took us lower and lower, the circle ever-tightening as we crew closer to the bottom. As I forced us into smaller, lower circuits, centrifugal force pressed us into our seats.

Finally I programmed an auto-sequence into the shuttle's propulsion system, and activated it. The craft twisted around toward the center of the basin, then shot straight up, accelerating so powerfully that Laney and I blacked out.

When I revived, I checked all systems — we were flying free, away from Callisto and any of the usual space lanes Callisto Base had established. Just as I had intended. Then I looked over at Laney, who had apparently awakened first. "Well," she said, "you've got the job — if you didn't kill us back there, you'll be pretty safe on any mission I can dream up."

Our "little jaunt" was the talk of Callisto Base that night, as a dozen of us sat around the base's commons drinking contraband bourbon someone had broken out for the occasion. But as the others spoke of vectors and fuel consumption rates, Laney and I traded smiles. There were still eight or nine people in the commons as Laney and I slipped away to her quarters to make love. She was as adventurous a lover as she was a pilot, and quite agile in Callisto's low gravity, just over a tenth of a G.

We began our first mission into Jupiter's clouds about a month later.

I've never believed in God; but I believe in Creation. It never fails to astonish. The discovery of life swimming in its atmosphere — the largest life forms in the solar system, dwarfing even Earth's blue whales or the long-dead dinosaurs — had captured the entire system's imagination.

As we hurtled through the giant planet's clouds of hydrogen and helium, our sensors strained to detect the electrical impulses the great beasts, some half a kilometer in length, used as their language. It was a difficult task to obtain a clear signal against the static Jupiter's own magnetic field generated. The "experts" (to use the term loosely) believed their language was even more complex than that of Earth's whales. Although we found evidence that they used language to sound warnings or make course changes in a herd, much of what they sounded had no practical meaning we could discern. Laney and others believed much of their meaning was cultural or intellectual. After all, they were in much the same position as Earth's whales — without manipulative organs or a way to create fire, they could not become a technological species. Such intelligences must find outlets somewhere, and what better ones than music or philosophy?

Deciphering that language fully, not to mention attempting to understand the culture of beings the size of houses who lived neither on land nor in seas would be the work of a lifetime. Somebody else's lifetime, not mine. I was merely a willing witness, content to remain in awe of the patient mental processes of the creatures who lived in Jupiter's skies.

The day those missions ended, Laney and I shared a drink in the commons at Callisto Base. I asked her, "What's next for you?"

"I don't know. I'm being considered to head the stardrive research group on Earth, but the funding may not be there."

I stared into my drink. "And what about me?"

Laney took both my hands into hers. "I'd like to be wherever you are. We share the same dream. I know that."

I nodded. "I'll wait with you — to see what happens with that position on Earth. I'll find a way for us to work together — we can go to the stars together."

I was impatient for the stardrive breakthrough. It hadn't come, and didn't seem to be on the horizon. The U.N. Space Council was about to cut funding for star travel research. Something had to be done quickly, to convince them it was vital to proceed, using cold sleep or whatever other methods might be necessary.

And I did find a way to help. My exploits had made me somewhat of a cult figure for a romance-hungry populace; I was willing to use that notoriety shamelessly. I had to return to Earth quickly, but without letting on I was coming — in the weeks my journey from Callisto Base would take, too much support against me might be mustered.

I remember: the return in secret to the water world that had so sparked my imagination; the surprise appearance as spacer spokesman before the U.N. General Assembly; the subsequent approval of funding to continue the stardrive research. It was an act of desperation, but it was worth it. Laney found herself head of the stardrive project.

But that project didn't need me. I was a working spacer, not a theorist. And I realized I wasn't ready to become an Earther, a flatlander full-time. I wanted to keep working in space. But I kept thinking of Laney.

Then the Arols came, and everything changed. Laney was part of the contact team, and I was shut out.

When I took that vacation in the Bahamas, I spent half my days wondering whether I should try to contact her. Then she tapped me on the shoulder as I walked down that beach. In my cabin, when we began to argue and Laney started back down the beach, naturally I ran after her. I'm not a total fool. We were married two weeks later.

*****

I looked at Laney's profile, her features barely visible in starlight and the glow from a crescent moon. She was more beautiful to me now than ever. "Chilly out here in this field," she said, looking into the clear skies.

I bent closer to the video monitor that received its picture from the portable telescope we had set up in the broad field behind our Florida beach-front home. "I like the cold," I said. "I like being outdoors. It still seems like a new experience to me."

The sun, unnaturally bright — the landscape frighteningly flat — eyes closed against the uncomfortably empty sky above.

"Can't you see the ship yet?" Laney asked. "Maybe the kids had the right idea, letting the A.I show it to them on the cube."

"There it is! Just barely. This isn't the optimum instrument for this, you know."

Laney looked. "It's still magnificent." The Tsiolkovsky II was a glorious sliver of light in the center of the monitor.

"Look quickly. It'll only be visible a moment before it goes out of frame. I can't be sure I'll be able to follow it. We need to buy a newer 'scope, one that tracks on its own."

"Oh, shush. It's still magical enough, isn't it? A pretty good payoff for eight years of work. It didn't take as long as we thought."

"Those years have passed quickly," I said. I looked toward the heavens. "I envy the starfarers so much."

"They have good reason to envy you. You were the father of all this. And you'll be here to find out what they've discovered."

"We'll be here. That's the important part."

Laney and I fought again after that day in the Bahamas — but there was never any question that we wouldn't be staying together to continue our battles. The Earth, after all, really is still an alien world to me. The Sistine Chapel and the Great Wall must surely be as wondrous as any alien artifacts.

Still, it's tough to stand out beneath the night sky and not look upward and wonder. The Arols are alien enough, but still almost disappointingly humanoid. What other beings are hidden out there on unseen worlds circling the stars? What physical laws have they discovered that we have not? What insights about life and death and love and God? What do they look like? Are the cat and lizard people and tentacled monstrosities of science fiction too bound to human ideas of biological development? Will we discover whole new categories of life when we find it out there — life not mammalian, nor reptilian, nor insectile, nor any other Earth type, but something utterly new and unanticipated?

I still wonder about such things, but the answers, if any, must still wait decades to be revealed. They may never be revealed, at least not during my lifetime. So much depends upon the Arols.

The Tsiolkovsky II's burn started. Laney and I looked upward — the ship's flare could now be seen with the naked eye. Even when its initial burn ended, it would still be visible to our 'scope, an ever-fainter star, a beacon of hope.

I'd given up on finding my loophole. I was luckier than many, however. I had Laney, and two beautiful daughters, Ruth and Tess. I had seen magnificence most humans only dreamed of and if I wanted more, that only meant that humanity could never rest until all the universe's secrets had been revealed. We could never be satisfied. I'd discovered my share. I realized that even if the Arols came up with a stardrive I could use tomorrow, it was time for others to take over.

I packed the telescope away and Laney and I ran down to the ocean and splashed each other in the surf, laughing and running like children.

After a while, exhausted, we left the water and collapsed onto the sand, as if we were new life that had just crawled up from the sea.

THE HUMAN EQUATIONS

Here's the first story of three in this volume featuring Leo Bakri —
someone I never thought would become a series character when I created him
for *The Human Equations*.

This is a post-9/11 story, in which I wondered how far we could take
"zero-tolerance" attitudes.

———————

As many times as I'd been called upon to banish Volatile people to
Earth, few of them had ever attacked me.

The final time it happened was within the New Lancaster Habitat,
home to 10,000 New Order Mennonites, known as the "Habitat of the Gentle
People." Moments after I arrived at the farm of Bishop Anna Troyer and her
son, Samuel, I knew it contained at least one exception.

As I stepped onto the porch, I couldn't help thinking that the Troyer
home looked like something out of history: wooden structure, metal gutters,
the porch sporting a swing and rocking chairs. An even more primitive-
looking building, the barn, stood in the rear. Between them was an electric
car, and a larger vehicle that probably harvested the crops. In fields both adjacent to the Troyer home and directly overhead, I could see people working in
the sprawling fields scattered throughout the habitat.

The heat and humidity of the habitat's interior washed over me. It was
only mid-morning and already conditions here were oppressive; why would
people work in those fields all day? I wished I could've come about a week
later when the habitat was due to turn colder. It was a practical measure; the
apple, cherry, and pear trees needed that cold snap to blossom.

I knocked on the flimsy-looking door, which was a thin frame of
wood surrounding a fine metal mesh. Out of the shadows within the house,
two figures resolved themselves. Bishop Troyer was dressed in a gray one-
piece dress beneath an apron of the same color, and wore her snow-white hair
up, topped with a finely pleated white hat. I knew she was only middle-aged,
about sixty, but her deeply lined face made her look decades older. Being a
Mennonite, I thought, must be a rough life. I knew it could even be deadly.
Bishop Troyer's husband Amos had died eight years earlier when a grain har-

vester rolled over on him — not an uncommon fate for farmers here, apparently.

Samuel was twenty, broad-shouldered, and with skin burnished by countless hours beneath reflected sunlight. He was wearing a farmer's overalls and thick-soled boots.

Bishop Troyer didn't speak, just glared at me, but she still opened the door — Congregationalist courtesy, no doubt. I stepped inside, grateful for the respite from the heat. "I'm Triage Officer Leo Bakri. I'm here to carry out the Order of Banishment on Samuel Troyer."

The only thing that saved me was that although Samuel was big, he wasn't a trained fighter, and that my New Human reflexes are faster than those of most Volatiles. His right fist swung at my face, and I grabbed it with my right hand and twisted sharply, measuring my force so I wouldn't break his wrist. Samuel yelped and sank to one knee. I placed my hand on the butt of my stunner but didn't draw it.

Bishop Troyer went to her son's side and held his shoulders. I wondered if she was trying to comfort or restrain her son.

I felt the chill of perspiration drying on my forehead. The house wasn't climate-controlled, but it was cooler than the habitat's current outdoor setting. Too much like a "natural" environment, too uncontrolled, I thought. Why should any environment be uncomfortable for the Humans living in it?

Bishop Troyer said, "You realize that sending Samuel down there is a certain death sentence?"

I said, "You know the seriousness of Samuel's crime."

"I still have trouble believing that Samuel would — "

"Attack someone the way he just attacked me?"

Samuel looked up at me. "You're taking me away from my mom, you bastard!"

"Samuel!" Bishop Troyer said. "Even in such a time, you'll not use that kind of language."

"Mom, he's taking my life away."

I said, "Samuel, you know the law. There are no appeals."

Bishop Troyer said, "Triage Officer Bakri, you must understand my son doesn't want to leave his home."

In my heart of hearts, I didn't think his home was anything to fight for. The many shelves and a mantle above the fireplace (now there was a danger!) here in the living room were crowded with, I believed the term was, "knick-knacks." They included small stylized figurines with vaguely Human form, tiny woven baskets of an unknown (at least to me) significance, and flat, unmoving pictures of loved ones. The paintings on the walls seemed to be originals by talented but untrained artists. The comp in one corner was a bulky console-and-monitor combination.

Samuel Troyer said, "You didn't prove anything — "

I told him, "We have cubes. They show you inside a shop within the Shosha Habitat, assaulting its manager, Saburo Endo."

Bishop Troyer stood. She held her hand out to Samuel, who took his place beside her and said, "That's not evidence to us. My people don't use that kind of technology."

"With all respect to your beliefs, the Shosha authorities do make decisions based upon that technology. We also have nearly a half-dozen witnesses to the assault against Mr. Endo. You know the penalty for traveling to another habitat to commit violence."

Samuel Troyer tilted his head and squeezed his eyes shut. "I didn't go there to commit violence." Then he looked me right in the eye. "I just wanted to see what it was like somewhere you don't have to get up in the middle of the night to milk cows. Or spend half your days just growing food. Where you have time to read and to think — "

Bishop Troyer shook her head. "It looks as if you've spent too much time thinking already, and it's allowed ungodly ideas to get into your head. I never should've agreed to that trip. You're too young. You don't understand why our way of life is so important to us."

Samuel's voice held a bitterness I guessed he'd been nurturing for some time. "You always said these places were so evil. I wanted to decide for myself. I always expected to come back here. And I did. I wanted to find a way to make a different kind of life for myself here, with you."

I said, "You knew you were here only on probation, awaiting your sentence."

"On something that wasn't a crime. I just wanted something nice for my mother."

"A gold necklace worth six months' pay on Shosha."

Bishop Troyer said, "My son had never been to another habitat. He had no concept of a market economy."

"You should have taught him, then. To let a Volatile — "

"I am so sick of hearing Samuel referred to by that term. I suppose you're what they call a New Human?"

"I am." I allowed a little pride to come through in my tone of voice. Nothing wrong with faster reflexes, added strength, or more immunity to disease. Not to mention the moral improvements. Less prone to violence. More inclined to find peaceful solutions. "I'm from Newton Habitat." Customarily, Banishment Orders were carried out by Triage Officers from habitats other than those involved in the original crime. The Earth-circling habitats have two common rules — live as you wish, but anyone can leave whenever they want. And anyone who commits the slightest physical assault is immediately banished.

Samuel shook his head. "Great. Not just a New Human, but a scientist. You think you're better than I am."

I shifted my weight from one foot to another. No one seemed likely to offer me a seat. And I wasn't sure I'd accept it — the Troyers' living room chairs were wooden, some upholstered with actual cloth, everything apparently hand-crafted. I supposed that was fine if you liked that kind of thing, but it all seemed unnatural and wasteful of time and resources to me. "Statistics show a Volatile is more likely to act inappropriately. A point you helped prove on Shosha."

Samuel wiggled his fingers in front of my face. "They were so upset that these hands touched their precious property."

"In Shosha, it's called stealing."

"And the shopkeeper —

"— Mr. Endo — "

"— was rude. He yelled at me in front of all those people in the market square. And he grabbed my arm so hard it hurt."

"You wouldn't let go of the necklace."

Samuel shook his head. "It was mine. I'd picked it up. I tried to tell them I'd send them something in trade later."

"That's when the real crime happened. When you struck Mr. Endo."

"He wouldn't let go of my arm. He started it."

I said, "And I'm finishing it. Get your things."

Samuel pointed to one of the upholstered chairs. "There's my bag." His shoulders slumped, as if having prepared the bag also meant acknowledging his crime. He picked the bag up and stood passively, his attention focused on his mother.

I told him, "You can see that I'm accustomed to dealing with Volatiles. If you try to assault me or anyone else again, I'm stunning you and carrying you to the port. If you give me your word you won't be violent, I'll let your mother come along."

Bishop Troyer folded her hands in front of her. "Thank you, Triage Officer." She looked meaningfully at her son. "We may be plain unaltered Humans, but we won't be any trouble."

I said, "My car's waiting."

*****

I insisted that both Bishop Troyer and Samuel ride in the rear of my borrowed police cruiser. The car mostly drove itself, which let me keep an eye on them on a heads-up vid display.

As we drove off her property, Bishop Troyer said, "All this for a trinket I wouldn't have wanted anyway."

Samuel said, "The gold was from what you call the good Earth. I know you miss it there, even if you never want to go back. The shopkeeper said it was hand-crafted, not replicated."

I said, "They just say that, Samuel. That's a typical ploy to get a little extra money out of a tourist."

Samuel's mouth gaped open. "He'd lie?"

"Plenty of shopkeepers in plenty of habitats will do the same thing."

Bishop Troyer said, "It's one reason we chose a different path in this place."

New Lancaster Habitat was a typical four-kilometer-long cylinder, its homes mostly single-family dwellings scattered across a broad landscape of furrowed fields. Most Human colonists brought workbots, nanotech, and grav pallets, along with virtualities and news nets. They desired the conveniences of Earthly existence even while they sought more living space or the opportunity to form a unique societal structure.

Not here. Workers harvested timothy and clover in the countless fields that curved upward and met two kilometers overhead. I didn't understand the pull of such an existence. The repetitive toil, the eternal cycle of artificially-generated seasons with the rituals of planting and harvesting, and all for what?

I supposed that was why we have dozens of habitats circling the home world. Live as you want, without anyone abridging your freedoms.

But that was just what Samuel Troyer had tried to do to Mr. Endo in Shosha.

I said, "If Samuel had struck someone here in New Lancaster, it would've been a purely internal matter. But it's gone inter-habitat. It's the equivalent of a diplomatic incident on Earth."

Samuel sat with his hands in his lap, as if waiting for his mother and me to settle this between ourselves. I had to wonder if the anger he'd shown just moments ago had been only momentarily suppressed.

Bishop Troyer asked, "Can't you give Samuel some leniency? He's never been in trouble before."

"Could I suggest you render unto Caesar that which is — "

"That is an inappropriate context for that reference, Triage Officer. And you will not use my religious beliefs as a pretext for taking my son from me."

I took a deep breath. "I apologize."

Samuel rolled his eyes at that, which I pointed out to Bishop Troyer. "You see his attitude? Haven't you glimpsed that before?"

Bishop Troyer cast a hard look at her son. "Only...aimed at me."

"With all respect," I said, "Perhaps Samuel found it all too easy in Shosha, a place where no one knew him, that he could intimidate anyone who challenged him as he committed his mischief. Add to that, not realizing his actions were being recorded in holographic vid and immersion sound."

Samuel said, "Perhaps you should take me away. I might finally find respect down there on Earth."

Bishop Troyer said, "Don't even pretend to feel that way. I'm still your mother, I'll always care for you the way no one else can."

I said, "You can still care about your son, Bishop Troyer. He just can't continue to live here."

Bishop Troyer turned a stern visage toward the vid input. "We're talking about a 20 year old boy who committed an inadvertent theft, and who struck a shopkeeper. Meanwhile, we don't seem concerned that we're about to send Samuel down to a planet where some countries still mandate the death penalty for non-violent crimes. The PacFed doesn't believe you have a soul, Triage Officer, or even that Samuel or I do, and it wouldn't be illegal to kill us for no reason. The Eastern Sword chops the hands off of thieves. Do you need more examples?"

I said, "A condition of establishing Human habitats in Earth orbit was that we could only ship back malcontents or criminals if a government agreed to take responsibility for them. That makes it difficult for us, but if Samuel doesn't go to Earth, that would mean someone who committed violence wouldn't be dealt with. Our entire system will fall apart, in every habitat. Samuel will leave. But he goes somewhere he's wanted."

"What kind of place will have me? What kind of people can I live near?"

I said, "Most of the world falls into two major categories, culturally."

Samuel frowned. "Yes, Euro-American and Afro-Asian. I've been to college, thank you."

"Your culture here most closely resembles Euro-American. I've gotten you a good job on the English Strait. Reclamation duty. They're desperate for manpower there."

Samuel asked, "Manpower? What's that?"

"People who perform physical labor, or sometimes skilled tasks."

"Why would anyone perform physical labor back on Earth?"

"Some societies there also reject nanotech, just as your own does."

"What if I refused to work? What could they do to me?"

"You wouldn't get paid. You wouldn't be able to buy food or clothes or shelter."

"Oh, I see, these are places like Shosha."

"Much worse than Shosha. Hard work, very little pay. Hard to get ahead. Harder still to save for old age."

"They don't even take care of old people?"

"You have to save enough so you can get by when you're too old to work."

We'd arrived at the habitat's southern cap. I flashed my Triage Services shield at the nearest lift, asking the civilians gathered there to take the next one. I didn't think Samuel would become violent again, but I wanted to keep things simple.

Aboard the lift, we all grabbed handrails as the habitat's floor, and the pseudo-gravity of its rotation, fell away. Looking across the four-kilometer distance to the northern cap, I saw people who had donned wings and were flying along the cylinder's center. "That surprises me," I muttered, and when Samuel tilted his head in a questioning look I pointed out the fliers.

"It's simple tech," Samuel said. "As natural as the flight of birds."

Then it was off the lift, in zero-G conditions now, and into the passenger waiting area. Both Bishop Troyer and Samuel glided awkwardly through the broad tube that led from the revolving cylinder of New Lancaster to its stationary hub. I'd made sure we arrived only minutes before departure; I didn't want to draw this out. I'd only allowed Bishop Troyer to come along because I thought her presence would help me deal with Samuel until I got him aboard the shuttle.

We reached the broad waiting area. About three dozen other passengers were also waiting to board the shuttle down to Earth. I'm sure my sigh of relief was audible. Gone were the organic smells and too-warm, too-moist air that had assaulted me when I first entered New Lancaster proper. I marveled at the small comforts I found in filtered air, smooth white surfaces, and decorative cube images of planets and galaxies that were the same in any such chamber.

Another flash of the shield, this time toward a customs officer. He said, "Don't worry, Triage Officer, we'll get you seated first, in just a moment.

As we all moved to one side and grabbed handrails, I sneaked a glance at Bishop Troyer. Her mouth had tightened into a narrow line that emphasized the wrinkles in her face. I'd seen similar expressions before, on dozens of frustrated parents' faces — she was coming to grips with the reality that she was about to lose Samuel. She couldn't prevent me physically from taking him, and they'd had no legal options or I wouldn't have arrived at their doorstep. "I know this is difficult," I said, "But look at the broader view — "

Bishop Troyer said, "I don't have a broader view. I only know I'm losing my son."

Samuel was grinning. "Let him spin his fairy tales, Mom."

Bishop Troyer's lips pursed and she looked at me. "Have your say."

"Human history, from the 19th Century onward. Conflicts between empires give way to the superpowers, whose disputes dominate the 20th Century. Some of those disputes involve intermediaries, often on the Asian continent. But after two global conflicts, wars became localized or internal. The world's countries were learning to live in peace. But in the very first year of this century, Humanity sees war waged by individuals."

Bishop Troyer lowered her gaze. "We're a sinful race."

"This is where it starts. With a simple assault, and the most basic disrespect for another person."

Bishop Troyer said, "You spout your theories of history and how Human society evolves as if they're as certain as the laws of physics you worship."

I said, "That's a good analogy. The laws of physics have been called the 'cold equations.' My job is to make sure legal consequences approach that same certainty."

"Then you, Mr. Bakri, are even colder than the laws of physics. Perhaps you embody the human equations. And if I refuse to let Samuel go?"

"I can take you into custody, too."

Samuel said to me, "I'll go to Earth."

Bishop Troyer said, "Samuel, no!"

"Mom, what kind of choice do I have? I'm young, I can adapt."

Like you adapted on Shosha? I thought, but wasn't about to say aloud.

Bishop Troyer asked her son, "Do you know the danger's you'll face there?"

Samuel said, "Radiation. Marauders. Leftover nanoweapons."

"We have to find you something somewhere else."

I said, "Most countries aren't interested in taking a Volatile. They don't want our — "

"Castoffs? Rejects?"

"I believe you're both good people. It's just that Samuel did something that can't be tolerated in this community."

Bishop Troyer offered me a sad smile. "I have my own beliefs about what can be tolerated and what cannot. As does everyone who has received our undeserved gift — God's love. We reciprocate that gift by building a community filled with Christ's attributes. Forgiveness is one of those attributes."

I didn't have anything to say to that.

"Don't worry," Bishop Troyer said. "I'm not a proselytizer. I'm willing to speak in the limited terms of everyday life. Did it ever occur to you that maybe Samuel thought he was in the right?"

"You've seen the vid?"

"I have. I don't approve of what he did, but I don't believe it's worth banishment."

Both of Samuel's eyebrows raised and his jaw dropped open. "How did you see it?"

"The farm's comp. It has HabNet access."

"But you never allowed me to — "

"To fritter away your time on foolishness — games and useless knowledge disguised as revealed truths or wisdom? No, I never did. But this is different. I had to see for myself what happened."

I kept quiet. I thought letting this little drama play out might be the best thing for me.

Samuel said, "You had no right — "

"I have every right to know about my son's actions. It was foolish to let you go there. I can only ask the Lord's forgiveness. If only your father had lived — "

Samuel wagged his finger before his mother's face. "It always comes back to that, doesn't it? The sacred Amos Troyer, who could do no wrong — "

Bishop Troyer knocked Samuel's hand aside, and by his reaction, you would've thought she'd slapped him full in the face. "You will respect your father."

Samuel recovered quickly, and his features hardened into an expression that belied his youth. "I've always respected my father. It's your attitude toward him that wears me down."

Bishop Troyer extended her hand toward Samuel's face. He flinched, then seemed to realize his mother's touch would be gentle this time. Anna Troyer caressed her son's face. "I'll always love you despite how you treat me."

Samuel said, "I know, Mom. It's just...I have to make my own decisions now."

The customs officer caught my eye and waved me toward the embarkation sleeve. I told Bishop Troyer, "I have to accompany Samuel down to the surface."

Bishop Troyer told me, "My son didn't understand."

"We don't care whether he understood. We care only that he not repeat his actions, whether in Shosha or here in New Lancaster."

"He wouldn't have. I'd have made sure of it."

"He's a Volatile. We couldn't be sure. Now we will be."

Mother and son embraced, held on tight, cried. I started to touch Bishop Troyer on her shoulder but couldn't bring myself to. I coughed softly. The Troyers took the hint and said their final goodbyes. Bishop Troyer told me, "I'll pray for him. And for you, and those who create our laws."

I thought it only appropriate to say, "Thank you." Then Samuel and I left. I didn't dare look back at the grieving mother.

*****

Samuel sat next to me quietly during the entire half-hour trip. I wondered how many of the other passengers might also be Volatiles, though I didn't recognize any Triage Officers from other habitats.

We'd be landing in the desert linking the sloping plain that was once England's Shakespeare Cliff to the ruins of the French village of Sangatte. It was only during the shuttle's final approach that Samuel said, "Tell my mother everything will be all right. Even if it won't."

This Volatile's concern for his mother stole at my heart in a way I hadn't anticipated. I could almost forgive Samuel for attacking me back in the New Lancaster Habitat.

Almost. I didn't respond to his request, and Samuel didn't make it again.

The shuttle settled to the barren ground and Samuel and I followed the other passengers, about six or seven, who were getting off.

Bright light and blowing dust made me squeeze my eyes to slits as I followed Samuel out of the shuttle and stepped onto dusty ground. Close to the horizon, I saw the reclamation facility that fought the losing battle to reclaim this strait as fertile ground. Nanotech conflicts had left the land full of unwanted surprises, from transformation mines to death-tech. The suggestion had already been made in some quarters to let it return to its "natural" state, to become the English Channel again. As if natural meant static, unchanging, safe.

A tall man in a crisp uniform and wearing a breathing mask walked up to us and introduced himself as StraitForce Lieutenant Phillipe Cassell. "I'll take the boy now," Cassell said, his voice stern and metallic through the mask.

"Where's my mask?" Samuel demanded.

"You'll get one when you earn one," Cassell said. He pulled Samuel toward a waiting personnel carrier. Samuel looked back at me and said, "Goodbye."

My mouth was dry and I choked back words. By the time I raised my hand to wave, it was to Samuel's retreating back.

That's when a sharp crack came from overhead and I was knocked to the ground. I lifted my head from the dust just in time to see the rear of the personnel carrier blasted away. Armed men and women were popping up from beneath the ground. They were aiming weapons and squeezing triggers, but I didn't hear discharges and didn't see flashes of light.

I got up and ran toward Samuel Troyer and Lieutenant Cassell, who were lying next to the carrier's wreckage. I pulled my stunner and got off a few shots, without hitting anyone.

Samuel pulled me down next to him, clearly glad to see a familiar face, even mine. He seemed unhurt; Cassell's chest and face were ruins. Before we could say anything to each other, Samuel slumped to the ground. Whether unconscious or dead, I didn't know.

A scuffling sound to my right, and I raised my weapon at a gunner advancing toward me.

Some New Human I was. The gunner was quicker and even though I still didn't hear a discharge or see a flash I slumped to the ground next to Samuel.

*****

I found out what happened when I woke up in the reclamation facility's hospital. A Channel Separatist raid on the reclamation facility had ended with nine raiders dead, but 52 workers killed and 142 others, including Samuel, suffering nano-infestation.

The Separatists had sprayed destructive nanotech over much of the facility. I was lucky; being a New Human gave me some resistance to such intruders, and my status as a Triage Officer meant I was one of the first attended to. Yes, I'm aware of the irony. The doctors flushed out my system successfully, and I was out of the hospital within hours.

Samuel, though, wasn't so lucky. The tiny disassemblers roamed through his bloodstream and throughout his nervous system, altering his body with an excruciating slowness.

I went to see him every few hours over a period of three days after the attack. Samuel's body was literally turning to dust. His feet crumbled away within hours of the infestation, and his legs were gone in a day. The nanotech made sure Samuel's skin closed around the parts of his body that remained, but did nothing to relieve his pain. "I'm bearing it," he told me through gritted teeth, "because I want to live." Once when I found him sobbing uncontrollably, he said, "I'm not crying for myself. It's my mother. I have to get better. I don't want her to know I'm suffering."

Doctors pumped him full of reconstruction nanotech and implanted temporary artificial organs as his intestines, liver, kidneys, heart, lungs, and other organs failed, then became dust.

Sixty-nine hours into his agony, doctors had given up on saving Samuel and were issuing frantic petitions to London and Paris for permission to euthanize him. The reply never came. He was, after all, only a Volatile.

The separatist attack told me no one was safe, and that it didn't matter who you were. Lieutenant Cassell had only been doing his duty. Samuel Troyer was a mixed-up young man who hadn't done anything that deserved a death sentence — something I'd realized in the final moments of Samuel's life.

All that remained of him was a head and an upper torso. He was breathing through artificial lungs and could still manage halting speech. Moments before he died, Samuel said he felt a comforting presence nearby, someone other than myself or the doctors. I knew he was a spiritual man, and I was glad that he'd received this vision in his final moments. But then Samuel's demeanor changed. His face contorted, and not from pain; his nerves couldn't transmit pain anymore. He forced one word out before he died: "Abandoned."

I couldn't speculate on what it was Samuel saw or heard, or who had abandoned him, though I had my own ideas.

*****

Within a day of Samuel's death I was standing on Bishop Troyer's porch on another sweltering morning, knocking on her door again. I considered it a mercy that she hadn't been allowed down to the Strait to see her son, because of the continuing separatist danger. I peered through the door's wire mesh, and saw a long wooden table set up in the living room, with plates and casserole dishes full of food spread across it.

The door opened halfway, and Bishop Troyer stood there, dressed in a white dress with a white cape. I'd expected her to look withered and worn, but she stood upright and sturdy. I wondered how long her newfound energy would last once the other mourners were gone. I wondered how long she might live.

The soft background conversations filtering through the doorway stopped one by one as guests noticed my presence.

"I know I'm probably not welcome here," I said.

Bishop Troyer's eyes seemed to perceive every wrong I'd ever perpetuated in my life, every broken promise, every petty insult. Every time I thought of myself as morally superior to a Volatile, because I was a New Human.

Never mind taking her only child to his undeserved death.

"Of course you're welcome here, Triage Officer."

"I'm not a Triage Officer any longer." At Bishop Troyer's questioning look, I said, "I've resigned. I won't be banishing any more Vol...any more citizens."

Bishop Troyer opened the door further. "Enter in the spirit of forgiveness."

I stepped inside, aware of all the eyes upon me. Mourners, most of whom would have known Samuel Troyer at his best as well as his worst. Bishop Troyer and I moved into one corner of the room and spoke quietly as other conversations rose again.

I told her, "I realized being a Triage Officer had only been my way of dealing with my own fears. I told myself others were responsible for them. Eliminate those others from my life, and I'd be secure. The fact that I operated with the habitats' laws on my side was only an excuse."

"And your new job?"

"Within a month, I'll be joining the Earth Alliance light cruiser *Solar Eagle* as chief security officer."

"Are you so eager to head out to the stars? Or are you leaving your past behind?"

"I don't think I'll know for a while."

Bishop Troyer looked thoughtful, not as haunted. "Then my son's death served some small purpose. Tell me how he died."

I hesitated, and Bishop Troyer said, "I'm sure he asked you to spare me the details. He always wanted to protect me."

I felt the corners of my mouth turn up just a little. "It was all he said to me on the way down to Earth. Tell you everything was all right, even if it wasn't."

"And as he was dying?"

"He didn't want you to know he was suffering."

"His suffering has ended, and he's with the Lord. You know you failed him."

I lowered my head. "Yes, I do."

I started at the touch of Bishop Troyer's fingers beneath my chin. "Then you mustn't fail me. I want to believe that the more he suffered, the more heroic he became."

"He did."

"Then don't give me the peaceful, sanitized version of his death."

So I told her, and she listened and didn't say anything, but her eyes closed tightly halfway through my description of Samuel's suffering and death. By the time I'd finished my tale she had one hand over her eyes and her chin was quivering. When she started to sob, her hand moved to cover her mouth, and she turned her back toward the friends and relatives who'd come to grieve with her.

Eventually Bishop Troyer composed herself. "I can't provide your forgiveness, Leo Bakri, and you won't find it out among the stars. It'll only be within your own heart. A lesson I've learned." Her mouth quivered, and she raised her hand to it again. I could hear her muffled voice. "Oh, Samuel, why was I so foolish?" Anna Troyer looked at me. "He promised he'd be a better, more respectful son. Just let him do this one thing, he said. It's all I'd ever wanted. That's why I let him go. Because of what I wanted."

She turned away from me then, and joined the other mourners. As I was leaving I paused in the doorway, aware that Bishop Troyer and I were embarking on a shared journey.

UNBOUND

Often, when I get an idea for a story, I try to imagine whether it would be a good fit for one of my many series characters; I like placing them in situations that might not have occurred to me in dreaming up a story specifically tailored to them. When I got the idea for *Unbound*, it occurred to me that Leo Bakri would be perfect to bring back — after all, he was about to join the military at the end of *The Human Equations*.

This is the only story I've published that takes place during the Great Human War, an event I've mentioned in other stories that take place later in my fictional timeline. I hope to document that conflict in more detail in later work.

One technical storytelling issue — it wasn't until much later that I realized that although Leo's first appearance in *The Human Equations* was told in first person, that *Unbound* presents his story in third person. Nothing wrong with that — I think each viewpoint is the proper one for each story. But I never used to believe it when other writers would claim they'd used a particular technique unconsciously. Now I know better.

"No other Galactic species is as unpredictable as Humanity. Their intense emotions lead them to unexpected heights of creativity, but also trap them within a subjective emotional state which prevents them from checking their basest urges."

— Omakuranek, excerpt from report to Arololularian Interspecies Relations Council, 2097.

As Leo Bakri stepped into the small passenger boat, it began rocking in the wake of a much larger freighter craft. The boat's pilot grabbed Leo's elbow to steady him. "Easy there, mate."

Despite his nervousness at what lay ahead, Leo smiled at his clumsiness. Imagine having to find your sea legs within a space habitat! He heard stifled laughter behind him and saw Marie Sovel holding her hand over her mouth. He reached up toward her. "Let's see if you do any better."

Marie took that hand and her fluid grace as she stepped into the rocking boat at just the right instant made him realize all the more why he loved her.

Marie Sovel was a stardrive tech aboard the Earth Alliance starcraft *Solar Eagle*. Leo was its chief security officer. They'd come to the New Queensland Torus to learn whether Leo would face charges of insubordination under fire. That judgment would come from the Earth Alliance's Strategic Planning Officer, Admiral Chen Ju. The very name made Leo's heart race. He rubbed his bare arms against a sudden chill from wind that rushed across the water's surface. *They've started calling this the Great Human War. It's barely started and I could be thrown out of the service. I couldn't bear that.*

The pilot glanced back and asked, "Alliance mission, is it?" Leo nodded and the boat eased into the channel. A spray of water from a pleasure craft gliding past splashed them all, and Leo was glad he and Marie had been told to wear standard ship's gear, pullover shirt and shorts, rather than anything formal, despite the seriousness of their meeting.

New Queensland was a donut-shaped habitat that circled a yellowish star, Radiance. It was one of the last outposts of Alliance authority in this region of Human space. The system had no planets Humans could colonize and no wealth of minerals or energy that couldn't be obtained more easily elsewhere. Its only value was its strategic position near Rebellion space.

The Alliance mission lay on a low ridge on the south side of the Middle River, where it rose upward before them.

"I've been aboard ship too long," Leo said, his voice hushed. "It's good to be in open spaces."

"To breathe moist air," Marie said, "to smell something other than shipboard scents — it's marvelous."

The Middle River flowed around the entire circle of the habitat, and was the basis for its commerce. Directly overhead, beyond the glare of the mirrors reflecting the sun's rays into living areas, beyond the non-rotating core where *Solar Eagle* was docked, the opposite side of the torus was nearly two kilometers away. Leo saw and heard the din and clatter of busy ports, the shouting of merchants in their markets, the laughter of children at play.

He squeezed Marie's hand. "This is the kind of life I hope you and I can have together someday." Marie looked at him and offered up a glorious smile. He told her, "I love it when you look at me like that."

Leo wouldn't have thought Marie's features could grow more luminous, but they did. She asked, "What do you see?"

Leo's gaze fell to the floor of the boat. Nothing in his past had prepared him for such a woman, for the possibility of sustained happiness. And just minutes from now, it might be snatched away. "I see everything that makes you precious to me. Affection. Trust. I think you find me...fun."

Marie hugged his arm and scooted her body against his. She glanced up at the boat pilot to make sure he wouldn't hear. "Don't forget that special hint of sexual adventures later on. I arranged to overnight here."

Leo face grew warm and he pulled Marie closer. "I'll love just being next to you. And not having to worry about anyone seeing us, or who's down the hall, or...I just hope we're still in the mood later."

Marie held him tight. "You didn't do anything wrong."

Leo looked upward along the torus's curve, spotted the Earth Alliance logo on the mission building's roof. "We'll see if Admiral Chen agrees."

The boat thumped against a small inlet at the base of a ridge. The Alliance mission at the top of that ridge was a long, squat building made of the same pre-stressed concrete which formed the torus.

"'Ere you go, sirs," the pilot said. "Enjoy your stay. Bikes are on the street for the takin'."

"Thanks," Leo said, and he and Marie climbed out of the boat — Leo with a sure step this time — and picked two bikes from several available. Marie swung a leg over and rode confidently up the gentle slope of the paved roadway that led to the mission. He admired the movement of her leg and thigh muscles as she pedaled.

Leo was shakier. "Been too long," he muttered, trying not to see the bemusement on Marie's face. Truth be told, he thought, I'm grateful to be the comic relief. I don't believe in the religionists' ideas of Heaven, but to see Marie's smile, to hear her laughter, and to know you initiated it, must be close to what they have in mind.

Marie's right. We've been shipbound too long. She's good for me. We've got to create something new, just for the two of us. Something solid, where you know there's more beneath your feet than metal or vacuum.

Will we have the chance?

Marie reached the crest of the hill and waited for Leo. They stowed their bikes in a rack outside the mission. Once inside, an ensign took them to Admiral Chen's office. She didn't look up as the ensign left them there, closing the door quietly behind him.

Admiral Chen fulfilled the image Leo had expected: the tight bun, the neat uniform, the dour expression. A small, angled desk served as computer library and comlink. The room had no windows, and no personal touches — no artwork on the walls, no cubes of loved ones. The chair and couch provided for guests looked comfortable, but the admiral sat on a stool behind the desk. Neither Leo nor Marie made a move toward them.

Admiral Chen told Leo and Marie, "Sit down. This won't be a formal hearing."

Leo went for the chair as Marie sat in the center of the couch. Best they don't appear a couple by sharing the couch, even if the admiral knew better.

Especially if she knew better, Leo thought. Throwing that fact in her face — not a good idea. He kept his hands folded in his lap, tried not to notice them becoming slick with perspiration. Knew to remain silent until Admiral Chen spoke to him directly.

The admiral said, "Lieutenant Commander Bakri."

"Yes, Ma'am."

"Let's establish a few things right away. Perhaps relevant to this proceeding, perhaps not. You're a New Human?"

Leo felt his face flush. "That's what some people call us, Admiral."

"Faster reflexes, stronger than the norm, not as likely to succumb to disease."

"That's correct."

"Better morally?"

Leo blinked and said, "I've made my share of mistakes, Ma'am."

Admiral Chen steepled her fingers. "And the incident as the Star Rebellion attacked Earth? Was that one of your mistakes?"

Marie would've died, Leo thought. But that doesn't matter to an Alliance admiral.

"Well, Lieutenant Commander?"

Leo felt the same rush of adrenaline pumping through him as when that Star Rebellion craft broke through *Solar Eagle*'s defenses and blasted its Alcubierre Module on the propulsion deck. Marie's station. I had to do it, Leo thought. Override the corridor lockdown sequence that would've trapped her in that compartment. She was the only one in it left alive. I found her unconscious, dragged her out, and canceled my override, much more quickly than "normal" Humans could have done.

Admiral Chen said, "You risked the *Solar Eagle* and its crew, didn't you?"

Leo said, "Admiral, I'm here without my advocate, and given the possibility of court martial proceedings — "

"This meeting is off the record, and could prevent a court martial."

Leo's lips pursed before he could help it. "I took actions that were risky, yes." But Marie is alive.

"If *Solar Eagle* had blown, it could have severely damaged the other two Alliance starcraft in the vicinity — *Eyes of Justice* and *Laika*. Couldn't it?"

"Admiral, Captain Hendrik on *Solar Eagle* wanted to recommend me for a commendation."

"His objection to this proceeding has been noted. If *Solar Eagle* had blown, those other two starcraft could have been damaged."

"Yes, Ma'am." So that's how it is, Leo thought. A quick glance toward Marie, and Leo saw that these proceedings were as difficult for her as for him; she sat on the couch with her hands folded so tightly the blood was pressed out of the tips of her fingers. Her crossed legs, foot gently rocking, and piercing gaze spoke of fear and fury.

Leo said, "Do what you want with me. But none of this was Marie's fault."

Despite himself, Leo flinched as Admiral Chen demonstrated some fury of her own. "I will decide what is fair," she said. "*Eyes of Justice* and *Solar Eagle* survived, and went on to crush the attack at Earth. A victory that might never have been, because of your willingness to risk your ship and two others."

Leo bowed his head. "I can't say you're wrong. But everything turned out for the best."

"What about next time, Lieutenant Commander? You may beat the more severe charges. But don't discount the lesser ones. Inappropriate relationship between officers in a wartime situation. Detriment to morale. Potential favoritism. You'll be drummed out of the force. Given the current popular climate, that's a record that'll make it tough to find civilian employment."

Marie looked at him. "Leo. Are you sure...?"

Leo told her, "Popular opinion works two ways. If we get our story out — "

Admiral Chen said, "Your story will be a casualty of war. It'll never get out."

"Admiral, you can't — "

"I can, and will. Your feelings for this woman, pleasant and comely though she may be, are dangerous."

Marie blurted out, "Split us up, then. Put us on different ships. Please don't court-martial him."

Admiral Chen said, "That's the easy solution. But I won't allow it."

Leo leaned forward in his chair. "Why?"

"We have an experiment in mind. A form of conditioning. Nanites make the smallest adjustment to the limbic system, which generates strong emotion. They inject drugs, just the right amount, into the pituitary. Tiny electrical discharges make additional adjustments. Soon you forget your feelings for Lieutenant Sovel, and the time you spent together."

Leo felt as if Admiral Chen's voice was receding into the distance, as if all of New Queensland Torus had faded away except for this room. All that existed were Marie, the woman he wanted to spend the rest of his life with, and Admiral Chen, who wanted to take his love away from him, literally. He muttered, "Why do this? Why can't we take the 'easy solution,' as you call it?"

"If this technique works, we'll also create troops who don't feel fear, and starcraft commanders without emotional ties to their crew."

Leo said, "I thought we were fighting to preserve freedom."

Admiral Chen folded her hands on her desk. "Millions have offered up their lives for that cause. This is certainly a lesser sacrifice. You and Lieutenant Sovel are competent officers and work well together. I'd like to prove our conditioning concept in a benign setting aboard *Solar Eagle*. If we are successful in unbinding your emotional ties for a while, we can experiment further on personnel aboard other starcraft constantly on the front lines."

Marie said, "What do you mean by 'for a while?'"

"The process is completely reversible. Think of what it means. Neither of you will be demoted. You can remain together, though neither of you will possess the feelings for one another you have now."

Marie looked at Leo with a hopeful expression. All Leo could hear was his own rhythmic breathing. "Sorry, Admiral," he said. "How do I know this process is everything you say it is? That it really can be reversed? That you really will reverse it when it's time?"

Admiral Chen place her hands flat on her desk and gave Leo a glare that he suspected could've annihilated a Rebellion starcraft. "You're questioning the word of an Alliance admiral?"

Leo shot his best imitation of that glare, inferior though it was, back at her. "No, Admiral, I'm questioning the information you've been given."

"If you doubt my information, you're doubting me. Don't you think I'd check it out?"

"If you're so certain this will work, why not just order us to undergo the procedure?"

Admiral Chen took a deep breath. "Even military discipline has its limits. To be allowed to test the procedure, we had to agree to use volunteers."

Some volunteers, Leo thought. Let doctors into your brain to play with your deepest, most personal memories, or face court-martial. "Sorry, Admiral. No deal."

Admiral Chen didn't respond at first to Leo's refusal of her offer, and Leo was determined he wasn't going to speak again until she did. Let her make the next move, he thought.

Admiral Chen said, "Lieutenant Commander Bakri, I've no choice but to schedule an immediate court-martial."

Leo said, "I understand, Admiral."

"I'm not sure you do. You won't be the only defendant. Lieutenant Sovel will join you."

Marie gasped, and the fear Leo saw in her face struck at his heart. He said, "She was a victim in all this — "

"But also a perpetrator," Admiral Chen said. "All the lesser charges apply to her, and all the penalties. I think you know which way a military court I convene will decide."

Marie's features stilled, and she looked at Leo with a determined expression as she addressed Admiral Chen. "Then that's how it'll be."

This is why I can't spend my life with anyone but Marie, Leo thought. I've never known anyone, within my family or among my closest friends, who would make such a sacrifice.

Which is why I can't let her do it.

Leo stood to give his decision, and as he spoke his consciousness narrowed again — he heard his voice grow louder over Marie's protests, felt his arm twisting from her desperate grasp, and watched her fall from his field of vision as he turned away from her and toward Admiral Chen.

It was as if he'd already lost her.

Security officers escorted Leo and Marie to a waiting area in a medlab next door to the Alliance mission and told them they'd have a few minutes alone before the procedure.

Leo held both his hands out toward Marie. She stepped into his embrace and they held one another without speaking for a time. Finally Leo said, "I'm sorry. But I couldn't let them charge you when you weren't at fault."

Marie took a step back and looked at Leo. Moisture glistened at the corners of her eyes. "It's not permanent. We'll be together after the war."

"If we both survive. If the admiral's telling the truth."

"It won't work, you know. Trying to make me stop loving you. We'll have that life together."

Leo took her hands in his. "You have to be right. It can't work. I know it can't."

Marie stepped into his arms again and kissed his cheek. "Then we don't have anything to worry about."

"It'll be our secret."

Another kiss then, on the lips, and longer. Then the techs arrived to escort them to separate exam rooms.

Leo's room was filled with polished metal surfaces, bright lights, and polite, professional doctors and technicians. Off with the uniform, a detailed physical, a quick injection, and the lead doctor pronounced himself done and dismissed the techs.

Leo rubbed his bare arm, though the injection had been painless. "So when will it take effect?"

The doctor flashed him a bland smile. "It should have already."

Leo started dressing. "I'm supposed to report back to *Solar Eagle* when I'm done here."

The doctor said, "Then go report."

Outside the medlab, Leo met Lieutenant Marie Sovel. They retrieved their bikes and headed back toward the dock. The boat pilot was waiting for them, and soon they were sailing on the Middle River toward the large passenger lift that would take them to the hub of the torus and the waiting *Solar Eagle*.

The boat trip was pleasant, though he sensed the trip toward the mission had been more enjoyable. But the more he tried to recall why, the farther away that memory receded; instead, images rose up of a day back on Earth when he was nine years old, memories of a rare north Georgia snowstorm and how its beauty had entranced him. Odd, he thought, as the boat continued down the Middle River. I haven't recalled that day in years.

He glanced over at Lieutenant Sovel. She sat with her legs crossed away from him, elbow on her arm rest, slender fingers beneath her chin, taking in their surroundings. She hadn't said a word since they'd boarded the boat. Not rude, just...aloof.

Leo turned his attention away from his colleague and toward his surroundings. Din and clatter of busy ports. Merchants shouting. Children laughing.

THE DAY THAT REVEALS

Another post-9/11 story, which looks at how religion, violence, or the threat of violence, and tolerance toward others' beliefs often intertwine.

I went to great pains to do the research to portray Islamic rituals in this story as accurately and respectfully as I could. My intent here was not to criticize any particular religion, but how some people interpret it and act upon that interpretation. Christians, for instance, who believe their co-religionists are only devoted to peace, should look up the history of the Crusades.

Later, when one tragedy after another befell Sadiq Salim, he comforted himself with thoughts from that last morning he spent with his wife Aasim, who was to deliver his son within a week.

As he entered her room, the midwife, a young veiled woman named Bahira Aban, was tending to her. Aasim's hand was rubbing her swollen belly and Bahira was handing her a glass of cool water and a damp washcloth to place upon her forehead. He worried that this first pregnancy was putting too much of a strain upon her.

For that reason, Sadiq made sure to keep his voice light-hearted, his expression optimistic as he asked, "And how are you feeling this morning, my darling?"

Aasim wiped perspiration from her forehead and returned Sadiq's smile with one that emerged from obvious discomfort. "I feel as I do every morning — as if I am a princess — your princess."

Sadiq's expression turned sly, teasing. "And to those outside our little habitat — who say our women live in a gilded cage, fancy and fluffy?"

"I'm content with the gild. I don't see any bars on our doors."

Sadiq placed his hand over Aasim's. She grasped it tightly. "You have to leave so early?"

Sadiq frowned. "An unpleasant task. But the Earth liaison's work is often such." He leaned over to kiss his wife's hand, to place his palm briefly on her belly. "I look forward to kissing my son, as well. I can hardly wait for the next week to pass. I'll be home as soon as I can."

As Sadiq turned to leave, he caught a glimpse of the midwife Bahira's eyes above her veil. The girl looked away, as was proper, but Sadiq couldn't place the emotion he saw there — concern for Aasim, perhaps, or anxiety over the coming birth.

Later, he would perceive it as guilt, or perhaps raw deceit.

*****

Once the detectives said it was safe, Sadiq Salim exited the darkness and safety of the police van. One step onto the rough gravel of the driveway, and he lifted a hand to shield his eyes from the sun's reflected rays. Part of him praised Allah silently, as his raised hand also kept him from glimpsing the half of this habitat — his world — that hung overhead.

He was grateful not to suffer the disorientation and blurred vision that greeted him whenever he first stepped outside, that feeling that he'd either taken a step into nothingness or that the upper half of his world was about to collapse onto the lower half. It was a constant, even though Sadiq had lived over half his life within this giant Earth-orbiting cylinder that was True Faith Habitat.

Sadiq fought to control his fury as he walked down that driveway toward the ramshackle home where officers had discovered the captives and the men who'd taken them. How dare these men commit such a crime?

As Sadiq made his way around to the rear of the abandoned home where the officers were holding their prisoners, his position shifted and the sun's rays reflecting from the giant mirrors at the habitat's hub shone on his neck and back. *Allah's spirit brings light to comfort and guide me,* Sadiq thought, *and heat which reflects my burning anger.*

The commander of the police team was Sadiq's brother-in-law, Amrullah Ahmad. Amrullah nodded at him, then indicated the prisoners, who were sitting on the ground with their hands bound behind them. Amrullah and the dozen officers with him were heavily armored and carrying energy rifles. Sadiq wondered if those weapons even had a non-lethal setting.

The prisoners squinted up at this new, unfamiliar face. Sadiq saw their frightened features harden into angry expressions and knew that despite his generous mustache, his otherwise unshaven face was an affront to them. Each man was in his forties, Sadiq noted, and each sported bruises and nasty cuts on his face. Several had blood caked on their cheeks and in their mustaches and beards. The police hadn't been gentle.

Good, Sadiq thought. No reason to have sympathy for this rabble. He looked down at them where they sat in the dirt in their filthy, tattered clothes. He told them, "I am Sadiq Salim, True Faith Habitat Liaison to Earth." He noticed the surprise on their faces; they undoubtedly hadn't expected a man in his mid-20's to have such an important position.

They don't know me, Sadiq thought. They don't know of my ambition, or my determination to preserve our way of life. "You men have brought shame to our world. And to our religion."

The man to his far left spit onto Sadiq's shoes. Amrullah was there in an instant and kicked the man in the face. The man toppled over, groaning and bleeding into the dirt from his mouth and nose.

"Anyone else care to comment?" Sadiq asked. No one did. "If those women are from another habitat, as I've been told, you'll be deported to Earth before the day is through."

Amrullah told Sadiq, "They're bringing the women out."

The officers stood aside respectfully as the women exited the building. All ten were dressed in long black robes, with scarves covering their heads. Sadiq's face grew warm with embarrassment as he saw most of the women had allowed their robes to fall open, revealing Western clothing underneath — bare necks, bare legs. They all looked frightened, and most had bruised faces.

Then two of the women, seeing their former captors, went to them and began kicking them, one shouting insults in Arabic: "Bastards!" "Dogs!" Sadiq couldn't help but grin at the sight, especially when all the other women joined in. Besides, it wasn't as if he or any of the police officers could possibly touch women they weren't related to, so he let the confrontation play out. He thought of the anger he would feel if Aasim had been mistreated as these women had been.

Once the women's anger was spent, and all four of the prisoners were even more bruised and bloody, Sadiq approached one of the women, the one who had first attacked the prisoners. She was short, with mousy brown hair, but penetrating brown eyes that revealed what seemed, to Sadiq, an odd inner peace.

"Salam alekum," he said. Peace be on you." He introduced himself and said, "May I ask your name?"

The woman replied, "We alekum salam." And on you be peace. "I am Hajna Tawil."

Sadiq's breath caught. Perhaps there was hope, perhaps this woman was native to the True Faith Habitat. "So you do speak Arabic!"

"I learned it in my childhood. My mother was originally from this habitat." She pulled on a necklace that hung down beneath her blouse. Sadiq's eyes were drawn to that movement, but he looked away from the inappropriate sight of this non-relative's naked neck, the hint, even, of cleavage.

He started as the woman touched his arm to get his attention. "It's all right," she said, "it won't hurt you," and held up the pendant dangling from the bracelet. A Star of David. "I'm from New Jerusalem now. I converted when I moved there. All these other women were born there. That creates a problem for you, doesn't it?"

Sadiq closed his eyes for an instant in silent prayer. "Enshallah," he said. If Allah wills. Not just Jews, but a Muslim who converted! When he opened his eyes, Hajna Tawil and all the other women were walking away from him, toward the safety of one of the police vans. The other officers would talk for weeks about the scandal they created as they doffed their robes and scarves on the way.

From overhead, Sadiq could feel the weight of his cylindrical world bearing down upon him.

*****

Sadiq didn't get to speak privately with Amrullah for a while after they arrived at the main police complex. His brother-in-law was kept busy processing the prisoners and arranging transport for the former captives back to New Jerusalem.

Sadiq used the comp in Amrullah's office to file a quick report with authorities back on Earth. At the call for the noon prayer, he kneeled toward Earth, and Mecca.

A couple of hours later, Amrullah entered his office, sat in his plush chair behind his wide desk, and asked Sadiq, "Those men — they'll likely be deported to Earth because those women were from another habitat?"

"These men smuggled women from another habitat into our world. They beat them and abused them sexually. Yes, they'll be deported."

Amrullah rubbed his beard. "These men may represent our future."

"If so, we have no future. Besides, I heard the stories of such men from our fathers' and grandfathers' time. They led our people into useless wars, the wars of jihad. I desire peace, the spiritual jihad."

"That desire is to be commended. But can we allow ourselves to become too weak?"

"By refusing to kidnap and abuse women?"

"By giving up our heritage. Were our grandfathers wrong to abandon the wars of jihad, in return for a safe haven?"

"When you marry, and have sons, you'll feel different."

"New Jerusalem will use this incident to open up two millennia of lamentation. Which our fathers established this habitat to escape."

Out of respect to his brother-in-law, Sadiq kept irritation out of his voice. Amrullah, after all, wasn't a diplomat. "New Jerusalem exists for the same reason. And you must understand, Amrullah, that it is possible for a Muslim to perform a wrong against a Jew. That is what happened here, and we must deal with it in a way that brings us honor."

Amrullah dismissed that idea with a casual wave of his hand. "You deal too much with outsiders. You see their side of things too easily. It's not healthy."

"Allowing men who kidnap and torture women to remain here is not healthy."

"A woman exists only to provide a man comfort. Your own wife is bearing you a son. Aren't you proud to receive that blessing from Allah?"

Sadiq tapped his finger against his chest. "I am proud, Amrullah, and rightly so. But I also want my son to be able to take a bride when he becomes a man. Just a generation ago, 100,000 people lived here. Now it's fewer than 40,000."

"Those who left were the unfaithful. It was Allah's will that they go."

"Is it Allah's will that we barely have enough people to sustain ourselves economically? That only about 15,000 of our population is female? My son may have to live alone, because too many young girls are leaving to live on other habitats, or even on Earth!"

"It should have never been allowed," Amrullah muttered.

"You know the provisions." Earth allowed an orbital habitat to maintain any culture it desired, as long as any citizen of that habitat could leave at any time.

Amrullah waved that concern away, too. "They should be forced to stay, anyway. Too much freedom's not good for a stable society. Look at your bride. She's content."

A smile tugged at the corners of Sadiq's mouth. "She seems to be." Unbidden, came thoughts of his most intimate moments with his wife. She's so beautiful, he thought, and that beauty is reserved for my eyes. Her touch, so tender....

Amrullah said, "The pregnancy, it goes well?"

"By all accounts."

"You're sticking with the midwife, aren't you?"

"Yes, of course. She's inexperienced, but she's the only one available. It goes with the shortage of women."

Amrullah said, "I feared you'd consider a male doctor."

Sadiq raised his eyebrows. "The Earth liaison take to the black market? And his brother-in-law a police commander? Not advisable." God is where I must find comfort now, Sadiq thought, not in continued argument. "Forgive me, Amrullah. I have much to think about. If I begin walking home now, I can reach the mosque down the street from me by the mid-afternoon prayer."

"That's the best thing to do. Get these foreign thoughts out of your mind. Think of God in all things."

I will think of God, Sadiq mused as he left the police complex. But those "foreign thoughts" will remain my burden.

*****

As Sadiq passed beneath the broad entrance arch of the mosque, he removed his shoes and placed them on the shelves provided for that purpose. Then he made his way to the men's washroom to perform the cleansing to remove sins and prepare for prayer. As he washed his right hand, then his left, Sadiq's thoughts were primarily of the day's events — the suspect spitting on his shoe, the faces of the abused women, the revelation that they were from another habitat.

As he gargled, and washed his face, the cold water focused his thoughts on the here and now, on the presence of God. By the time he'd washed his forearms, ears, and feet, all other concerns had faded. He entered the prayer room just as the call to prayer sounded: "There is no god but God, and Muhammad is the messenger of God...."

He gave no thought to anything but God until prayers were over and he exited the mosque to walk home. The sun was so bright, and Sadiq was so determined not to give himself up to blurry vision, that he started down the street squinting and shielding his eyes. That's why he never saw Amrullah until his brother-in-law grasped his arm so tightly he feared he was being assaulted. "You must hurry," Amrullah said. "It's Aasim. Your neighbor called. The birth has begun."

Sadiq said, "But it's not time."

"Allah sets the time, you fool. Therefore it is time."

"The midwife — "

"Nowhere to be found. Hurry!"

When they arrived at Sadiq's house, and Sadiq rushed into the women's area, the neighbor woman who'd called Amrullah wouldn't let Sadiq into the bedroom. It had all happened so quickly, she told him, the increasing pain, the screaming, Aasim saying her confession when she realized she wouldn't survive, the final throes, then drawing her last breath without giving birth.

Sadiq's body nearly doubled over from grief even as his consciousness tried, and failed, to recoil from the reality of Aasim's death. He stumbled into his home's courtyard and focused on his rapid breathing and on Amrullah's comforting arm around his shoulders. It was easier than embracing his anguish over his wife's suffering, or the realization that his son would never have a chance at life.

The midwife, it seemed, couldn't be found because she'd left True Faith Habitat that morning to travel to Shosha Habitat, to create a new life for herself.

Preparations for the funeral, with Amrullah's assistance, consumed all of Sadiq's time and consciousness for the next 24 hours. The neighbor woman volunteered to perform the ablution of Aasim's body, and to shroud her in the required layers of white cloth, and the veil. As that work proceeded, Sadiq contacted Earth Alliance military headquarters down in Brussels. He had to get word to his mother. We've often been at odds with one another in recent years, he thought, but we must set that aside now. And, to her credit, Mother always enjoyed Aasim's company, and honored her.

To Sadiq's amazement, he discovered that the medical craft she commanded, Galen, was due back in Earth System within a few days. The low-level bureaucrat he spoke with wouldn't give him more details, citing security considerations, but promised to get a message for Captain Salim to call Sadiq as soon as possible.

The next morning, Sadiq drew cold comfort from the prayers for the dead at the mosque, and the chanted confession as Aasim's body was carried to the cemetery.

That night, in his house, Sadiq sat alone, counting off the 99 names of God on his prayer beads. "Al-Malik, ar-Raheem, ar-Rahmaan." The sovereign lord, the merciful, the beneficent and compassionate.

I'd feared it would be my son who ended up alone, he thought, but this burden has fallen onto me instead. Truly God is great, but how much more wonderful to have a wife, a son, to share God's magnificence!

Sadiq continued counting beads: "Al-Mu'men, as-Salaam, al-Quddoos." The keeper of faith and giver of peace, the source of security, the holy one.

As he counted, strands of thought slipped into his consciousness, carrying the growing possibility that he'd been a fool to embrace the ideals of freedom and spiritual jihad.

Perhaps Amrullah is right, he thought, and society must embrace these old ways again.

*****

Sadiq pulled himself along a series of handholds within the True Faith Habitat's zero-G hub. He paused at an entryway and watched as passengers made their way through the embarkation tube from the just-arrived shuttle. Sadiq wished he could be as graceful in weightless conditions as many of those arriving seemed to be. Forever a groundling, he thought.

Then he saw his mother, Rabi Salim, and all the old anger and animosity from years past came rushing back.

There she is, Sadiq thought, wearing pants, and not wearing a veil. Her Earth Alliance uniform shouts that she has educated herself, that she holds down a job, that she speaks regularly with men who are not of her family. And she commands a starcraft. A woman!

His mother saw him now, and with that envied grace in weightlessness, she came to him and took his hands in hers. "Salam alekum," she said, and embraced him. "Sadiq, I'm so sorry," she whispered into his ear. "Aasim was such a joy, so caring and pious."

Sadiq felt a deep shame. My mother returns here for the first time in many months, and what are my first thoughts of her? Unworthy ones. This should be a time of healing. "Wa alaikum assalam, Mother. Let me take you home. We have much to talk about, and not just about Aasim."

*****

Sadiq sat with his mother in his home's library, awaiting the call he'd requested from Habitat Relations back on Earth. He found her presence in his home oddly comforting, despite her strange ways.

"But isn't that appropriate?" he thought. She is, after all, my mother, and therefore to be honored.

After a few moments, though, he couldn't sit any longer. Too much was riding on this call. Sadiq rose and paced the floor.

His mother sat calmly, hands folded on her lap. "Why do you want me here for this, son?" she asked.

Sadiq stopped pacing. He looked toward the blank wall screen where his contact's image would appear, then toward his mother. "I'd hoped you'd be supportive, even after all this time. Whatever you think of us, this is still your home. I'd have thought you'd want to preserve it."

"We've been through this. The Prophet encouraged women to learn."

"To learn how to heal others! How to farm for their families."

His mother said, "I do heal others. I may be a starcraft commander, but I'm still a doctor, as well. As for the Prophet, his youngest wife led an army after he died."

"One day, Mother, I believe you will be the death of me."

"Please, can we not talk of other things — especially at such a time?"

"I want to settle this before the envoy from New Jerusalem arrives this afternoon. Another complication in my life. And a moment of shame. I'm tired of shame. I want to make this a proud place again."

Rabi Salim looked down at her hands, and didn't say anything. My own mother, Sadiq thought. How can she be so frustrating? She was always adept at saying more with silence than most people could attempt with speech. He told her, "I have to attempt this. For Aasim's sake."

His mother looked up at him again. "For her sake, I'll be here with you. And I'll remain quiet."

Then the image Sadiq had expected appeared on the wall screen. A woman of Western descent, in her 50's, her uncovered hair just starting to turn gray. She smiled at Sadiq as if he were a family member and spoke in lightly accented Arabic. "This is Margaret Newell, Habitat Relations Liaison, calling from Brussels. How may I help you?"

From the corner of his eye, Sadiq was aware of his mother's presence. And aware that she would be examining him and how he dealt with this woman so much like herself. He said, "Liaison Newell, I'm proposing an exception to our habitat charter."

Liaison Newell's smile transformed into something more formal. "What sort of exception?"

"You're aware of the incident earlier this week in our habitat? The kidnappings and abuse?"

Liaison Newell looked as if she were trying to divine the nature of his soul right through the view screen. "I am."

Of course you are, Sadiq thought. Your so-called "news" media take any opportunity to criticize my habitat. He said, "We realize such incidents are symptoms of larger problems. We wish assistance in solving that larger problem."

He noticed that Liaison Newell's features grew rigid as she asked, "How may we help you?"

"We wish to be allowed to repeal one of the terms of our habitat charter. It's a rule that is destroying families by separating husbands from their wives, sometimes from their children."

"I see. And what is that rule?"

"Certainly you anticipate me. The rule which allows any resident of this habitat to leave at any time."

Sadiq saw that Liaison Newell's expression now was stone. She told him, "That's the one rule that makes the habitats possible."

Sadiq took a deep breath. "I'm sure you're aware how rapidly our population has fallen in recent years, despite our tradition of large families. Most of that is due to emigration."

"That's how people find the freedom to choose the life they wish within the habitats. That's the essence of the system."

"Our freedom on this habitat requires a balance of males and females, as it does anywhere."

Liaison Newell asked Sadiq, "Could I make a suggestion?"

Sadiq willed himself to remain calm. "That is the purpose of my call."

"Look at it as a practical matter. For your culture to survive, it has to be one which enough people want to live in. Part of your population problem is caused by the lack of medical care women receive. You must know that often women die in — "

"Madam, I do know women die in childbirth. I buried my wife this week, and my unborn son."

Sadiq found a morsel of comfort in the genuine shock and sympathy that washed over the woman's face. "Oh, dear," she said. "I had no idea. Well, then certainly you can see the need — "

Sadiq's hands tightened into fists. "It's forbidden for a man to touch a woman he's not married to, and for a woman to become a doctor. And it's not your place to criticize our religion. You talk of freedom. What kind of freedom is it when men feel they must kidnap and smuggle women into their world to find a wife?"

"Liaison Salim, I've seen this before, in many habitats, religiously based or otherwise. You're obviously polite and well-read, but you walk a narrow path. If you could identify with these women — "

Sadiq wanted to scream. The impertinence of this liaison, this woman! "Liaison Newell, this conversation is ended." He went to his desk and punched the control that blanked the screen.

He was immediately ashamed at what his features must have revealed to that impertinent woman, with his furrowed eyebrows and the veins on his neck popping out. He purposely did not look at his mother as he said, "It's unseemly. Asking permission to run our lives in a certain way."

His mother sat stock-still. Her voice was not without sympathy. "I knew that conversation would end in anger."

"As did I. Yet I chose to have it anyway. I wanted to exhaust all possibilities before I speak to the envoy from New Jerusalem."

Sadiq's mother cast him a doubtful look. "You sound as if you're looking forward to that meeting."

Sadiq said, "Now that I've confirmed that I cannot depend upon anyone else to alter the rules, this person may be the key to preserving our habitat's culture."

Sadiq savored the sight of his mother's expression as she reacted to that assertion.

*****

Sadiq was waiting for the liaison from New Jerusalem at True Faith Habitat's zero-G hub. Then he spotted a short woman in Western dress pulling himself along the exit tube. As she approached him, he saw that she was short, with brown hair and eyes and familiar features. He felt his heart race, his cheeks flush. What did it mean, to send this woman? "I remember your name," he told her. "Hajna Tawil, is it not?"

The woman let go of one handhold while gripping another tightly; apparently she was as unaccustomed to zero-G as Sadiq. "I am," she said, in virtually unaccented Arabic. "Salam alekum."

"Once again, I am True Faith Habitat Liaison Sadiq Salim. Uh...shalom. Was your trip a pleasant one?"

Liaison Tawil's smile was open, inviting, which Sadiq found vaguely irritating. "The best kind of space trip. Uneventful. Though it's good to be back in warmer temperatures. That shuttle's cabin was quite cool."

"May I ask if you have a family? Are they well?"

"A husband and two daughters," Liaison Tawil said. "And thank you, they're quite well." Sadiq felt a deep pang within his heart that this woman had achieved a goal he had not. I'd prefer sons, he thought, but to have daughters would be far preferable to having no children at all.

Liaison Tawil said, "I was sorry to hear of the tragedy within your own family, especially at such a trying time for your habitat. I've thought of your wife and son in my prayers."

Sadiq gripped his handholds so hard he started to drift out of control. He corrected quickly, which gave him a moment to decide how to react. Was Liaison Tawil as sincere as she seemed? Certainly he was touched by her gesture, to the point that he was blinking back moisture at the corners of his eyes. "Liaison Tawil, shall we go down to my office?"

Liaison Tawil said, "Could we find a place where we could overlook the entire habitat, and sit and talk?"

Sadiq found that a puzzling request but not an unreasonable one. "I have an excellent place in mind," he told her.

It was ten minutes' work for Sadiq and Liaison Tawil to take the main passenger lift down to the habitat's surface. He was somewhat nervous to stand so closely to a woman not of his relation. But, he thought, the Earth Liaison must do many unusual and uncomfortable things.

A broad residential street ended at a narrow, well-worn path up a gentle slope through some woods. Soon they reached a clearing that gave an unobstructed view of the True Faith Habitat's interior. They were just high enough that G-forces were reduced slightly.

Liaison Tawil reached the top of the hill just ahead of Sadiq and turned around to take in the sight. Sadiq stood next to her and slowly lowered his hand to allow himself the full view of the habitat's interior. Liaison Tawil noticed the gesture, and asked, "Are you in distress?"

Sadiq's mouth curled upward in amusement. "My spirit lives here, but my body is that of a groundling."

Liaison Tawil nodded her understanding. "I'm more fortunate. I've only lived within New Jerusalem for a year, but I find the view bracing every morning."

"Give me a few moments, and I adjust. Especially as it is such a beautiful sight." Sadiq looked down slope to where an irrigated desert plain filled with fruit trees led to Lake Medina. The villages of Gabriel's Point and Sawdah's Sorrow were on the opposite side of the lake. It was a pattern repeated to either side and overhead, with only the nature of the crops changing. Heavy industry was concealed within the habitat's lower levels. To maintain the habitat's self-sufficiency, that industry fastidiously recycled its wastes, keeping the habitat's interior pristine. True Faith Habitat was ten kilometers wide, two across, and rotated once in just under a minute to create its Earth-standard grav.

Liaison Tawil said, "It is beautiful." She took out a handkerchief and wiped her brow. "Reminds me of much of New Jerusalem. We, too, created a desert only to irrigate it."

"It reminds us of our fathers," Sadiq said, as a warm breeze washed across his face. "Such things are important."

"Indeed they are."

"It's especially important for me. I lost my father last year."

"I'm sorry to hear that," Liaison Tawil said. She indicated a flat grassy area. "May we sit and talk?"

Sadiq considered for a moment, then decided, why stand on ceremony? He waited for her to sit so he could settle in next to her at a comfortable distance.

"Liaison Salim, about those men who kidnapped me and the other New Jerusalem residents — "

"They've been deported to Earth. As has the customs man they paid to smuggle those women into our world."

"Where to?"

"The usual places. The English Strait. The ruins of Florence. They're forced to work on rebuilding rather than destroying. On behalf of the people of my habitat, I apologize for their actions."

Liaison Tawil let out a breath she'd obviously been holding awhile. "I thank you for that apology. And on behalf of my people, I accept it."

"I believe the families of the victims have made demands. Individual apologies. Financial settlements. We'll honor those, as well."

"Liaison Salim, you're a most agreeable man to deal with."

Sadiq placed his hands on his knees and sat up straighter. "This has been a difficult thing, Liaison Tawil. The sooner taken care of, the better."

"I hope I didn't sound condescending. Sometimes, you'll admit, this habitat speaks with...well, let's say, a harsher voice."

"We follow Muhammad's ways as we see fit."

"Of course."

Sadiq rubbed his hands together. They were sweaty, and not just from the heat. "I must admit, Liaison Tawil, I wondered whether your presence here was a challenge to my authority."

Liaison Tawil said, "We considered it a sign of trust. For me to return here, assuming I would be safe...this has not been easy for me, either. But it was important, for both our peoples."

Images of Aasim's beautiful face, and of her still form, welled up into Sadiq's consciousness. He told Liaison Tawil, "I've been waiting to approach you, with respect, regarding another matter."

"Then let us discuss it."

Sadiq took a deep breath. This must not go as the conversation with that damnable Liaison Newell went, he thought. "True Faith Habitat has been experiencing a decline in population."

Liaison Tawil picked up a seed from the ground and examined it. "A problem many habitats are coping with. Including my own."

"This habitat to a larger extent than the others."

Liaison Tawil's eyes were still focused on the seed as she rolled it between thumb and index finger. "It's unfortunate for you."

"Perhaps your people can help us."

Liaison Tawil's fingers stopped rolling the seed. She looked at Sadiq with an expression he realized was silently asking why she would want to help this habitat.

"You've seen what happened in this kidnapping incident," Sadiq said. "Such emotions need an outlet."

Liaison Tawil sat silently for a long moment before saying, "Tell me what you propose."

Such doubt, such mistrust I hear in her voice, Sadiq thought. Though if our situations were reversed, wouldn't I be the doubtful, mistrusting one? He said, "I propose that New Jerusalem and True Faith habitats combine."

Liaison Tawil's eyes went wide and she blinked furiously. "Tell me, Liaison Salim, how would this work? Do you think everyone in True Faith Habitat would want to come live in New Jerusalem?"

Sadiq was too thunderstruck to form words for a few moments. Finally, he said, "We cannot abandon our sacred mosques here. You would come to live in this habitat, of course."

"I see. And how will you explain this to both our peoples?"

"We control our media. We'll say it's being imposed upon us by outside forces."

Liaison Tawil asked, "Your government would lie so blatantly?"

"All governments lie."

She flicked the seed away. "I suppose our charters don't address that."

"There are legitimate societal forces at work here. Both our peoples understand ourselves in relation to each other. Your mere presence on our habitat will rally my people together, give this habitat new life. We'll discuss the nature of God in cafes, we'll have spirited governmental debates."

"We'll denounce one another as unbelievers and barbarians."

"Such anger, Liaison Tawil! How do you justify it?"

"Many of the women on my habitat wear Western clothing. Will that be allowed among your people?"

"Not appropriate, Liaison Tawil! We barely tolerate it for one such as yourself."

"And we'll want to remove the mosques in our half of the habitat, of course."

"Impossible!"

"We'll have to change the name, to reflect its new status."

"You're being unreasonable!"

"You see my point, Liaison Salim. Both our peoples left Earth and created our own, separate, societies to be done with such conflict."

"These conflicts have always been with us, and they make us stronger, your people as well as mine." Sadiq examined the woman's features as she looked out across the cylindrical landscape of the New Faith Habitat, saw emotional turmoil there that he suspected was similar to his own. "Please, Liaison Tawil, I come to you as someone who believes as Muhammad did. He respected Jews as People of the Book. He married a Jew, something many of my people don't know or will not acknowledge."

"Muhammad executed hundreds of Jews in the year 627 when they wouldn't convert."

Sadiq stood and looked down at Liaison Tawil. Images arose again, of Aasim's doll-like features, of her mouth forming words without sound, and of an impossible future, where his son took his first toddling steps toward him. He forced those images away as he asked Liaison Tawil, "Why do such people as you exist?"

"Jews, you mean?"

"No, you damnable woman! I mean those who twist words until they have no meaning."

Liaison Tawil stood and faced Sadiq. "My people won't be the focus of a new intifada."

"That was never my intention — "

"Liaison Salim, you've been kind enough and reasonable enough regarding the kidnapping incident, so I'll take you at your word. But you have to see that would be the unintended result."

"We simply want to live as we wish."

"And so you shall. But you'll live alone."

Liaison Tawil started down the slope then, back toward the lift that would return her to the hub. Sadiq didn't follow.

Moments after the woman left, the call to prayer echoed across the landscape. "There is no god but God, and Muhammad is the messenger of God...." Sadiq answered the call as he kneeled at the top of that gentle slope.

*****

When Sadiq opened his eyes, he saw his mother just down the slope from him, also kneeling in prayer. He watched as she stood and made her way up the hill toward him.

Sadiq stood, out of respect to his mother though he would have preferred to sit and think, and consider the nature of God. He asked her, "Did you meet Liaison Tawil as she left?"

Rabi Salim said, "I was kneeling in the path as I prayed. She stood there as I finished. Didn't say a word. Excused herself as she went past."

"She's an honorable woman."

His mother's eyes widened. I'm proud of you for saying that, son."

"Mother, I must ask you something. There is no God but God. But does every man — or woman, I suppose — carry around an individual perception of God?"

"I've always supposed God simply 'is,' independent of how we perceive Him."

Sadiq made a fist and held it before him. He said, "Those kidnappers believed in a God that allows men to take women captive and abuse them. My brother-in-law Amrullah believes in a God that approves of the armies of jihad over the spirituality of jihad."

His mother looked at him with both affection and concern. "And what do you believe in?"

Sadiq considered. "I believe the quick, simple solutions I sought will not work. I cannot count on others, whether from Brussels or New Jerusalem or anywhere else, to help us."

"So if you don't have a quick or simple solution, you must embrace a long, complex solution."

"Clever words, Mother. Without Aasim, I see a future in which I personally am alone. Enshallah. I'm determined, however, that my people will endure."

"Then our people must change. A new path can be...well, enlightening. I've found it to be so."

Sadiq barely heard his mother's words as a warm breeze blew dust into his eyes. He squinted and brushed at his face.

Eyes closed tight, the only light Sadiq could perceive was the pale pink of daylight that filtered through his eyelids. Against that backdrop, a familiar form appeared to him. He opened his eyes wide, but without really seeing his surroundings — fortunate, since he didn't want to experience his typical blurred vision or dizziness — and stood gap-jawed.

His mother gasped and took him by the hand. "Are you all right, son?"

Sadiq looked at her. "I don't know. I may have had a vision."

His mother frowned. "You know I don't believe in such things."

"I'm not quite so superstitious, Mother. I'm willing to admit it's an image my own mind placed within me. But it's no less disturbing. I saw Aasim."

Sadiq heard his mother's quick intake of breath. She asked, "What was she doing?"

Sadiq said, "Doing? She was dead. Still beautiful, even so. Skin like brown porcelain. Her expression, resigned and calm."

"Son, I know that had to be upsetting. But perhaps you should take your cue from that image of Aasim. From her calm, her acceptance of death."

"Don't you understand? In the image, hers was a cold beauty. An unchanging expression. It doesn't reflect the desert warmth, the human vitality our habitat requires to survive."

Sadiq's mother said, "The Qur'an speaks of the day that reveals. Much has been revealed to you this day. Do those revelations lead you into the same dark vision that led to Aasim's death?"

"The narrow path, as Liaison Newell referred to it?"

"The very same. You should reject it. You should travel down the path opening outward. The one in which women may enter childbirth without fear, and our sons may take wives in peace."

Sadiq tried to pull away from his mother, but she gripped his hand all the more tightly and told him, "Don't sacrifice yourself to that other vision. Holding families together by force? Keeping women and girls on a habitat in which they're far more likely to die an early, agonizing death? Kidnapping and abusing women? Could you really do that?"

Sadiq jerked his hand away. "If I believed it the proper path."

His mother slapped him, hard. He turned to her with his hands in tightly clenched fists, his jaw set. But he told her, "You know I could never strike you back."

His mother reached for Sadiq, and he stepped away from her. "I'm sorry," she said, lowering her eyes. "I'm so ashamed."

Now Sadiq also felt shame, and he reached for his mother and took her into his arms. "No, Mother, I provoked you, and I apologize."

"That's the Sadiq I wanted to see."

"What do you mean?"

"I see it in your eyes. The Sadiq who grieves over Aasim and your unborn son. The Sadiq who abhorred what those men did to the women from New Jerusalem."

"Yes, yes, I am that Sadiq."

"And you're the Sadiq who spoke to Liaison Tawil with respect." His mother's eyes narrowed and took on a familiar expression from his childhood. "You did treat her with respect?"

"Yes, Mother." As Sadiq considered what his mother said, it was as if a veil lifted itself from his consciousness.

"Let's go home. We'll speak more."

"That's good, Mother. I expect you'll like what you hear from me. I've chosen between the narrow path and the one that opens outward."

"What do you intend to do?"

"Liaison Newell was correct. You cannot know how it hurts me to say that. But we are free to choose where to live. I can only be certain of changing myself, but I hope to inspire others to change, as well, to join me in that path that opens outward."

"And where will you do that?"

"The warm vistas inside this world have always inspired me. It's here I intend to stay."

Rabi Salim said, "I believe you've chosen the proper path. But also the more difficult one."

"There is no God but God. And I can be no other Sadiq in the manner in which I serve Him. If I'm damned for that, so be it."

Sadiq and his mother began walking down the slope, through a dark and narrow wooded path. As they were about to exit the woods, without thinking he started to raise his hand against the blurred vision he knew would come.

In the instant before his hand shielded his eyes, however, he caught a glimpse of his world: the irrigated fields, the wide, clear blue lakes, the villages filled with homes that greeted you with broad arching entrances and enveloped you in courtyards filled with greenery and the love of family and friends. This manmade cylinder, in turn, envelops my world, Sadiq thought. As God envelops it in his commands for obedience and righteousness and as his spirit brings light to comfort and guide me, and heat which reflects my blazing love for all within.

Sadiq lowered his hand as he followed his mother from the darkness of that narrow path and saw the world that opened out before him more clearly than ever before.

INFINITY'S FRIEND

A few years ago I was looking through some old *National Geographics* and came across an article in the October 1983 issue titled *Pitcairn and Norfolk: the Saga of Bounty's Children*. As I re-read the article, Pitcairn Island came to fascinate me. Its population at the time of the article's publication was a mere 45 people, and may now be up to about 50.

Pitcairners work hard in the fields growing sweet potatoes and avocadoes, and on the ocean catching fish. The island's only established religion is Seventh-Day Adventism.

I thought it would be the perfect place for someone to grow up honoring the community that raised him but yearning for something beyond it — the perfect place for a space explorer to come from, someone like Matt Christian.

And what kind of world might Matt be likely to explore? A world just like Welkin, of course, in the story that follows.

Matt Christian was guiding his skimmer down toward an active volcano jutting up from the planet Welkin's ocean when Sarbin contacted him over the datalink to confess he'd beached himself again.

Matt shook his head in frustration as he halted the skimmer's descent well short of the looming plume of the volcano's smoke and ash; as much as he admired the Aquatile, this was becoming a bad habit. "Can't you make it back into the water?" he asked.

Matt envisioned his native friend much as he'd discovered him twice previously — his broad, walrus-sized body flopped over onto its back, stubby arms flailing, wet round eyes taking in the brilliant, moonless night sky and all its wonders (the name Welkin meant "arch of heaven").

"I'm sorry, Matt. I cannot," Sarbin said. "The stars above — they were so wonderful, and I cast myself high upon the shore so the waves wouldn't pull me back. But it was too far."

Matt understood the pull the stars exerted upon Sarbin — that same pull had brought him to this planet after all. He cast a wistful eye down at the volcano — any secrets it possessed as to how Welkin had formed with so little land area would remain hidden a while longer. He eased the skimmer back the way he'd come, toward the spit of land, not a kilometer across, that Sarbin favored for his contemplation of the stars.

Then he thought of something. "Sarbin."

"Yes, Matt."

"How long have you been beached?"

"I...don't w...want to tell you."

Matt wanted to pound the control console before him, as he realized the datalink translation was passing on hesitation in Sarbin's voice. Was it just nervousness, or was Sarbin finding it more difficult to speak? Matt forced himself to remain calm. "How long?"

After a pause, Sarbin said, "A...couple of hours. And the sun will be coming up soon." Matt stifled a curse. This beaching had become an immediate danger, not just an inconvenience. The Aquatile, though an air-breather, could not remain out of the water for long. Removed from the ocean, Sarbin's slick skin would quickly dry out and crack, even on a cool, humid night. Gravity's pressure would strain his muscles and could even rupture his internal organs.

Yet he'd taken this chance again!

When Matt checked and saw how long it would take him to return to that tiny island half a world away on Welkin's night side, he felt grief and regret over Juliette's death four years earlier wash over him anew. "Sarbin, I may not make it back there in time. Is there any way you can return to the water?"

"I...have tried, Matt. I'm exhausted. Outside the water...it's so tiring."

"Even at this skimmer's top speed, it's going to take me the better part of an hour to reach you. And...."

"And in an hour," Sarbin said, "I could well be dead. I understand."

Matt muttered, "Sarbin, I will not put myself in that position again. You have to hold on."

Sarbin didn't speak again for a moment, and Matt wondered if the Aquatile had fainted, or worse. Then Matt heard, "What do you mean 'again?'"

Matt didn't say anything. He busied himself with the skimmer's controls and checked its trajectory again.

"Matt?"

"I'm here, Sarbin."

"What did you mean?"

Matt said, "I was...just wishing I had someone else from the crew here to help out." He was a contact specialist aboard the Earth Unity exploratory craft Haldane. That craft was in the outer system exploring some interesting-looking gas giants. He'd promised Captain Blackwell he'd be careful while here on Welkin alone. Besides, he'd told her, the skimmer had a fully-equipped nanodoc program. What could go wrong?

Now he knew. As he often did when he thought of death, Matt longed for Christ's resurrection, which would also be Juliette's. The Seventh-day Adventist beliefs they and the rest of the population back home on Pitcairn Island shared had been another bond between them. He also felt a deep sadness that Sarbin, if he were to die now, could never be part of that resurrection.

For now, though, the Aquatile was telling him, "If anyone can rescue me in time, you can. After all, you're infinity's friend."

Matt suppressed a groan. The very concept of "infinity" had been one of the most difficult to explain to a being he'd originally thought of as "confined" to an ocean. Once he'd taken a few swims with Sarbin, and followed him into the deeps of that ocean in Haldane's small submersible a few times, he'd learned better than that! If an environment was much larger and varied than an individual could explore in a lifetime, wasn't it, in practical terms, "infinite?"

Sarbin, though, had eventually grasped the concept, understanding that when he was lying on the beach staring at the stars he was staring at the equivalent of more oceans than any one being could even count in a lifetime, let alone explore.

"Sarbin," Matt said, "tell me how you're doing."

"As well as could be expected. The more you speak to me, the better I am."

"I'm growing closer with each moment."

"Matt, I was just remembering the days when we first met."

"That's a fond memory for me, as well." And much preferable, Matt thought, to dwelling on a previous tragedy.

He and Sarbin had spent the first few days upon Matt's arrival on Welkin fine-tuning the translation tech. Sarbin's datalink was implanted next to the two small bones at the back of his head that produced the clicks and low tones that were Aquatile speech. Those sounds were feeble whenever Sarbin was out of the water, though, and the link had to amplify them for transmission. Submerged, Aquatiles could communicate for many kilometers.

With Sarbin beached, however, that ability was useless to him. And no other Aquatile had yet agreed to an implanted link, so Matt couldn't call for help, either.

Sarbin said, "Do you remember the first time you spoke to me when part of me was sleeping?"

Despite himself, Matt smiled. "We were swimming together, just a couple of days after we'd met." he said. Matt remembered how new everything on Welkin seemed to him then — the freshness of the air, the lighter .85 grav, and especially Sarbin. Matt had had little contact with other Galactic species other than the occasional Kanandran or Arol.

Sarbin, with his sad wide eyes offset by his dolphin-like eternal smile, was an endless fascination to him, an otherworldly manifestation of the passage from Romans that referred to "gifts differing according to the grace that is given to us." Certainly Sarbin's gifts differed greatly from a Human's, and were perfectly suited to his environment.

The Aquatile's arms, so weak on land, along with the singular fluke of his muscular tail, could propel him through the water with a shark's swiftness. The two of them were swimming together one day, well within sight of the strip of land where Matt had landed his skimmer. Sarbin was amused at Matt's breather mask, with its nanotech that extracted breathable oxygen right from the ocean's waters. "We're both mammals," Sarbin said. "And I don't need a breather."

"I can't go without breathing for more than a few minutes, either." Matt knew Sarbin could take deep, deep breaths into his broad chest and remain underwater for nearly an hour if he wished.

Sarbin said, "I want to visit Earth."

That was a surprise! Matt said, "I never knew that you thought about — "

Sarbin interrupted Matt. "I want to go right now. Wait — there it is. Just land. Hardly any water anywhere."

"Well, actually, most of Earth's surface area is — "

Sarbin interrupted again. "I could grow legs. I could walk on earth...on the Earth as you do."

Matt stopped swimming to tread water while he tried to figure out what was wrong with his friend. "Sarbin, you seem confused. What can I — "

Then the Aquatile's fluke flipped toward the sky and Sarbin was gone — Matt could just make out his body's form flashing through Welkin's waters before losing sight of him. Matt swam back to the tiny island and sat on the small strip of beach, waiting. After the first hour, he began to pray. Where had his friend gone so suddenly, and would he ever return?

At the end of those two hours, he did. Matt splashed into the water and embraced Sarbin. "I was afraid I'd never see you again!"

Sarbin's eyes grew even wider and the vertical slash of his single nostril opened and closed rhythmically. He took Matt by the shoulders and gently but firmly broke the embrace. "Why were you concerned?"

Matt was puzzled; even through the translation, he sensed a lack of affect in Sarbin's words. And that business of refusing his touch — Matt walked up onto the shore again and sat.

Sarbin said, "You look as if you have never spoken to someone who is asleep before."

That's when Matt realized what was happening. "The two halves of your brain take turns sleeping!" He felt foolish for not realizing that sooner. Dolphin brains back on Earth pulled the same trick — part of their consciousness had to be awake constantly, otherwise they risked "forgetting" to swim, and could sink and drown.

"Which half was I speaking to earlier?" Matt asked. "You weren't making a lot of sense. And when you swam off like that — I was worried."

"You shouldn't have been. If a real danger had been present, that side would have come awake. You were speaking to the part which controls emotions and conjures up ideas."

"In Humans," Matt said, "That would be the right brain."

Sarbin slid up onto the beach, but not so far that his stubby arms couldn't push him back into the water again. "In Aquatiles, I am not certain. The particular idea the emotional half mentioned, visiting Earth, is not one this side of me would consider."

"I'd take you there if you ever wanted to go."

"Then perhaps this logical half's objections will be overcome. So, tell me how Human brains control their sleep patterns."

"Both halves of our brains sleep at the same time."

For an instant, Sarbin's gaze lifted upward in thought, as his lips, three times the length of a Human's, pressed together. All in all, an oddly Human expression. "Interesting," Sarbin said. "I wondered why, when you would say it was time to sleep, that you would excuse yourself and enter your skimmer. I would imagine sleep is a vulnerable time for you. Did you fear I would harm you?"

"Sarbin! Never! It's just that my species prefers quiet and darkness while sleeping."

"Do not feel offended at my suggestion. Remember you are speaking to the purely logical side of me. No doubt my emotional half recognizes that you are benign, and in fact appear predisposed to my welfare."

Matt, remembering that as he piloted the skimmer to rescue Sarbin, frowned the same way he had that day. "Benign, huh?" he thought. Though I suppose it's better than being some sort of alien menace.

"Matt," Sarbin said. "I'm worried."

"I'll be there within twenty minutes."

"The sun is coming up."

Matt knew how difficult it was for an Aquatile to withstand direct sunlight. Sarbin's skin would dry out more quickly, and his eyes, adapted to the deep ocean, often found sunlight blinding. Aquatiles had little reason to scan daylight skies, and the only reason Sarbin ever beached himself was to be able to contemplate the stars at night.

The first time Matt had discovered Sarbin lying on his back on dry land, he'd admonished him not to do it again, and Sarbin had promised he wouldn't. Matt hadn't believed him,

Just a week later Matt was nearby as Sarbin pulled himself onto the shore of the tiny island and flopped himself over. In a sense it was a moment of pure wonder for Matt, as if he were seeing the Welkin equivalent of life first emerging from the sea onto its new home, the land, just as it had happened upon the Earth. Never mind that the image was more metaphorical than literal; Sarbin was a large sentient being, not the slimes and molds that would have been the first travelers from Earthly seas onto the land. Matt had yelled at Sarbin again, but he'd feared the lesson hadn't sunk in.

And now Matt's worst fear was coming true. "You have to concentrate, Sarbin. Keep talking to me."

Sarbin didn't answer for a moment. When he finally replied, his confusion was apparent even over the translation. "Is that to help me, Matt, or reassure you?"

Matt ran his hand through his hair. "A little of both, I guess."

"I have little to talk about except my own pains and fears."

"Pick something else. Some story passed down through your pod, or something."

"Such stories usually involve dodging sharptooth or avoiding being entangled in trapweed. Or failing to dodge or avoid."

"Dammit, Sarbin!"

"You tell a story. Tell me what you meant about being in this position again."

Matt said nothing, only made another position check. Less than ten minutes away, he thought. Dear Lord, don't let me be late...

"Matt. Please."

He tried to keep the growing impatience out of his voice. "What is it?" he asked Sarbin.

"Tell the story. For me, in what could be my final moments."

The skimmer's nav display showed the tiny island just on the horizon. With max magnification, Matt would even be able to make out Sarbin soon. "I never talk about it," Matt said.

"If it's something secret, it may die with me."

Matt considered. "You'd forgive me for something that happened years ago?"

"Just as I forgive you in advance if I die before you arrive."

"Don't say that."

"Then tell me."

"I was thinking of my twin sister. Juliette."

"I didn't realize you had a twin. Our current situation reminds you of her?"

Matt thought of Sarbin lying helplessly on that small stretch of land, with only the stars for company. "Throughout our childhood, we spent many a night together behind our home on Pitcairn Island."

Sarbin interrupted. "You did not live on one of the large land masses you described to me?"

"Hardly. Pitcairn is home to only a few dozen people. Many of our ancestors were mutineers, come to live far from other Humans. Juliette and I, we would sneak out of our rooms on many a night and lie on the ground. We'd stare outward into clear, starry skies. We couldn't grow up quickly enough. We awaited wonders beyond measure. And each of us promised the other that no matter what, no matter who we married, we'd also explore the galaxy side by side, partners forever."

Sarbin said, "But that didn't happen."

"We were only twenty-two years old, not spacers yet. But an expedition to Earth's South Pole needed a shuttle pilot."

"A skill you had."

"But Pitcairn's so remote. No maglev trains go there, there's no starport."

"I don't understand those references, but I perceive the problem."

"Our people had one skimmer among us, and no other transportation off the island. I took the idea to our parliament. They agreed I could leave as long as I came back right away if the skimmer was needed."

Sarbin said, "And when you left..."

"Just days after I arrived, the expedition was stranded on an ice shelf that came under a snow squall. Do you understand what that is?"

"I've never seen one myself. But others of my pod have described them to me."

Another position check. Matt said, "I'm so close now. Just a few minutes."

"You have to speak quickly, now. I..."

"Keep calm. The more excited you get, the more energy you use."

"My...logical half is losing consciousness. My emotional half is all that...is listening."

Was that possible? Matt wondered. Could this being have that much awareness of his own mind? "Sarbin."

"I'm so frightened. Tell me the story."

Matt blinked away the beginnings of tears. Were they for Juliette four years ago, or for his helpless friend right now, whose fate was still open? "Juliette fell ill."

Sarbin asked, "What happened?"

"The doctor back on the island said she had food poisoning."

"And you couldn't leave because of the squall."

"The expedition's shuttle could have lifted, but it was designed for transporting cargo, not for a long-range journey."

"And your island's skimmer?"

"Couldn't lift out of the storm. I wanted to try it anyway, but the expedition leader wouldn't let me."

Sarbin asked, "And your twin sister?"

"We didn't have modern medicine. No nanodocs. The doctor made a mistake. Juliette actually had a ruptured appendix."

"I'm sorry, Matt, that didn't translate."

"A vestigial organ attached to our colon. Such a rupture is rare. I got to talk to Juliette over the net. And...what she said to me was so terrible."

"She blamed you because you couldn't reach her?"

"Not at all. She told me there was nothing I could have done. She told me I was following our dream, and that I should keep following it no matter what. Sarbin, I'm only about a minute away."

"You have to keep talking. I can't stand just to lie here."

"Sarbin — I see you now." Matt set the skimmer's autopilot to make the landing on its own.

"I...can hear the skimmer. Matt — I feel myself slipping away. If you don't — "

"Shut up!" Matt said as he grabbed a portable nanodoc kit. I will make it!"

"Juliette was right. You should listen to her."

"She's dead," Matt said, as he strained to keep his voice cracking from grief both remembered and anticipated. "Part of me died with her."

"Your brain must be addled from keeping both sides awake all the time. You have it backwards...."

Matt was out of the pilot's chair and punching the control that lifted the skimmer's hatch even as the craft settled onto the island's surface. He swung himself down onto the beach with one hand while clasping the medkit with the other. He blinked against wind-blown sand and the sun's glare on the horizon. He could just make out Sarbin's arms and his fluke from behind a low rise. Matt ran toward his friend. "What do you mean, Sarbin? What's backwards?" I don't care what he meant, Matt thought. I just have to keep him talking.

He topped the rise, and Sarbin's form was still. His eyes stared unseeing into clear skies.

I never got to see Juliette's eyes again, he thought. By the time I arrived for the funeral, she was lying in her coffin with her eyes closed.

Matt didn't hesitate. No use taking a sensor reading or trying to inject nanodocs. He has to get back into the water, he thought.

Sarbin was only about ten meters from the water. A shallow channel showed where he'd dragged himself onto the beach. Matt tossed the medkit onto the beach. Then he pulled off his shirt and dipped it into the ocean waters, went back to Sarbin, and squeezed the shirt over Sarbin's body. The Aquatile's skin soaked up the water like a sponge. Matt did that a couple more times, then slapped the wet shirt onto Sarbin's body.

Then he grabbed the Aquatile's fluke and pulled — to no effect. His body didn't move even a centimeter.

OK, Matt thought. Different tactic.

He went to Sarbin's side and tried to roll him toward the water. His spirit leapt when the Aquatile's body turned over, but fell when Sarbin's outstretched arms dug into the sand.

Help me, Lord, Matt thought. I need all your strength now.

He grasped Sarbin's fluke. The Aquatile was too heavy to pull straight back, but yanking him first to the right, then to the left, let him make a zigzag path toward the water.

Progress was slow but steady. Matt had to hope the moisture from his shirt gave his friend a fighting chance. Within three minutes he had Sarbin in the water. He cradled the Aquatile's head in his lap to keep Sarbin's face above water. Ocean waves lapped against his chest and water splashed his face.

Sarbin's eyes blinked, and he came to awareness. "I knew you would arrive in time."

Matt grabbed the medkit from where he'd thrown it and took a reading, holding his breath the entire time. When the kit told him Sarbin's condition, he smiled. "You're going to be fine with some rest and a good meal." Matt patted Sarbin's side. "Your logical side wasn't really asleep, was it?"

"I'm sorry I misled you. But you are only infinity's friend, Matt. You are limited, as am I. I did need to hear your story. But I knew my emotions would suppress yours until it was right for you to express them. It is time, my friend. Part of you did not die with her. Part of her stays alive within you."

Matt set aside the medkit, held Sarbin tighter, and wiped away the salty moisture stinging his eyes, unknowing and uncaring whether it was sea water or tears and recalling that whenever he'd looked into Juliette's eyes he'd always had the feeling he was looking into his own.

ON THE WELKIN SHONE THE STARRES BRIGHT

In this follow-up to *Infinity's Friend,* I wanted to explore the ecology of the planet Welkin in more depth, as well as the culture of the Aquatiles in general and Sarbin's personality in particular. It's easy for a character like Sarbin to be the idealized sidekick, and I wanted to hint that he could have his darker side, too.

————————————

Matt Christian guided the flying submersible over the planet Welkin's seemingly endless ocean. Other than the occasional speck of land, motile islands, and the distant polar caps, water dominated the planet's surface.

He guided the small craft a couple of times around one of those motile islands. Matt wanted to know why it had not moved from the path of the tropical storm due to arrive in the area within a few hours. Sensor readings confirmed his fears. He told his Aquatile friend Sarbin, who swam in the submersible's hold, "It's worse than we thought."

"What's the problem?" Sarbin asked. Over his datalink, Matt heard water splashing as the Aquatile spoke. He knew his friend, a native of the planet, ached to swim free again. Aquatiles possessed broad, smooth bodies that reminded you of a walrus, only without fur. Sarbin also had stubby arms and a muscular tail that could propel his meter-and-a-half long swiftly though the ocean.

Matt performed a preliminary sensor check. "The island's injured," he said. "But I can't tell what caused it." Welkin's motile islands were masses of thick, taut weeds and other vegetation, often kilometers across. They provided most of the oxygen in Welkin's atmosphere. Several native life forms lived on them, mostly smaller animals dwelling within the complex intertwining of the islands' vegetation.

Sarbin said, "I wonder if the Sprinters did something to them. Believe me, Matt, you never know when to trust them. They're big and fat, and their body hair is disgusting. And half the time they live on dirt."

Matt frowned. He hated hearing that kind of talk out of Sarbin. *He's better than that,* he thought.

The Sprinters were another of Welkin's major aquatic species. If Aquatiles reminded Humans of walruses, Sprinters resembled aquatic dinosaurs — larger and fiercer than Aquatiles, but not as mobile. A pod made up of hundreds of Sprinters protected the eggs its females had laid on the motile island.

Matt said, "There's a 'real' island — actual land — about two K distant. Why don't I set down over there and we'll approach underwater?"

"An excellent idea," Sarbin said. "If these Sprinters haven't seen Humans before, the submersible may frighten them. Frightened beings can become violent. And the storm is approaching. I can smell its presence. I'm sure when we enter the ocean, I'll feel its pressure against the water. If the island is injured, those Sprinters are all in danger."

"I'm glad you're concerned about them."

"I'm not, Matt. But you are. That makes this mission important to me, as well."

And that, Matt thought as he guided the submersible downward, may be about all I can hope for.

*****

Matt released Sarbin through the large hatch underneath the submersible. He could tell his was pleased to return to his natural element. Matt landed the submersible on the tiny island and put all its systems on standby.

Matt put on a skintight and a breather mask that extracted oxygen from water for him. His knife and stunner were on a belt around his waist. He had his wrist sensor, and a medkit strapped to his chest. He left the submersible and splashed into Welkin's ocean.

Sarbin's short arms and broad flippers held tightly onto Matt's body as the Aquatile's tail propelled them both just beneath the water's surface at about two or three meters per second. Matt knew if he came under attack by the Sprinters, his nanotech lifesuit would harden into nearly impenetrable yet lightweight armor, the same as a spacesuit.

But Sarbin doesn't have that kind of protection, Matt thought. I have to make sure he can make a run for it if something happens. He told Sarbin, "A successful mission for us should be a nice tribute to why Humans named your sun after a writer named Chaucer."

"'Writer?' What does that mean?"

"It's someone who...well, puts down information or a made-up story so that others can read it. But I guess reading isn't something you know about, either."

"I've seen you look at your small machines and learn from them even though they don't speak to you."

"That'll do for now. And I know your people tell stories about made-up people and events."

"Mostly in teaching our young."

"Many Humans read such stories all our lives. Chaucer's best-known work was The Canterbury Tales. In one story, a husband torments his wife so she can prove her love for him by putting up with his bad treatment. Eventually he realizes that's wrong. When he decides to love her without reservation, the story explains how, 'on the welkin shone the starres bright' — meaning things have gotten better."

"You've told me 'welkin' means 'arch of heaven.' I think I understand."

"It's how I expect to feel after you and I save this island. The stars will seem that much brighter, I think."

"That should be a very good tribute, indeed. But I must wonder about the Sprinters themselves. Why would they want to remain on this island when it's in danger?"

Matt said, "On my world, occupying land gives you power. My people often battle one another for control of it."

"For breeding purposes, like the Sprinters?"

"In part, I suppose. But we also make our homes on the land, raise our children there, and grow our food on it. It's where we make our lives."

"Aquatiles are in constant movement. Humans remain in one place."

"Humans move around a lot, too. But we like having that one unmoving place waiting for us." Matt thought of Earth, of his own home on Pitcairn Island. He recalled his mother making bread pudding and fried banana burgers, his father creating a kite of cloth or plastic and watching Matt run fast as he could to make it soar high into the heavens. The food was a known quantity, safe and secure, even as the kite held the possibility of new adventures, new places to fly.

Then a sensor protocol beeped in Matt's ear — a life form approaching rapidly! And Matt had only the briefest glimpse of a dark shape flashing through the water before it struck both him and Sarbin a glancing blow. Sprinters! The Aquatile's body spun around, his arms holding tighter to Matt to keep from losing him.

Then a second shape slammed into them, and Matt and Sarbin went flying in different directions.

Matt spread his arms and legs so his body would stabilize more quickly, the whole time keeping an eye out for their assailant, for Sarbin, for which direction led to the ocean's surface.

Then he saw one of the shapes again, this time in more detail — a dark body half again as big as Sarbin, with flippers thrusting it forward and a short tail whipping back and forth for guidance.

And strong-looking jaws lined with impressive rows of teeth!

Matt drew his stunner, but before he could aim he was struck from behind.

It was Sarbin snatching him away from the Sprinter. They broke the surface of the ocean with a huge spray of water. "Put away your weapon," Sarbin told him. His wide eyes and eternal dolphin-like smile would've belied the seriousness of his words if Matt wasn't accustomed to them. "A stunned Sprinter would sink to the ocean floor and drown. It's not as if I would mind that, but then we'll never make peaceful contact."

"Did those teeth look peaceful to you?"

"They're protecting their young." Sarbin upended himself and disappeared into the ocean's depths, leaving Matt to tread water.

He put away his stunner and ducked his head into the water to see what was happening. Sarbin was leading the two Sprinters on a merry chase, taking advantage of his smaller body to make tighter turns and repeatedly evade them. Once the two Sprinters even crashed into one another.

One of the Sprinters separated from its companion and rose toward Matt, its two-meter-long body growing larger by the second. Then Sarbin broke away, too, and he was faster. The Aquatile overtook the Sprinter and rammed his snout into its side. The Sprinter twisted around to try to strike Sarbin, but the Aquatile was quicker and made a tighter turn every time.

Matt grinned, and yelled encouragement to Sarbin as the Sprinter all but turned itself into knots trying and failing to gain an advantage.

Then he realized — I don't see the other Sprinter.

Matt spun around just in time to see it only seconds from ramming him. He pressed the middle finger of his left hand into his palm to activate his lifesuit tech. In an instant, Matt's body was coated in a silvery material that normally served as a spacesuit.

But he didn't want Sprinters to get the idea they could attack Humans without consequences, either. Matt pulled his stunner, aimed, then waited for the Sprinter to get within about five meters — any farther away, and the beam might be too diffuse.

Now! Matt fired, and the Sprinter went limp and its body began to tumble. Matt was about to swim aside and dodge it, but instead grabbed it and dog paddled to keep its head and blowhole, above the surface. "Sarbin," he said, "get that Sprinter you're dancing with to look up here."

"I'm heading your way," was Sarbin's reply.

Matt held tighter to the Sprinter — a difficult task, given its slippery skin and great bulk. Matt stared into the being's left eye, which stared back without consciousness. He wondered how much intelligence resided behind that eye. The Sprinters don't seem to be as bright as the Aquatiles, he thought. Why would one such species become sentient, while another doesn't?

Beneath him — the swift approach of the other Sprinter. Matt pushed himself away from the unconscious one even as a glancing blow sent him tumbling through the water.

By the time Matt righted himself, the other Sprinter was swimming laboriously toward the motile island, its companion's right fin clasped in its powerful jaws.

Another touch in the palm of his left hand, and Matt's lifesuit tech faded. It makes me feel too much like I'm in space, he thought. I like feeling the waves against my body, catching a whiff of salt air.

Sarbin glided up next to Matt. "That was a difficult encounter." The Aquatile flipped himself over and Matt saw several bloody streaks down his belly. "That Sprinter was just grabbing onto me when I got away."

Matt gasped. He grabbed his sensorpak, and did a quick scan. "It's not serious, but some of those cuts are deep. I'm sure it's painful."

Sarbin flipped upright again. "I'm sure it is, too."

Matt asked Sarbin, "Can you get us to the shore of that motile island?"

"I believe so. I haven't seen any more Sprinters, and I think we can beach ourselves on the opposite shore from where their mates have laid their eggs."

"Very good. I want to examine your wounds. And I want to get a look at the Sprinters' nests before we travel beneath the island."

Matt let Sarbin grasp him again and they proceeded toward the motile island. He noticed that Sarbin held him well away from his belly.

*****

Matt went clambering over the thick masses of weeds that made up the two-kilometer-across motile island as Sarbin watched from the water's edge. It was rough going, even in Welkin's .85 grav, as his feet broke through thin patches or sank into soft areas. Easy to break an ankle here, he thought. The Sprinters have an easier time of it. They slink across this surface with their wider bodies distributing their weight.

Matt opened his medkit and grabbed a nanodoc injector and a dermal wand, both of which he had already loaded with protocols for Aquatile physiology. He went back to Sarbin and pressed the injector against Sarbin's skin. "What did you put into me?" the Aquatile asked.

"Tiny machines that will go into your bloodstream and keep you from getting infected. They'll also help you heal faster, and not hurt so much."

"Are you allowed to give me such a miracle?"

"My religion tells me to believe in miracles," Matt said. "But these are just tools. Turn onto your side." Sarbin did, and Matt ran the dermal wand's healing field over the Aquatile's wounds. It cleared the damaged area of dirt and other residue and promoted healing. It also, Matt thought, captures any tissue or hairs the Sprinter left behind. I'm eager to take a look at them.

"I already feel better," Sarbin said, "I can't thank you enough."

Matt ran his fingers along Sarbin's belly. The Aquatile barely flinched. "That's going to be tender for a few days." Matt stepped back onshore and put his med gear away. He asked Sarbin, "I'm going to get a closer look at the Sprinters. Will you be all right?"

"I'll wait here for you. But be careful. You're far from home, and have no fins or family."

Matt blinked at the reference. Sometimes idioms didn't translate well. "I'll be back in a few minutes."

"I'll stay here in the water," Sarbin said. An Aquatile risked injury or death by staying out of the water too long, especially if exposed to the sun — their skin cracked, and their bodies risked straining muscles and internal organs when not supported by water.

"You know what to do if the Sprinters attack again — run away."

"Unfortunately, I cannot run."

Matt frowned in mock anger. "You know what I mean."

"I do. And I will. You'll be standing here talking to yourself. In the meantime, my emotional side will take a nap." The two sides of Aquatile brains, like those of dolphins on Earth, took turns sleeping, since they had to remain conscious constantly to keep returning to the ocean's surface to breathe.

Matt walked along the shoreline until he judged he was close to the Sprinters' nesting area. He went onto his hands and knees to get to the top of a small rise. The thick layer of vegetation settled slightly beneath his body as he got down onto his belly to catch a glimpse of the Sprinters.

He saw dozens from this vantage point. Some of them moved their bodies across the beach as if they were giant caterpillars, slinking their way over the packed vegetation. Their front flippers were broad enough that they served as "hands," able to grip holes in the island's surface or grasp thick strands of vines and pull themselves along. Others gliding out of the ocean had water rippling off their short, dark brown fur. That fur protected a Sprinter from Chaucer's rays as an Aquatile's slick skin could not.

And so many gathered around their eggs! Matt could catch only an occasional glimpse of an egg or two as one or another of the females shifted position; but he recognized the quiet determination in the large round eyes of each of the females. Any lingering frustration or anger he'd had at the males who had attacked him or Sarbin swept itself away. They're just protecting their next generation, he thought, as anyone would.

The Sprinters weren't alone here. Birds called amblers, thin-beaked and fat-bellied, wheeled overhead. Matt knew other beings called such motile islands home — bracken-mites, dancer slugs, sargassum drones. But his interest was in the Sprinters, and in saving them before the storm bore down upon them.

But they don't seem concerned about saving themselves, Matt thought. Shouldn't they be trying to abandon this island?

What if nothing in their instincts tells them to do that? What if they're not intelligent enough to figure it out for themselves?

Matt eased his way back down the rise and returned to where he and Sarbin had come ashore. Sarbin swam in slow circles in the shallow water. Azure heavens vaulted over bright blue waters for now, but to the west loomed darkening skies. He could smell rain — a sensation he'd loved since childhood.

Welkin's sun, Chaucer, was still a few hours away from setting. The planet was slightly more distant from Chaucer than Earth from Sol, but the star shone down with about a third more radiation. Without the nanodocs in his bloodstream, Matt could develop skin cancers or worse.

He told Sarbin, "I wish I could let the Sprinters know I'm concerned about them — especially since it looks like the island won't be able to get out of the way of the storm."

"We should go," Sarbin said. "It would be rare for Sprinters to attack anyone on land, but it's not unheard of."

Matt could make out the concern in Sarbin's voice even over the datalink. He waded out into the water. "Let's see what we can find underneath the island, then. I'm afraid that's our last hope."

*****

Human and Aquatile dove deep into the waters around the motile island. As always, Matt was impressed with the variety of life beneath Welkin's waves. The farther down he and Sarbin went, the more life forms proliferated

— familiar seekerfish and sargassum drones, and many others he wished he had the time to examine more closely.

Sarbin skimmed the underside of the island, and Matt aimed his wrist sensor at the thousands of long, thin appendages hanging down beneath it. He flinched as one of the longer ones brushed his head. Swarms of seekerfish emerged from within them and swam past him. I must've spooked them pretty well, he thought.

"Don't be afraid, Matt," Sarbin told him. "Those seekerfish cannot harm you."

"Yeah. Just startled me." He asked Sarbin, "Is there a way to communicate directly with the island?"

"My people know of none. And you must understand, the island is not quite...I don't have a word for it."

"Humans would say 'sentient.' It's means being intelligent and self-aware."

"A marvelous word. But not one meant for these islands."

"These things hanging down cause the island to move, correct?"

"They do," Sarbin said.

"Ah — then they're called flagella."

"You have such things on Earth?"

"Not nearly this large," Matt said. "And not hanging from islands. Of course, we don't have motile islands."

"They should be moving it by now. Can you tell what's wrong?"

Matt glanced at the wrist sensor and frowned. "Not just yet. Once we get back to the submersible, given more computing power and a little time — we'll see."

As Sarbin grasped Matt tightly and propelled them both through the warm ocean waters, the Aquatile said, "I don't understand how you can work to save Sprinters after they attacked you. Doesn't that show you that they're disgusting, just as I told you?"

"I don't like that we were attacked. I especially don't like that you were hurt. But they thought they were protecting their young."

"If Humans had never come here, that storm would wash the Sprinters off that island. It might be damaged, but could probably heal on its own. If you help the Sprinters live, you favor them over Aquatiles."

"No, I don't," Matt said. "I want you both to live. And what about all those Sprinter females? Should they die, along with all their eggs? My experience, and my religion, tell me they should not."

"Humans know a lot of things. But I wonder if they know what it is to be a friend."

Matt, gripped beneath Sarbin's belly, wished he could look into the Aquatile's eyes. "Sometimes I wonder myself. But I think you're teaching me."

*****

The submersible still sat on the nearby, "real," island as dark clouds obscured much of Chaucer's brilliance, bringing an early twilight. Matt left Sarbin at the shoreline and went inside. So. Set the computer to working on the problem at hand — what's wrong with the motile island, and can it be "healed" in time to get it moving away from the coming storm?

Matt also had an idea occur to him, one that he realized he had a unique opportunity to test. In helping Sarbin heal more quickly, he'd gathered tissue both from him and his Sprinter assailant.

Time to compare.

The comp finished that latter task, the simpler one, first. At his first glimpse of the results, he gasped and his eyes went wide.

"How will I ever tell Sarbin", Matt wondered. He'll give birth to kittens, right in front of me!

Then the comp finished its tougher, more important task, and Matt concerns about Sarbin faded, replaced by a much more immediate concern — and deep regret.

*****

Matt left the submersible and went down to the shoreline to speak to Sarbin. The winds whipped at him with enough force he had to lean slightly into them to walk. He squinted against the salty spray continually blown into his face. Sarbin hadn't quite beached himself, but was lying where frequent waves washed over him.

Matt knew that Sarbin could hear him easily over the link, despite the rush of wind all around them, so he spoke quietly: "The large flagella on the island's underside are damaged. What could've caused that?"

"I understand now," Sarbin said. "You remember the many seekerfish we saw beneath the island. Sometimes they hide from predators there. They have protection and food. But if they're discovered, the seekerfish fights the predator among the..."

"Flagella."

"The flagella, yes, and they — and the island — can be injured."

"That doesn't seem as if it would cause so much damage."

"The flagella don't just propel the island. Since they hang down in the water, they also understand changes in temperature and pressure, and realize when the island needs to move." Sarbin looked up at Matt. "Can you heal them? As you did me?"

The salt air stung Matt's eyes and he wiped his face. "The island's so big, it would take days, or weeks. We only have hours."

"I'm sorry, Matt."

"So you feel for the Sprinters, at least a little bit."

Sarbin's stubby arms splashed water to one side, as his gaze left Matt. "I wish I did, for your sake."

"Then you need to hear this," Matt said. "Sprinters and Aquatiles are related."

Sarbin's hands stopped their splashing. The Aquatile looked up at Matt in disbelief. "You can't mean that!"

"I compared your flesh with that of the Sprinter who attacked us. The connection is clear. You had common ancestors far in the past."

"How can I believe that?"

"Perhaps it's difficult to want to believe it."

"Being this close to the land is weighing me down," Sarbin said. He waddled backwards until his tail fluke was in deep enough water to let him swim away from Matt. "And I'm hungry and now my brain's logical half could use some sleep." Sarbin didn't say anything more. He slid backwards into deeper water and with an abrupt tail flip was gone.

Suddenly Matt felt very alone here on this slip of land — and concerned that his friend had disappeared beneath the waters so quickly. "Sarbin!" he shouted, though he knew the Aquatile could certainly hear him over the link.

The darkening sky and blowing wind were Matt's only answer.

*****

Matt retreated into the submersible — the wind and water were kicking up enough that he was grateful for the shelter. He sat in the pilot's seat and looked out at the storm.

I didn't like the way Sarbin left, he thought. Too abrupt. And that business of being hungry, and needing to let half his brain sleep? Excuses.

Matt reached toward the submersible's sensors, but hesitated. Then he said a silent apology for invading Sarbin's privacy and homed in on Sarbin's datalink.

The Aquatile was out there, about three clicks away, circling. Vital signs normal, Matt thought. Probably feeding. And I'd bet he's still angry.

To call again would be an insult. Whatever he and I have to work out, it'll wait.

Another sensor reading. He's on the move now, Matt realized. Wait a minute — headed toward the motile island! What's he up to?

And does he have any idea he's swimming right into a pod of Sprinters?

"Sarbin," he said over the datalink. "Listen to me — you've got to turn back. I don't know what you think you're doing — "

Sarbin's reply revealed his desperation even through the datalink. "Got to help them — they're going to die!"

"Sarbin — you've got Sprinters about to attack you."

"Got to save them!"

The logical half of Sarbin's brain really is asleep, Matt realized. He's not thinking, just reacting. Quickly as he could, he powered up the submersible and lifted toward the ailing motile island. The winds from the tropical storm gained strength by the moment — Matt could feel them buffeting his small craft. For now he stayed airborne, though, since he could make better time in the air.

A quick sensor reading confirmed that Sprinters were patrolling the waters around the island in force. It's as if the storm were something they could repel, Matt thought. They'll consider Sarbin an intruder.

The submersible reached the skies above Sarbin's position. Sensors picked up several Sprinters circling the Aquatile warily, as if working up the courage to approach. After a couple of swift passes, a single Sprinter came from below to strike Sarbin. It was a much stronger blow than the Aquatile had taken in his earlier fight with the Sprinters. Matt thought, I've got to get to him now.

Matt activated his craft's internal gravitics — he no longer felt the winds' buffeting. He was also protected from harm as he arced the submersible downward, sending the craft plunging into the ocean. He opened up its hold, letting it fill with water even as he passed an amazed pod of Sprinters. Two individuals were about to catch up with Sarbin. Not a time to take chances, Matt thought as the Sprinters bore down on his friend. But I don't want to kill them if I don't have to.

A quick thrust from the submersible's gravitics, and its nose struck both Sprinters from behind. They went tumbling away even as Matt called out to Sarbin: "Look above you! Get into the hold."

Sarbin's reply still revealed his intense emotions. "I've got to help them!"

"Sarbin, dammit, wake up your logical side." Matt didn't wait for a reply, but tried to center the entrance of the hold at the bottom of his craft above the Aquatile. Sarbin kept evading him, though, and Matt wished the submersible had an enticement field that would let him pull Sarbin into the hold.

Matt looked forward, and saw the underside of the motile island was less than a click away. And sensors told him more Sprinters were gaining on them.

Matt shook his head in regret. Sorry, Sarbin, he thought, and applied another rapid thrust, striking his friend from behind.

"Matt!" came the anguished cry over his datalink. "Why? Why would you...." Then came only silence.

Please God, Matt thought as he steadied the submersible over the Aquatile's body. I know your greatest desire is for me to see you clearly. I shouldn't ask such a thing, but tell me your design means I haven't killed my friend.

Matt set the submersible's controls to "hover" here beneath the ocean's waves, and went back to the hold. He worked the controls that quickly drained most of the water, grabbed his medkit, then passed through the airlock into the hold. He waded over to Sarbin, who looked up at him with plaintive eyes. "Matt," the Aquatile said. "You..." And Matt waited for the accusations, the anger.

"...saved me," Sarbin said.

Relief flooded Matt as he placed his left hand against Sarbin's side to comfort him as he worked the medical sensor with his right hand. "Thank goodness," Matt said. "Sarbin, you're fine. Not even a broken bone. Just some bruises." He felt around in the medkit for the dermal wand, found it, and passed it over Sarbin's body. "This is starting to be a habit," he said. "What happened? Why wouldn't your logical side wake up?"

Sarbin said, "I was very disappointed in you. The emoting side of my brain was so overloaded, I could barely form words. That left my logical side helpless for a while."

Matt smiled. "My brain works differently, but I understand the feeling."

"I take so much for granted since I met you. It doesn't seem strange anymore to be lifted high into the air, or to speak to Humans, to hear your strange speech translated into clicks and tones."

"But much of what I say is still strange, I'd bet."

"Never apologize for speaking truth, Matt. If I cannot cope with it, the problem is my own, not yours. And you see how well you changed my mind. I nearly killed myself for the Sprinters."

"If we'd realized earlier that the Sprinters couldn't save themselves, I could've had a fleet of submersibles here for them."

"Can't we save any of them?"

"You saw how difficult it was just to rescue you. The Sprinters wouldn't cooperate any more than you did. The submersible doesn't have stunners. Can you see us trying to chase them down, either in the water or at their nests, especially since they'd think we were trying to harm their eggs?"

"You're right," Sarbin said. "But I had to ask."

Moments later, Matt lifted the submersible and flew several hundred meters over the motile island. Winds whipped across its thick vegetation. Leaves and clumps of weeds were propelled across that living landscape and into the air. Matt saw several ambler nests torn apart. The adult Sprinters huddled around their nests, trying to protect their eggs, mostly unsuccessfully.

From the hold, Matt heard Sarbin over the datalink: "The Sprinters count on the island to protect them. They don't know what to do when it fails."

Matt had nothing to add. He brought the submersible into a wide turn to take it out of the storm. Chaucer's brilliance was just barely apparent in the east.

Sarbin said, "You spoke about wanting to see the stars when this mission is over. I'd never cared much to look at the stars until I met you. Now I beach myself all the time just to regard them."

Matt grinned. "And I've had to rescue you more than once when you got stranded once the tide went out."

"I remember the story you told me. And its happy ending."

"I wish today's story had such an ending."

Sarbin said, "We'll remember this day as the one in which the stars didn't shine quite as brightly over Welkin."

Dave Creek

STEALING ADRIANA

When I got the idea for *Stealing Adriana,* as usual I looked to see whether any of my regular series characters would fit into this story. None of them would without some pretty significant shoehorning, so I got to create a new character — Carrie Molina, the "fish." I haven't dealt much in my fiction with people altering their physical form, so it was a fun exercise for me.

I also enjoyed the idea that in sticking to a simpler lifestyle, Mennonites had still advanced technologically over the decades, allowing themselves to move toward a time of fax machines and cell phones.

———————

As Carrie Molina was about to step into the Humboldt River, she saw Jacob Troyer looking at her, and noted the concern in his expression. Jacob told her, "Don't do anything foolish."

"Not unless I really have to," Carrie said. She ignored Jacob glaring at her as she took several deep breaths to prepare herself, then stepped into the river, which curved all the way around the interior of the New Lancaster Habitat.

Carrie ducked her head beneath the surface and paused to allow her bio-engineered body to adapt to existence in water. She didn't breathe water, didn't have gills; the term "fish" was a misnomer. She had to surface to breathe the same as a dolphin or whale. That was because water didn't have enough oxygen absorbed in it for the physical exertion she required, and it didn't transfer oxygen into the bloodstream well enough. There were reasons many of the largest sea creatures were mammals. Her heart rate sped up to pump blood furiously through her body to keep it warm, and her lungs expanded to half-again their usual size.

Carrie swam downstream, toward Malcolm Vicari's compound. She shivered slightly as the micro-dermal ridges of her skin, a trait she shared with dolphins, opened up — a goose-bumply feeling. Though barely visible, they trapped a thin layer of water molecules against her skin. That let her glide through the water with less resistance, since liquid flows against another liquid more smoothly than against the Human body.

Carrie only shivered for an instant, though, as her body made even more severe adaptations. Her blood coursed even more quickly through her veins, and her skin actually thickened slightly. Her legs ached for an instant as they prepared to steal more of her body's energies if Carrie required a sudden burst of speed.

Having blubber like a whale or dolphin might have been more efficient. But, she thought, that would make it tough to get a date on a Friday night back home in Madrid.

Not that I'd worry about it here. I can tell the nightlife here in a Mennonite habitat wouldn't be what I'm used to.

*****

Earlier that day, Carrie was undergoing a brief ritual anyone entering New Lancaster Habitat was obliged to submit to.

"Ow! That hurts like hell!" Carrie rubbed her neck just below her left ear.

"Please, Officer Molina," Detective Jacob Troyer said as he lowered the cylindrical instrument that had just extracted Carrie's datalink. "Language." He placed the instrument and the link on his wooden desk, which was covered with stacks of paper, a ceramic container filled with pens and pencils, and a small phalanx of rubber stamps. Not a comp in sight, not even the simplest vid or graphic readout.

Without her link, Carrie felt cast adrift, separated from the rest of Humanity. Not that there was anyone to communicate with here in New Lancaster. But there'd always been the possibility of a communication from Earth or another habitat or an orbiting spaceship. Not any more, at least while she remained here. "I'm not an officer," she said. "And was that actually offensive to you?"

Jacob looked down his nose at Carrie. He was a tall man in his thirties, and already a bit of gray was showing at his temples. He wore a black vest over a plain white shirt and gray trousers, but his face was clean-shaven. "You believe just because I'm a Mennonite — "

Carrie felt her face grow warm. "I never meant — "

"— and because I live in a single-culture orbital habitat, that I'm unsophisticated." His eyes narrowed. "I'm not shocked. But I don't intend for you to make a habit of such talk while you're here."

Carrie ran a hand through her short black hair. They stood in Troyer's office in the small police headquarters building at one end of the ten-kilometer-long habitat. 15,000 New Order Mennonites lived here in the "Habitat of the Gentle People."

Family farms formed a series of neat and orderly rectangles that curved upwards and met 1.2 K overhead. Peppered among them were paved roads connecting small villages containing single-family homes of wood and stone and family businesses that tanned leather, darned socks, or repaired electric cars or telephones.

Carrie said, "Maybe we should start over."

Jacob asked, "So, if you're not a Unity officer, what exactly are you?"

"A freelance troubleshooter. A fixer. One week I might be searching for an artifact on a world Humans haven't explored before. The next I might be helping colonists find just the right asteroid to make their new home."

"Which makes you the person to confront and capture Malcolm Vicari."

"Detective, I can turn right around and go back down to Earth. That's when Unity officers will come up here. They'll have subpoenas, issue press releases, and the whole thing will be a P.R. disaster for this habitat." Carrie stopped when she saw the mounting fury registering on Jacob Troyer's face.

He said, "Do that, and it looks as if you're interfering with our culture. Then the Unity has a P.R. disaster of its own."

Carrie made herself smile. "Then we understand each other."

"We know Vicari as a godly man. Yet you believe these reports he's abused several women?"

"On Earth, and in several orbital habitats."

"In Shosha last year, I understand? And Newton?"

"Yes," Carrie said. "And New York and London."

"And this year, in Minerva Habitat and right here in New Lancaster?"

Carrie fought not to let her emotions rise at thoughts of Adriana as she said, "And one more. On the Moon."

"Most of which embrace advanced tech. Yet he abused people without being discovered."

"For every tech capability, there's a counter-capability. He's a nanotech engineer, apparently a genius at it. The same tech that allowed him to commit his abuse also protected him from leaving DNA samples, odor residue, fingerprints, anything. And he always found places where there was minimal recording surveillance. All the evidence is circumstantial in these neural attacks."

"Pardon me, the...what?"

"Vicari's body is embedded with nanotech — much like a lifesuit for going outside a spaceship. If he touches you, he can send electrical charges through your limbic system. That's — "

Jacob said, "I know what the limbic system is — modulates emotional responses, memory, sexual desire.'Mennonite' isn't a synonym for 'uneducated.'"

"I'm sorry."

"You're actually better than most visitors. So — a neural attack?"

"An electrical discharge in your limbic system can cause symptoms similar to psychosis, or psychotropic drugs. Specifically it affects the amygdala, which helps process emotions. He can evoke a particular emotion in his victim. And he can...well, the unscientific phrase is that he can absorb it."

"How's that possible?"

"A feedback effect of the electrical discharge. It sears the emotions he captures from others into his memories. He can relive them anytime he likes."

"But...Malcolm Vicari. I've sat next to him at Sunday service. He's contributed money to my neighborhood school. Everyone acquainted with him knows he's a godly man."

Carrie said, "Not everyone. Helena Penner, for instance."

Jacob rubbed his chin. "I believe I've met her."

Carrie muttered, "Small habitat, I guess."

"Plenty of barn raisings, you mean. She lives on a farm several lots down from mine. About twenty, lives with her parents, Abram and Maria. What's her connection to this?"

"She's the one who got away. She was working on his farm, supposedly helping with his bookkeeping. But he assaulted her there. It was the first time he's made that kind of mistake. Ironic, I suppose, that it's the low-tech society where he's discovered."

"How'd the Unity learn about this?"

Carrie shook her head. "There's a lot we don't know. Somehow she got away, sent a message down to Earth. Some sort of link in her home."

"Forbidden tech? In that family's home? I'm surprised."

"By the time authorities on Earth started looking into it, Helena was back on the link begging them not to do anything, it was all a misunderstanding."

Jacob said, "Not unusual for many victims, unfortunately."

"Which is why the first thing I want to do is see her."

"I agree." Jacob rummaged through one of the stacks of paper on his desk. "Oh, here it is." He handed her a sheet of paper and a pen. "If you'd sign here?"

Carrie looked at the document. "What the he...I mean, what am I signing?"

"All very straightforward. Acknowledges that I removed your datalink safely."

Carrie rubbed her neck again. "I guess that amounted to 'safely.'"

Undeterred, Jacob continued: "It also acknowledges your agreement that while you're here in New Lancaster Habitat, you've brought in no other high technology."

Carrie bent over the desk to sign the paper. "This would be a lot easier with some sensors or nano-searchers, or even that datalink. And I'd sure feel a lot safer with a stunner."

"A pity," Jacob said, taking the document from Carrie and returning it to its stack. He opened a desk drawer and pulled out a pistol the likes of which Carrie had never seen before. A fat cylinder ran beneath its barrel. Its grip was made of wood. "This is the only weapon you'll be allowed here."

"What the...heck...is it?"

"An air pistol. This reservoir beneath the barrel holds the compressed air. It can power over a hundred shots, but the clip only holds twelve, so that's plenty." He handed her the pistol.

Carrie turned the weapon from side to side. "What's it shoot?"

"Rubber bullets. They're meant to stun you — not as a stunner does, mind you, but by sheer impact. They can break bones or even kill."

"And you think this will be enough firepower to take on Vicari?"

"I can assure you he doesn't have any advanced weapons. Besides, I'm an excellent shot." Jacob handed over a leather belt and holster. After a bit of fumbling, Carrie figured out how to fasten it securely just above her hips and fasten the flap properly. "Sort of screams that I'm armed."

"It's called a duty holster for a reason. Making it clear that you're armed is one of the requirements for a law enforcement officer here.

"Fine," Carrie said. "Oh, there's one bit of advanced tech I can't change."

Jacob regarded her with suspicion. "What might that be?"

"I'm a 'fish.'"

"Beg pardon?"

"Bio-engineered to exist underwater for long periods without breathing equipment. Vicari's compound's on the Humboldt River. I might have to make my way there without him realizing it." She made her expression as bland as she could. "I hope that isn't a problem."

Carrie had to admit Jacob easily defeated her when it came to bland expressions. "Our habitat charter doesn't allow discrimination based on your physical characteristics, whether natural or acquired," he said. Which, Carrie thought, is a long way from saying whether it's a problem or not.

"Speaking of which," Jacob said, "Does it bother you that I'm acquainted with Vicari? You may think I'm prejudiced in favor of him."

Carrie thought of ashes, of an end of dreams, of a golden face she would never see again. "That's all right," she said. "You'll balance me perfectly. Vicari's latest victim was my big sister Adriana."

*****

Jacob remained silent as he led Carrie out of the police HQ and to an electric car to head to the Penner farm. His features were unreadable as he pulled away from the curb and drove down a broad paved road through a tiny village and into the countryside.

Carrie still expected Jacob to demand an explanation from her — how could he trust her to apprehend Malcolm Vicari in a professional manner when she had such an emotional attachment? How could he know she wouldn't lash out violently, perhaps get them both killed?

But he didn't. Didn't say anything, in fact, as they rode away from the southern end of the habitat, and soon approached the Humboldt River, which was a bright blue band bisecting the habitat. Carrie glimpsed both pleasure boats and larger cargo craft transversing its waters, some heading straight across, others taking the much longer trip "up" and around. A small stream that wound its way through the other side of the habitat, down from a highland area, ended in a waterfall that dropped about thirty meters.

But not in a straight line. "I get it," Carrie said, pointing out the curving trail of water curving to the west. "The habitat's rotating away from the falling water."

Jacob said, "The water's actually falling in a straight line. It just doesn't look like it." After a moment, Jacob spoke in a more serious tone. "How did Vicari get away with his crimes for so long?"

"A lot of it was brute force computing — looking at who had visited each of those cities or habitats during the time frames when women were assaulted. There were more than you might have thought. And in Shosha, he was nearly caught."

"What happened?"

"He apparently bribed his way off."

Jacob's expression turned sour. "Someone would let a man like that go free just for greed?"

"Shosha doesn't pay its security workers very well. If someone's wondering how to pay that month's rent or put away money for his child's education, a big enough bribe can be quite a temptation."

"So we take him into custody, just like that."

"That's Plan A."

"And if it's not that simple?"

"Then you'd better hope I have a Plan B."

Farmlands rose before them now, soaring "up" until they met overhead. They glided past fields tended by large electric combines and threshing machines and by men and women using rakes and hoes.

It was difficult for Carrie to rid herself of the impression that the car was standing still and the habitat was rolling beneath her, as if she were a gerbil in a plastic wheel. She blurted out, "Whatever you have to say about me, let's get it into the open."

For an instant, Jacob's focus of concentration appeared to be on guiding the car smoothly around a sharp curve. But Carrie saw his jaw clench, saw the tips of his fingers whiten as he gripped the steering wheel. "I'm trusting you not to let what happened to your sister affect your judgment. Which means I'm taking responsibility for you. Do you understand?"

Carrie sat up in her seat. "It means I have a responsibility toward you, as well."

Jacob gave the smallest of nods. "That was the right answer."

"You can have faith in me."

"I have faith only in the Lord. You'll have to settle for trust — and conditional trust, at that." Jacob continued driving, and Carrie was once again lost in the image of the cylindrical world rolling around her.

*****

As Carrie continued swimming toward Vicari's compound, she came up for another quick breath, rode the wake of a passing barge, then continued the sharp strokes and kicks that propelled her through the water more swiftly than even the most accomplished non-modified Human swimmer. And in this habitat, she thought, I don't have to worry about heat detection sensors or sonar or cameras discovering me, about energy bolts or even slug-throwing weapons targeting me.

Maybe I could learn to like it here after all.

She paused again, allowed her head to break the surface, looked around. Darkness had fallen more deeply than she was accustomed to in other habitats. No metropolitan areas blazed with light; the only illumination came from farmhouse windows and the occasional security spotlight or streetlight.

A world without a moon, Carrie thought. Or even stars.

The sound of a dog's barking carried from a homestead beyond Vicari's, then was obscured as a pleasure boat glided past on the still river.

Carrie drifted downstream the final few meters, approaching Vicari's property without having to make strokes that might have been heard from above.

She floated smoothly and silently until she was even with Vicari's property, then eased her head just above water level and looked around. Two boats were there at the dock. Each a nice comfortable size, Carrie thought, without being ostentatious. A wooden stairway zigzagged its way up a twenty meter cliff to the house.

She looked up, but a wide rock outcropping blocked her view of the house until she let herself drift to one side. Light shone from a wide picture window overlooking the river.

There sure is a lot of activity up there, Carrie thought. Lots of people moving around — what the hell?

He's bugging out, Carrie realized. I misjudged him. I thought he'd try to bluff his way through, or even confront us physically.

And I don't have time to get back to Jacob.

*****

Earlier, as they pulled up to the Penner farm, Carrie felt as if she'd been transported back a couple of centuries. The house was modest but sturdy, wood construction, painted white with a red roof and trim. Behind the house stood a barn, its paint job not as recent, it's broad wooden doors standing open. Past the barn, she saw several cows in a wide field, some grazing, others lazing on the ground. A rich combination of smells wafted from that field — animal fur, hay, manure, and some odors Carrie couldn't identify.

As she walked toward the Penner home, she heard an odd sound and stopped in her tracks. "What's that?" she asked.

Jacob also stopped and listened. "What's what?"

Carrie looked more closely at the cows. "Oh, they're mooing! I've never heard that before."

Jacob favored her with a grudging grin. "It's called 'lowing.' That sound they make."

"How do you know that?"

"This is my home," Jacob said, and proceeded toward the house.

As they stepped onto the unscreened porch, Carrie thought it curious that no one had taken notice of them. Jacob knocked on the front door and when no one answered, he went to a window, leaned over, and peered inside.

"Isn't that rude?" Carrie asked.

He looked up at her. "It's neighborly enough."

A voice behind them, male and gruff: "How can I help ye?"

Carrie started, turned, and thought: Now this is the real thing, the pure stuff. The man standing there sported a full beard. His coveralls were dirty and worn, real workman's clothes and not a retro fashion statement. The pitchfork he was leaning against completed the picture.

Carrie's initial impression was that the man was close to a century old — his hair was nearly all gray, and his face was deeply wrinkled. But she quickly revised that, realizing here was a man who was living his natural life span, not one augmented by medical or cosmetic biotech — he may not have been older than 45.

Jacob bounded off the porch and extended his hand. "Mr. Penner, we've met at a couple of barn raisings, I believe."

Penner shook Jacob's hand. "Troyer's your name, isn't it?"

"Yes, sir, Officer Jacob Troyer." He indicated Carrie. "And this is Carrie Molina, from — "

"From Earth, I'd gather," Penner said as he shook Carrie's hand.

"Yes sir," Carrie said. "When did I start wearing a sign marked EARTHER?" she wondered. Never mind that it's probably apparent in every word I speak, the way I walk, probably even in how I shake hands.

Penner's face revealed a deep suspicion. "You're here about Helena, aren't you?"

Carrie was about to speak up, but Jacob beat her to it. "We are, sir."

"She's in the fields working. As she should be."

Carrie said, "You know how important this is."

Penner's expression was unyielding. "I know how important my daughter is to me. I won't have her be...disturbed again."

"Sir — your attitude toward your daughter is admirable. But there's plenty of other fathers who should be just as concerned about their own daughters."

"That's their responsibility. Helena is mine."

Carrie let her shoulders slump and her hands fall to her sides. She lowered her head for a moment, then looked Penner in the eye. "I want to respect your wishes, sir. But I have a duty here, just as your duty's to your family."

Penner addressed Jacob. "And what is your responsibility here, Officer? Obviously not to protect my family from unnecessary prying by outsiders."

Jacob said, "Mr. Penner, what would you think of another girl's father who could've allowed her to speak up but didn't? How could you not blame him if something happened to another girl?"

Penner grasped his pitchfork's handle with both hands and thrust its prongs into the dirt before him. "The time for blame is past — long past. My blame arrived when I allowed Helena to work for that man."

Carrie said, "Mr. Penner, she's twenty years old, she can do what she wants."

"That's what I told myself then. I can't change it. But I won't let it happen again."

"But, sir — "

Jacob took a step in front of Carrie. Heat rose to her face and she nearly pushed him aside but at the last instant thought better of it. Jacob shook Mr. Penner's hand and said, "I thank you for your time, sir. We won't bother you again." He strode off toward the car.

He's just assuming I'll follow, Carrie thought, like some nice little girl.

I'll follow, all right, Carrie thought as she jogged to catch up to Jacob. But I won't be nice about it.

*****

Carrie was still fuming as Jacob led her back to the car. "What the hell was that all about?"

Jacob wagged a finger at Carrie as if she were a child whose mouth he was about to wash out with soap. "Now, now. Language again."

"Well, then, whoop-de-do or kiss-my-whatever. You'd better have a damned good reason for that."

Jacob opened the driver's side door but paused with one foot inside. "By 'that' I suppose you mean abandoning a conversation that was going to yield us exactly nothing."

"Well, uh...yeah. I guess."

"Fine. As long as you know what you're complaining about." He got into the car. Carrie took a deep breath, then eased in next to him. Jacob pulled the car away from the Penner farm. He said, "I did as much as I could for Mr. Penner. I let him know I respect him and his views. Now we talk to Helena anyway."

Carrie grinned. "So your idea for a Plan B was the same as mine!"

"I'm more concerned about what happened to Helena than I am about Mr. Penner's feelings."

Carrie let her grin fade. "I have to admit, you surprise me."

"Because I don't approve of a man abusing a woman? Because I'm willing to violate a father's wishes to find out what really happened here?"

"It's not that, it's — "

"What? My not wearing a beard? Not speaking in 'thees' and 'thous?' I'm a man like any other. There are as many different shadings of Mennonite belief as there are individuals in this habitat."

"You're being unfair."

"Perhaps you just think that because you don't believe."

"Actually, I rather do. But your beliefs seem more personal than mine."

Jacob's smile was...beatific was the only word that came to Carrie's mind. She'd never seen such peace reflected in a man's face. He said, "My relationship with God is indeed personal. And intellectual and emotional. Even though I live in a man-made structure, this Human handiwork reveals His own."

Carrie said, "I might be convinced to envy you for that."

Jacob slowed the car as they passed another field where several men and women toiled. He pulled to the side of the road and took a small handheld device from his pocket. A flick of the wrist, and the top part levered upward, forming an "L" shape.

"Some sort of communicator? I'm surprised."

"Just a cell phone."

"A...what?"

"A cellular phone. It...never mind." Jacob punched several numbers into the phone's small keypad, then put it to his ear and listened. "Looks like her calls are blocked."

"You had her contact number the entire time? Why didn't you just call her before we got here?"

"I was sincere about wanting to go through her father first." He selected a different series of numbers. "But did she block texting?" Seeing Carrie's puzzled expression, he explained: "It's one thing to block calls. But young people love to text-message, and can do it more unobtrusively than talking." More number-punching and he was done. "Well, it looks like it went through. I told her who we are and where we are."

Carrie looked out toward the field again. "What are they harvesting out there, anyway?"

Jacob was still staring at his phone. "Timothy and clover, mostly."

"So they harvest that, and form those bales of hay?"

Another grin from Jacob. "Someday I'll have to meet you down on Earth and we'll take a look around. I can just hear myself: 'So, I press the button on the replicator and food just appears?'"

"So you know more about my society than I do about yours. But — "

"Wait — here comes a reply. We're to meet Helena on the northern end of the Penner property."

"Let's go, then," Carrie said.

Jacob guided the car down the road, then turned north at the first intersection.

*****

Helena stood at the edge of the roadway next to a low rock wall, leaning against her pitchfork in a stance eerily similar to her father's. Her work clothing seemed newer, less worn, but Helena herself, at age twenty, seemed closer to her father's age. Her face was dusty, she had the beginnings of lines at the corners of her mouth and eyes, and her eyes were sunken. Damn, she thought, life in the fields ages you.

When Carrie and Jacob got out of the car, Helena's posture stiffened even more. She said, "I didn't believe it. My first time seeing an Earther."

"Beg pardon?" Carrie said, utterly flummoxed that a woman she'd just met would go out of her way to insult her. "Listen, young lady, I'm here to help you."

Helena spit on the ground, just centimeters from Carrie's feet. "That's what I think of your help."

Jacob said, "I understand, Miss Penner, that you're still upset. But you're the one who called for help."

Helena leaned her chin on the pitchfork's handle. "Oh. That was a mistake."

"The mistake may have been using forbidden tech to make that call."

"I...wasn't thinking. Please don't make us get rid of the comm. My father...he uses it to talk to his brother down in Iowa, that's all."

Jacob said, "So now we're telling truths."

Helena lowered her chin from the pitchfork handle and held it close to her chest. "Yes sir."

"And a little respect toward our guest from Earth would be good, too. Your father raised you better than that."

Helena's eyes flicked toward Carrie, then away. "I'm sorry, Ma'am."

Carrie said, "Helena, we don't care about the tech. We just want to know what happened between you and Malcolm Vicari."

Helena looked at Jacob. "Could you walk down the road a ways?"

"Of course."

Helena watched until Jacob was out of earshot. "There's some things a man shouldn't hear."

"I understand," Carrie said.

Helena raised her pitchfork, then stuck it into the ground. She sat on the low rock wall, back straight, hands in her lap, fingers interlaced. She looks like a schoolgirl about to recite a story, Carrie thought.

Helena stared at the ground. "What do you want me to tell you?"

"The truth."

Helena sniffed, and wiped her nose with her hand. "The truth will set you free. John 8:32."

I won't respond, Carrie thought. Sometimes silence is the best way to get someone to talk. Let the other person want to fill that empty space.

And Helena did: "I only wanted a job. Something to let me be on my own. My father considers me an old maid, you know. But he hardly lets me out of the fields or away from the house — how in this world can I ever meet my husband?"

"How'd you start working with Malcolm Vicari?"

"He heard during services one week that I was good with numbers. And I'd taken bookkeeping in our habitat's college. He was willing to give me a chance, though he couldn't pay much."

"How did...."

"It happen?"

"Yes."

Helena said, "I was staying late one night. It was near dark, but Mr. Vicari said he'd give me a ride home. I called my father and he didn't like me being out late, but Mr. Vicari spoke to him and...and told him he'd keep me safe."

"How far is his house?"

Helena pointed up and to the right, on the opposite side of her inside-out world. "Just on the other side of the Humboldt River. See the red barn with the white roof?"

"So not far. And this strikes me as being a much safer habitat than many."

"I wouldn't know about that. I've never been to another." Helena looked down at the ground again.

Carrie spoke up quickly to keep Helena from winding down. "Then what happened?"

"He came into his study, which was where I worked during the day. It was dark out now, and just one light was on. When I looked up and saw him, I 'bout jumped, 'cause of how shadows fell across his face."

How did Adriana react when she first glimpsed him? Carrie wondered. She forced that thought down and asked Helena, "What did you do?"

"Just...sat there. He said he was sorry he scared me. Then he...are you sure you want to hear this?"

I'd rather hear anything else in the world, Carrie thought. "It's what I have to hear. To do my job."

Helena's interlaced fingers tightened until her hands shook. A tear fell onto one wrist and when Carrie looked at Helena's face she saw more about to well over. Helena said, "I'm sorry I called you that before. You know, when I called you a — "

"You don't have to say it again."

"Yeah. I guess not. So Mr. Vicari came to me. He didn't say anything else. He...touched my face. And it was like an electric shock went through me."

"What did you do?"

"It surprised me so. I stood up too quickly, and my head began to swim. He told me to be careful and grabbed my shoulders. He never touched me before. His hands were as strong as I remember my dad's being when I was little and he used to pick me up and throw me up in the air. And I could smell him — Mr. Vicari, I mean. Not in a bad way, just...I don't know."

"You weren't used to him being that close to you."

"He held my arm with one hand and touched my face again with the other. It was like I was paralyzed, only...I wasn't."

"Not physically, you mean."

Helena turned her head toward Carrie and now the tears flowed, making little rivulets down her dusty face. "It was like I couldn't make myself move. Like he had some sort of power over me, something ungodly and evil."

"It's just tech," Carrie said. "Nothing supernatural."

Helena glared at Carrie. "I don't consider my idea of evil to be something 'supernatural.' Like it's not real."

"All I'm saying is that he's a man like any other. He hurt you using machines. That doesn't make him any less...evil."

Helena looked down the road, and Carrie realized she was making sure Jacob was still well away from them. "I haven't even told my mother everything."

"We don't want Vicari to keep doing this. He's assaulted other women, left them empty shells with no personality. He could have killed you."

Helena rubbed her eyes, as if trying to wipe away an image to terrible to look upon. "Like I said — it's as if I was paralyzed. There's something he did. Something I've had a hard time understanding."

Carrie waited. Helena looked around her, as if someone might sneak up on them to eavesdrop. "He stole an emotion from me. I'm a Christian woman. I'm expected to think kindly of everyone, even those who have sinned. But I can't anymore, not for someone like Malcolm Vicari."

"Because of the way he treated you."

"No, it's what he did with that...what is it, nanna-stuff?"

"Nanotech."

"Yes, that. He stole that feeling from me, took it for himself. He was looking for something else. Something to do with, you know, sex. Or just, whatever's in your brain that makes you feel good."

"How'd you get away from him?"

"He just stopped. Told me he was sorry, that he should never have done that to me. Then he left, and I ran away."

Carrie touched Helena's arm. "You're a brave young woman. You've done nothing wrong."

Helena stood. "Thank you." She leaned in close. "If you have to kill the bastard or rip off his balls, tell him to think of me while you're doing it." She grabbed her pitchfork and strode back across the field, leaving Carrie staring in astonishment. Damn, she thought. Language.

And she let her own tears flow as she thought of Adriana.

*****

When she arrived beneath Malcolm Vicari's compound, Carrie swam toward the dock, making each stroke as quietly as she could, conscious now of every splash, every breath. And she had no way of knowing how close Vicari was to leaving.

As she raised herself up onto the dock, her heart rate eased, lungs contracted, and she felt goose-bumply again as her micro-dermal ridges closed up. She wished she had a datalink, one of those damn phones, anything that would let her contact Jacob.

I bet this is that foolish thing he warned me against, she thought. Vicari bribed himself off Shosha. Godly as these people are here in New Lancaster, it just takes one customs official with worldly needs to let him get away again. If he's smart — and he is — he's already got one in his pocket.

Carrie decided it would be too risky to go up the stairway — she'd be trapped on it if Vicari or one of his men started down, with nowhere to hide. Instead, she made her way up the rocky hill, groaning with pain each time she stepped on a sharp rock. Dammit, she thought, I'm a water beast, not a land one — my feet are too tender. Twenty meters didn't seem so high when I wasn't climbing them straight up.

Halfway to the top, she sensed movement above her. She looked up. Malcolm Vicari and two other men, presumably a couple of his farmhands, stood there. They were all pointing air pistols at her. Carrie froze.

"You may as well come on up," Vicari said. "This pistol might not necessarily be lethal, but one shot could knock you off this little cliff. You could break your neck."

*****

Earlier, just after Carrie finished speaking with Helena, she heard Jacob's footsteps behind her. She wiped her face with hands that wouldn't stop shaking. Jacob said, "I was about to say that must've been difficult for her. But I see it was just as hard for you."

"I'm sorry," she told Jacob.

Carrie saw conflicting emotions play over Jacob's face. "Nothing to apologize for," he said. "I couldn't hear Helena's words, but I heard her tone of voice. I saw her face."

A couple more tears made their way down Carrie's face, but she didn't wipe them away. "I'm ready now."

Jacob went to the car and retrieved a pair of binoculars from a compartment just in front of the passenger seat. He handed them to Carrie.

"What am I looking for?"

"Whatever you can see from here."

Carrie raised the lenses to her eyes. "Well, I can make out his house — a very nice house, by the way. Dock down below. I see a couple boats down there, under a very big rock outcropping. I bet he just loves to sit on that rock and look out over the water and think big philosophical thoughts. There's the barn. Fields, lots of people working in them. Cows. Horses."

"It's all sort of generic to you, isn't it?" Jacob asked, a hint of humor in his voice."

"Sorry. Different life. Cities. Nanotech. By the way, when's the next cloudy day scheduled?"

"They aren't. We realized we had to accept weather tech, but we insisted it stay somewhat random."

"Then we can't count on being able to sneak up on him."

"No, we can't," Jacob said. "We'd best be on our way." He headed for the car, Carrie right behind him.

*****

Within minutes Jacob was pulling into a parking lot at a small marina. About a dozen craft of varying sizes bobbed gently in the waters of the Humboldt River. Jacob led the way and Carrie soon found herself stepping gingerly off the dock into a police boat. It reminded her of the water taxis she'd often seen while visiting her aunt in Venice.

The small cabin was just big enough for them to sit side by side. Jacob took the pilot's position and started the boat's motor. "Very nice," Carrie said. "I suppose your department has to patrol the river, as well."

"This river helps define the habitat. A lot of commerce travels on it. Some people think of themselves as southerners or northerners." Jacob pulled the boat out into the river, steering confidently while remaining alert for river traffic. He slowed as a towboat passed by, pushing a barge. The craft eased past them, its wake creating a minor roller coaster effect for the small police boat. When it was safe, Jacob pulled farther out into the main body of the river.

Carrie felt content to lose herself within her own senses for a time — the sweeping sight of the habitat's interior as it rose to either side then overhead, and the rhythmic slap of waves against the side of the boat.

It reminded her of watching the kilometer-long cruise ships come in at Barcelona. The scents of oil and sewage, even with the ship diligently employing nanotech to clean up after itself, would overpower the ocean's salt smell and the honey-like scent of Spanish broom, modified to flourish in a damp, salty environment, in a nearby field.

Jacob's voice broke into her line of thought: "Tell me about your sister."

At the thought of Adriana, Carrie's facial muscles relaxed even more and she even managed a wan smile. "She was a couple of years older than me, and I called her my guiding star when we were growing up. Other than my parents, she was the only person I ever loved unconditionally."

Carrie let herself get caught up again in the chug-chug of the boat's motor and the feel of the spray on her arm. Water that smelled more of chlorine than the sea.

Jacob asked, softly, "How did you find out what happened?"

"Not until recently. When the Unity approached me. All I knew before was that she was the victim of a neural attack."

"Like with Helena."

"Stealing emotions is how it starts. Then he ends up destroying the personality."

"How in the world does he pick the emotional response he wants?"

"From the way Helena talked, it sounds like he can't. It's as if he's accessing a series of computer files. My briefing from the Unity said the process can take anywhere from a few seconds to close to half an hour."

Jacob said, "Or like me flipping through my rolodex."

Whatever a "rolodex" is, Carrie thought. "It happened in Aristarchus City," she said. "She was with some friends having pizza at A Fall of Moondust."

"I've been there," Jacob said. "I get their special — it's one-sixth larger than the regular size, you know."

Carrie didn't want to smile, but couldn't help herself. "Yeah. They always got that, too. It was late and Adriana walked home by herself. No one thought anything of it. She'd done it a hundred times...when they found her, she was — empty."

"Empty?"

"Perfectly healthy physically. She likes to eat ice cream, or for me to run my hands through her hair. But there's no personality. Her body is there, but what makes her Adriana is gone. He stole her."

Carrie couldn't find any more words. She set her features against her grief, steeling herself against a full-fledged outpouring of the raw stuff, like she'd allowed all those nights in Aristarchus City or Madrid or closeted in her quarters on some starcraft, clutching her pillow, shaking uncontrollably, tasting the salt of the tears as they soaked the pillowcase, as the only thought her consciousness could retain was Adriana's unperceiving eyes within a living body.

Carrie realized the slapping of the waves against the boat's hull had filled the silence. She told Jacob, "You have to forgive me."

His expression was kindly, understanding. "That's not my place." He guided the boat toward another small marina at this opposite shore of the river.

*****

Carrie helped Jacob tie up the police boat at the dock. She was impressed to see that another car was waiting for them. "How'd you do that?" she asked.

"I asked HQ over here to provide a vehicle, and said I wouldn't need additional personnel. They trust me."

But as Jacob started toward the car, she grabbed his arm. "I want to get the lay of his land, so to speak, before we rush into anything."

"How do you intend to do that?"

"Let's go behind the marina office."

Jacob was clearly perplexed, but followed her all the same. She led him behind the marina's small office. It was a single story tall, and for some reason appeared sturdy enough to withstand a hurricane. "OK," she said, "You notice we can't see Vicari's compound from here. That means he can't see us, especially as it grows darker."

Jacob stood with his hands on his hips, and Carrie could tell he was becoming more impatient by the moment. "So what do you intend to do?"

"Sometimes I even have a Plan C. Hold my clothes while I take the plunge to get a closer look at things up ahead. Oh, you don't have to turn your back — I'm wearing a bathing suit, which is more than I usually do, for goodness sake." For goodness sake? Carrie thought? Where did that come from?

Jacob reached out a hand to accept her clothing. "Is this a good idea, Carrie?"

"I intend to get a closer look at his compound, from a direction he doesn't expect."

"That's all you'll do? You'll come right back?"

No, Carrie, better not say "swear to God." "Promise."

Jacob said, "I only have the one phone, and it wouldn't survive being underwater, anyway. We'll be out of touch."

"Vicari's compound isn't quite half a K away. I should be back in an hour," Carrie said. "If you don't see me by then, the original plan's off — call for backup."

*****

After marching Carrie up the hill, Vicari told the farmhands to stay outside the house. It's every bit as nice close-up as it was from a distance, she thought. Vicari marched her through a sun deck at the side of the house, through an elaborately furnished living room, and into the same office where he'd abused Helena. Quality wood desk, she thought, just like Jacob's. No comp. A keyboard attached to some sort of metal implement. Looks like you'd have to bang on the keys pretty hard. Lots of fancy wooden bookshelves, stuffed with volume after volume.

I admit it. I'm scared.

Once she reached the center of the room, Carrie turned to face Vicari. He was still pointing the pistol at her. To her own surprise, her fear washed away, and she knew only anger — part of it was that he was such an ordinary-looking man, dark hair down to his shoulders, clean-shaven, eyes bright with intelligence. A man who works in his office every day, Carrie thought, and probably spends much of his nights reading all of those books.

How dare he not be a monster? How dare he be so...mundane?

"Nothing to say for yourself?" Vicari asked.

Sorry, Adriana, was all she could think of. But mention her sister's name, Carrie knew, and he'd only be more likely to kill her. "We could play this out like one of those cube dramas. I could tell you there's no chance you'll leave this habitat."

Vicari took a step forward and centered his aim between Carrie's eyes. "Reality's a little messier. I'm trying to stop, you know. I almost have. But you've just made everything that much more complicated."

And that's when Carrie heard a chuffing sound, then heard it again, followed by two dull thumps. It can't be, Carrie thought. He wouldn't be that foolish — as foolish as I've been!

As Vicari turned toward the doorway, Carrie saw her chance — she leaped forward to grab Vicari's arms from behind. He bent forward to throw Carrie over his shoulder, but she managed a kick against the back of his leg and he fell to his knees.

Jacob appeared in the doorway even as Carrie reached for Vicari's pistol again. Vicari tore himself away from her grasp and fired at Jacob.

Even as Carrie saw Jacob was struck in the head, Vicari's other arm thrust back and struck her in the face. She fell backwards, stunned. She felt a hand touching her face, then nothing...

*****

...until she realized she was lying on the floor of Vicari's office. She sat up, rubbed her nose, and was glad to find it wasn't broken, saw Jacob lying in the doorway.

Not dead, please, Carrie thought. She went to him, touched his neck. Good pulse. "Thank your hypothetical God," she muttered. Now — where was Vicari?

She rushed back through the living room and the sun room, past the prone bodies of Vicari's two farmhands, and heard a motor start up behind the house. One of the boats, Carrie realized. A few steps brought her to the overlook. Sure enough, Vicari was starting up a boat, certain to pull away any second.

I can survive a twenty-meter jump into water, Carrie thought. And the water comes up to the dock, not to a shoreline — it's plenty deep.

But that damn rock outcropping's in the way. I'd splatter against it like a melon.

Vicari's boat left the dock, headed west. Carrie had about a second to react — no time to run past the outcropping.

Then she made the connection — he's headed west. The image of the curving waterfall flashed into Carrie's mind —

— and she jumped.

First came a horrifying instant in which the outcropping seemed to fill Carrie's entire frame of vision and she knew she was dropping straight down — then it was as if an unseen force pushed her smoothly aside and she cleared the rock easily and splashed into the river to one side of Vicari's boat.

The instant she struck the water, Carrie twisted around, retaining as much momentum as she could, and swam hard toward the surface. She'd been out of the water briefly enough that her body quickly adapted again.

Carrie marshaled all her strength and made a final push to break the surface and grasp the edge of the boat. As Vicari, standing at the boat's controls, turned toward her in surprise, she pushed up with her arms, got a leg over, and leaped at him. She struck him full-force with her body, slamming him into the boat's controls.

Carrie could tell Vicari had the breath knocked out of him, but he wasn't giving up yet — he reached toward her face, but she knocked his hands away, grabbed him by the shoulders, and pulled him around in front of her.

Then she gave him a shove and savored his look of amazement as he fell backwards into the river.

She dove after him.

Vicari was struggling to stay afloat as Carrie landed on him. She grabbed him around the neck and pulled him beneath the surface.

Vicari's hands swung at her, and Carrie took some pretty good blows to her head. Doesn't matter, she thought. I can stay under a lot longer than he can. Let him start using up the oxygen in his bloodstream, let the CO_2 build up, he panics, and I have him just where I want him.

When Vicari really began flailing about, Carrie pushed him away and looked closely at his face — the eyes wide with fear, mouth closed tightly as he fought not to breathe.

Maybe you know just a little of what Adriana felt, in the final moments when she could feel anything at all.

Just a little.

Carrie twisted around again, let her strong legs propel her beneath Vicari, grasped him from behind, and rushed him back to the surface.

*****

Jacob was coming down the wooden stairway as Carrie was pulling Vicari onto the dock. He kneeled down to help her. "Is he alive?" he asked.

"Yes," Carrie said. Vicari coughed up water. She rolled him onto his side until he stopped.

Jacob asked him, "Mr. Vicari, are you all right?"

Vicari spit out more water and indicated Carrie. "No thanks to her — she tried to drown me! I want — "

"I was only asking so I could know to cuff you." Which he did, then pulled Vicari to his feet. He took his prisoner by the arm and led him up the stairway.

Carrie followed them, saying, "Jacob, I can't thank you enough for — "

"I told you I was an excellent shot. I had you figured out from the beginning, by the way. I knew your plan D had to be ditching me and taking on Vicari by yourself."

"Plan D? I never have a plan D."

They approached the front of Vicari's house, where Jacob's car waited. The farmhands were already cuffed and in the back seat. Jacob put Vicari in with him and shut the door.

That's when Carrie saw the haunted expression on Jacob's face. "What's wrong?"

Jacob put a hand to his face and Carrie could see he was fighting back tears. That's when she realized: "Vicari touched me just as I blacked out. Sheer spite, I guess. I can't tell that he did anything to me, but if he touched you, too...."

Jacob lowered his hand. Tears streamed down his face. "I...told you my relationship with God is personal, intellectual, and emotional."

"You did, but — "

"He stole that emotional connection." Jacob made a fist and stared at it. "It's as real as this. But anyone you tell about it has to take your word — you can't quantify it."

"What will you do?"

Jacob stared toward the river. "Keep living my life as I always have." He looked at Carrie. "Does that surprise you?"

"You said you had faith only in the Lord. That's more than something you feel, isn't it? For you, it's knowledge."

"Maybe you do understand after all. Com'on, I've got your clothes in the car. Let's get you dressed again, and these guys back to my office. Are you sure Vicari didn't harm you when he touched you?"

"It doesn't feel like it," Carrie said. "Remember — the length of time it takes him to gain access can vary quite a bit."

"So maybe I was just unlucky."

"I'm sorry."

Jacob told her, "You'd better hope it isn't something you only realize later."

"I'll be fine once we get Vicari on the way back to Unity custody."

*****

A week later, Carrie entered Adriana's bedroom. Her sister didn't look up, but continued staring out her window. Since Adriana's "window" was a hundred meters below the lunar surface, it was really a holo of a village in the La Apujarra region of southern Spain. White-walled homes spread across a steep hillside, the occasional church steeple jutting out from among them. A series of mountain ranges stretched to the horizon, seemingly acting as protectors for the village and its inhabitants.

Carrie sat on Adriana's wide bed. *She's still so beautiful,* she thought as she ran her hand through her sister's jet black hair, the same as her own, and across the smooth skin of Adriana's face, then cupped her chin.

Adriana looked at Carrie, but without recognition. Her face was set in a smile that hadn't wavered since Vicari's attack. *I wish I could know whether that reflects a real happiness within her,* Carrie thought. She took Adriana's hand and squeezed, without receiving a squeeze in return.

Carrie's tears arrived, as they usually did at this point in her visits. *I can only hope I'm giving her some comfort,* she thought. *I guess I'm kind of like Jacob in that respect. He can't feel the presence of his Lord, and I can't feel whether Adriana is really with me, or if I'm all alone.*

I suppose that's...

Wouldn't that be ironic?

Except it doesn't feel — wait a minute! That's the only thing could manage in the instant he touched me? My sense of irony?

And that's also...except I can't feel that, either.

"You son of a bitch!" she said, and lost herself to full-throated laughter even as she shed tears for her smiling sister.

MIDWIFE CRISIS

In reading a *National Geographic* article about blue whales, I was struck by a description of their arteries that said they were wide enough that a person could swim through them. Well, there's an SF story if I ever heard one!

Remember how I look at an SF idea and see if it's suitable for any of my existing characters? In *Stealing Adriana* I didn't have anyone who fit, so I created Carrie Molina.

Well, when I started considering the idea for what became *Midwife Crisis* (*Inside Job* was an early title), I knew I needed a water world, and the planet Welkin certainly filled the bill. All I had to do was establish the species called Leviathans, which are even bigger than blue whales, and I knew Sarbin would soon be swimming around inside one.

But I didn't want Matt Christian in there with him — I needed a person with special skills that Matt doesn't have. That's when I realized Carrie would be the perfect recruit for the job — I like doing these kinds of crossover stories anyway, because it adds to the "reality" of my future history.

"So let me get this straight," Carrie Molina said. This was only about five minutes after landing on the water world called Welkin. She stood on a landing pad where her small shuttle barely fit next to a submersible craft. The pad stood next to a small Earth Unity base perched upon a motile island. She heard waves splashing ashore and caught a whiff of salt spray. "You brought me here to inject me into a creature called a Leviathan so I can treat its unborn child? What am I, some sort of antivirus, or something?"

Carrie saw Matt Christian's grimace and knew she wasn't making a good first impression, but she didn't care. *You opened the door with this crazy idea for a mission,* she thought, *and you take whatever comes through it.*

"Not at all," Matt said. He was a tall, slender man in his late twenties, just a little younger than Carrie. "It's all fairly straightforward. The Leviathan's not quite fifty meters long — "

"That's about twice as big as a blue whale back on Earth!"

"Exactly the analogy I was about to use."

"And the medical problem it's having is...what?"

Carrie watched Matt take a deep breath. "Why don't you come see her for yourself? And as soon as he gets here, I can introduce you to your partner."

"Partner?"

"He's someone I work with closely," Matt said. "And he should complement your own unique abilities."

*****

Carrie followed Matt down to the shoreline and a dock. No boats were tied up there, but her eyes widened as she spotted a dark presence floating just at the surface of the water. Matt said, "Meet the Leviathan — Varis. She has datalink access, but she doesn't care to speak to Humans much. She's a little prejudiced against landside life forms."

He didn't exaggerate the size, Carrie thought. No wonder they're called Leviathans. I've traveled aboard ships that were smaller.

A closer look, and she found herself staring into eyes the size of bowling balls. Eyes with an amazing intelligence behind them, she thought. And I don't think I'm anthropomorphizing. Just behind those eyes was a pair of blowholes — Varis was, like an Earthly whale, an air breather, not a fish. A mouth the width of a small shuttlecraft opened and Varis chomped down on a clump of vegetation provided for her at dockside. The chewing sounds were prodigious.

Matt said, "Your partner should be here soon." He shed his clothing except for swim trunks and jumped into the water. He placed both his hands upon the dark form of the Leviathan. Carrie didn't hesitate, and removed her own clothing — she wasn't wearing a swimsuit, but was accustomed to casual nudity — and moved toward the edge of the dock.

Even as she stepped off, Carrie was conscious of the differences between Welkin and Earth. Its .85 grav meant she fell just an bit longer than she would have on the home world, and when she dove beneath its waters, she was aware that the water didn't press against her as much as she was accustomed to.

She took a moment for what Matt called her "unique abilities" to assert themselves. They were, after all, why she was here. As her bio-engineered body adapted to her environment, her heart rate sped up to pump blood furiously through her body to keep it warm, and her lungs expanded to half-again their usual size.

Carrie didn't breathe water, didn't have gills; the often-used term "Human fish" was a misnomer. Water didn't retain enough oxygen absorbed in it for the physical exertion she required, and it didn't transfer oxygen into the bloodstream as efficiently. There were reasons many of the largest sea creatures were mammals.

She shivered slightly as the micro-dermal ridges of her skin, a trait she shared with dolphins, opened up — a goose-bumply feeling. Though barely visible, they trapped a thin layer of water molecules against her skin. That let her glide through the water with less resistance, since liquid flows against another liquid more smoothly than against the Human body.

Before heading to the surface, Carrie took this opportunity to check out the rest of the Leviathan's gigantic form. She saw what must be an incredibly strong fluke at the Leviathan's rear. She wondered just how fast it could propel itself through the ocean's waters, despite its massive bulk. Varis's sleek underside was interrupted by a round bulge of considerable proportion. That has to be one big baby, Carrie thought.

Toward the front of Varis's body, just behind those wise-looking eyes, were appendages that looked more like hands than flippers. They were webbed, and she was impressed with the four digits that looked as if they could manipulate objects much as a Human hand would. Tool-using aquatic forms. How did they arise here?

Before she could consider that question further, the Leviathan's body began to shake violently, sending out strong underwater waves that pushed Carrie away. The surface of the Leviathan's rubbery skin rippled again and again until the seizures subsided.

Carrie barely had time to react to that when another aquatic form, about the size of a walrus, but much faster, zoomed past her. I never even saw it coming, she thought. What the hell is it? She kicked upward, breaking the surface next to Matt.

Who caught the slightest glimpse of her naked body, blushed, and looked away.

Damn, Carrie thought. One of those. I hate nudity taboos.

Carrie was still figuring out how regain Matt's attention when the walrus-sized creature surfaced between them. Over her datalink, she heard, "You must be Carrie Molina. I'm Sarbin."

Matt turned back her way, though he seemed relieved that Sarbin mostly blocked his view of Carrie. Poor man, she thought. Can't even enjoy the sight of a good-looking woman.

"Sarbin," Matt said, "is an Aquatile." His broad body featured stubby arms, different in detail but apparently similar in function to the Leviathan's. His wide, bright eyes spoke of an intelligence at least equal to a Human's. His snout ended in a single nostril. "I've heard of your people," Carrie said. "I'm pleased to meet you."

"And I'm pleased to be your new partner," Sarbin said. Carrie heard clicks and low tones that she realized much be the Aquatile's true speech, which her datalink translated.

Matt said, "Your temporary partner, Sarbin." Carrie tried not to react to the firmness she heard in Matt's tone, or what she believed was a note of jealousy. To Carrie, he said, "Let's get back on shore, and I'll let you know what little we've figured out about Varis's seizures."

*****

Carrie expected Matt to escort her to the Unity base for a briefing. Instead, he excused himself to go inside the submersible shuttle on the landing pad. She would've preferred to sun herself awhile and dry off before getting dressed, but decided not to shock Matt's sensibilities any more than she had to and put her clothes back on. They'll dry soon enough under this sun, she thought.

Matt's hand, holding a towel, thrust itself through the submersible's hatchway. His voice was muffled a bit since he spoke without sticking his head outside. "I thought you might want to dry off."

Carrie didn't try to suppress her grin. "That's OK, Matt. A little late now, but I appreciate the offer."

Matt's head moved cautiously from behind the hatchway. "Oh. Sorry."

"A little water's the last thing that bothers me. You were going to show me what's wrong with Varis?"

Matt came down the shuttle's steps with a holopad under his arm. "Let's go back down to the water. I don't want to leave Sarbin out."

That's why we didn't go up to the base, Carrie thought. She followed Matt down to a shallower area of the island's waterline, where Sarbin had beached himself. Matt sat down next to the Aquatile, and Carrie settled down on the other side. Matt made a couple of adjustments to the pad, and a cutaway image of the Leviathan Varis appeared among them, its internal organs clearly visible, along with the outline of the unborn child she bore.

"Damn," Carrie said as she leaned forward to examine the Leviathan's insides more closely. "I've stayed in hotel rooms smaller than Varis's heart."

Matt said, "As large as she is, you've seen how her seizures affect her."

"And what causes them?"

Sarbin said, "The Leviathans believe they become ill because they're sinful."

"What do you believe?"

"Aquatiles don't believe in sin."

Matt said, "The Leviathans do, though, and they banish from the open ocean those who become ill. They make them come to these motile islands and follow them around awhile. Usually they get well within a few days."

"Which makes it seem as if the banishment actually works."

"And which is reinforced by the fact that sometimes they get sick again once they come back to their families."

Carrie said, "But Varis hasn't gotten better yet."

"Not quickly enough. We suspect the pregnancy is the problem."

"How close is she to delivering?"

"She's about sixteen months along — so about another three months."

"Damn," Carrie said. "That makes my belly hurt just thinking about it."

Matt said, "We're not sure how to treat Varis herself — it's been difficult analyzing what's wrong with such a large being. But doctors and scientists here at the base have come up with tech they believe can protect the child from further infection, and strengthen her against Mom's seizures."

Carrie ran a hand through her dark hair, which was nearly dry. "So I'm the delivery system."

Matt pointed within the holo to the unborn child's position deep within Varis. "We don't know enough about Leviathan physiology to design a self-propelled delivery system."

"I read up on them as much as I could on the way here," Carrie said. "I understand the difficulties. How will we even be able to see while we're traveling inside her veins?"

"You'll be wearing goggles that combine infrared imaging technology and sonography. Some things might be a little blurry or indistinct, but you'll be able to see where you are and where you're going — especially given your enhanced eyesight and echolocation abilities."

"But how wide will a needle have to be to inject me?"

Matt grinned mischievously. "That's been its own technical problem. But we think we have a solution."

*****

That solution amounted to Matt leading Carrie into his submersible shuttle, lifting off, and heading out just far enough over the ocean to settle into its waters just beyond the spot where Varis floated. Even from within the submersible's small cabin, the Leviathan's size was intimidating. Although, Carrie thought, the bigger the better if I'm taking a trip inside there. She told Matt, "When the Unity recruited me for this mission, the briefer told me I'd be taking a fantastic voyage. I thought that meant some kind of ocean trip."

"At least you won't be alone. Sarbin's going in with you." Matt turned and peered into the cargo bay behind them, which was filling up with water.

"With all respect to Sarbin, why?"

"Varis doesn't trust Humans. She's sentient, but she believes the superstitions about sin causing her illness. Sarbin, being a native and a fellow aquatic being, is the one who's tried to convince her otherwise."

"Except you don't have a good explanation."

"Which doesn't help our credibility much. But we can't wait for research breakthroughs here. Varis's child will die unless we can protect it against whatever is making his mother sick."

Carrie said, "Having a Human — an alien life form crawling around inside your own body — has to be a frightening proposition."

"Which is why Sarbin will be there to reassure Varis that everything's fine as you get this job done."

Carrie stared upward at the dark mass of the Leviathan. "Let's hope everything really is fine."

"The Unity asked for you because of your abilities in a liquid environment — plus you have plenty of endurance, and you've shown that you keep your head in a tough situation."

Carrie turned back toward Matt. "That sounds like you're quoting from my file."

Matt looked away from the submersible's controls just long enough to glance back at her. "Well — I did read it."

"You're worried about Sarbin."

Matt's kept his gaze forward. "He's my friend. I never expected I'd become this close to someone who can't even live on land. I've saved his life at least once. And he's risked his for me."

Carrie returned to the co-pilot's position. "I know what it's like to lose someone close to you. I'll take good care of him."

Matt's expression hardened. "If you don't mind — who was it you lost?"

"My sister. Adriana. A man named Malcolm Vicari hurt her badly. She died a few weeks ago."

"Oh." Matt's eyes seemed to lose focus, and it was a moment before he said, "I'm sorry."

"Being here, working, is the best thing for me. Like I said, I'll take good care of Sarbin. More likely, he'll take good care of me."

"Thank you for being here, then. One more thing...."

"What is it?"

"Something I have to tell you before we allow Varis in on our datalink transmissions. Even Sarbin isn't hearing this. It's about what I might have to do if the two of you get into trouble while you're inside Varis."

"What you might have to do?"

Matt shook his head. "I'm a deeply spiritual man. The idea of killing anyone is disgusting to me. But my orders from the Unity say that if Varis gets worse — if the seizures grow worse enough that it's clear she's dying, and you're in trouble, I'm to use the submersible's disruptors to cut you out of there."

"Me? What about Sarbin?"

"I don't have any orders regarding him. But I consider his life as important as yours."

"As you should," Carrie said. "But I wouldn't want you killing Varis and her child to save me."

"I don't claim to know how anyone might choose to face death. I can't even say how far my faith could take me if I were in there and in danger. But my orders are independent of your wishes, or...Sarbin's."

He was about to say, "even Sarbin's", Carrie thought. She said, "Then I guess Sarbin and I will just have to make sure Varis and her child live."

*****

Carrie stood at the entrance to the cargo bay as Matt continued holding the submersible steady, just behind and beneath Varis. She touched her left middle finger into her palm and her lifesuit tech activated, at a lower level than the usual spacesuit function. It covered her entire body and provided her with a bubble helmet.

Sarbin was in the water-filled cargo bay now. He wore a tight-fitting Aquatile variation on her lifesuit. "Varis is still nervous about this," he said. "She's decided to speak only to me."

"Is she only listening to you, as well?"

"That's right."

"That's good to know. You've got the medical pouch?"

Sarbin flipped over, faster than Carrie suspected would have been possible for someone of his bulk. "Strapped right to my belly," he said. The pouch also contained some simple medical instruments in case either she or Sarbin had to perform an incision or seal up a wound.

"Sounds great," Carrie said, and slipped into the cargo hold.

Carrie couldn't help grinning as Sarbin nuzzled her with his snout. Her body began adapting to the watery environment even within her lifesuit. Her chest expanded (Not that Matt would let himself notice, she thought) to allow her to take in more oxygen, her blood coursed more quickly through her veins, and her skin thickened slightly. As usual when her body underwent its transformation, she felt more alive than she ever did on land.

Sarbin emitted a series of clicks, and Carrie's datalink translated: "I'm so eager to leave — Matt, are we over Varis yet?"

"Just about," came the answer from the submersible's control cabin.

"'Over' Varis?" Carrie asked.

"She's submerging," Matt said, "and I'm going to settle us down so we're just touching her back. Ah — we're there."

"So now what?"

"So now this." A circular portal about two and a half meters wide irised open in the bottom of the cargo deck, and Carrie saw Varis's skin rippling slightly at the bottom of it. "The edges of that portal are rimmed with medical tech. It'll anesthetize that area of her skin and provide an entryway into her bloodstream at the same time — she shouldn't feel more than a pinprick."

That's what doctors always say, Carrie thought. And they're always lying. "How thick is her blubber?"

"The better part of a meter. But don't worry. You'll zip through it in a flash. And a coagulant follows you, so she shouldn't bleed much."

"How will we get out when we're done?"

Carrie could hear the tension in Matt's voice even over the datalink. "Just the same way. But we'll have to pick a spot. Your datalinks will let me keep a position on you at all times. I'll be your capcom, right here the whole time."

Sarbin said, "Varis is ready, though she's still fearful."

She's not the only one, Carrie thought. "Let's get started."

Matt said, "Both us you, float facing the incision area. Carrie first, Sarbin right behind her. You're positioned right above a vein in Varis's back. At the moment of injection, I'll create a burst of positive pressure in the water around you."

"Which should pop us right into the vein."

"It should be quite a ride. And don't worry, I won't do any jokes about Jonah. Hold on...in three, two — "

I hate countdowns, Carrie thought.

"— one!"

A flash of light blinded her, a giant hand threatened to squeeze the life out of her, and Carrie felt as if she were falling from a high tower while simultaneously being pummeled by giants.

And, as promised, in a flash it was over and she was riding within a smoothly flowing current down a pink tunnel filled with bright red liquid.

Damn if it didn't work, Carrie thought. She checked the size of the vein by extending her arms to either side — she couldn't quite touch them as long as she stayed in the middle. Sarbin was a tighter fit, but still had room to move back and forth.

Her suit glowed, providing just enough illumination to let her see a few meters in any direction. It also helped that Carrie's bio-engineering included increased light sensitivity and an echolocation sense. But as Matt had said, everything was pretty blurry. "Sarbin — are you OK?"

"I'm right with you."

Then came another push from behind them, and the vein's walls rushed past that much faster for a while before they slowed again. "What the hell was that?"

Matt spoke up over the datalink. "Just a little boost from Varis's pulse. You'll feel it every twelve seconds or so."

Carrie realized she must be blushing about as red as the rich oxygenated blood all around her. "Sorry. Wasn't thinking."

"Perfectly understandable. You and Sarbin are on a good path from Varis's back to her belly. But it's not a straight route — it curves around her body. It could become a bit of a roller coaster ride."

Carrie encountered one of those curves and slammed a shoulder against one side of the vein, bounced off it, and nearly tumbled out of control. Only her bio-engineered reactions and strength let her straighten out and force her way back into the middle of the steadily pumping bloodstream. "It already has," she gasped.

Sarbin asked, "Are you all right, Carrie?"

"Getting there," she said, trying to anticipate the vein's next curve as she approached it — she took the bounce with her right arm and her hip this time. "That was better. You have to let the impact work for you. The sides are actually pretty resilient."

"It's too bad you don't have a fluke," the Aquatile said. "It makes the journey much easier."

"It's hard to tell how much progress we're making."

Matt's voice came over Carrie's datalink: "You're not traveling as quickly as you might think. But it's constant."

"With that little bump from the pulse. Sarbin — how's Varis doing?"

"Fortunately, she cannot feel us inside her. But the very idea still worries — "

Sarbin's voice broke off as Carrie was tossed against one side of the vein, then the other, as a vast, deep rumbling assaulted her ears. A third collision knocked Carrie's breath out of her, and for a while she let the bloodstream take her as it would, accepted the pummeling it gave her.

Matt's voice over the datalink: "Carrie — Sarbin — Varis is having a seizure — are you all right?"

Carrie had her breath back and started anticipating each collision with the vein walls. "I'm starting to get the hang of it," she said over the persistent reverberation that surrounded her. "It's just rolling with the punches — except they don't stop. Sarbin — what about you?"

The Aquatile replied, "In different circumstances, this could even be — fun."

"Your idea of fun and mine are considerably different."

"Really, Carrie? What's fun for you?"

Some wine, some cheese, and a healthy specimen of manhood who is... "Let's not worry about that right now, Sarbin. Matt, how long do these seizures last?"

"It depends. Sometimes several minutes."

Carrie took another hard blow against the side of the vein wall. "Well, I wish this one would hurry up and — "

The rumbling ceased and Varis's bloodstream quit trying to pummel her against the vein's walls.

"— finish."

Sarbin caught up with Carrie nearly effortlessly. "You really should consider having that fluke installed."

Carrie couldn't help grinning. "Matt — how close are we to the child?"

"You're most of the way there. The trick's going to be holding yourself against the blood flow while you insert the pouch."

Sarbin said, "That's another reason I'm here, Carrie — to brace you as you work."

Matt said, "I wanted to be there with you."

That jealousy again, Carrie thought. "Matt, I know you've worked quite a bit with Sarbin. But you couldn't have done this. You don't have the swimming skills or the body strength. Please realize I'm not bragging. I was made this way."

No response for a moment, then Matt said, "Point taken. I'm glad you're there to help Sarbin in ways I couldn't."

Can't fault his loyalty, Carrie thought. "Thanks. How's the baby doing?"

"Vitals are a bit rocky. We need to get that pouch to her."

"By 'we,' you mean me and Sarbin."

"Well, uh — "

"Just giving you a hard time, Matt. How close are we?"

"About fifteen meters."

Sarbin said, "I'm going to move ahead of you, Carrie, to get into position to steady you."

"Sounds great — uh-oh — hang on!"

Varis's body roiled again, and Carrie found herself crashing hard against Sarbin before she could dodge him. She rebounded off the Aquatile and found herself getting into the rhythm she'd discovered earlier — bounce off the vein wall, try to stay in the middle of the bloodstream, anticipate an upcoming curve....

I'm starting to get the hang of it, she thought. It could be worse —

Varis's body jerked again, Carrie struck the vein wall —

And it gave way and she went tumbling head-over-heels and crash-landed against something smooth and rubbery. Whatever it is, at least it cushioned the blow, she thought. But blood spurted from the hole in the vein, covering her and whatever body part she was lying against.

*****

Sarbin's voice came over her datalink: "Carrie, are you all right?"

"I'm fine." More low noises all around, and Carrie laid herself flat against the rubbery flesh beneath her. Last thing I want is to start bouncing around inside Varis. Then the Leviathan's body grew still again. "I'm worried about the hole in this vein — it looks like Varis is losing a lot of blood." She rolled to one side to get clear of the flow.

Matt broke in. "It looks like you landed against Varis's bladder.

"Oh, great," Carrie said. "I'm going to forgo the obvious jokes. Sarbin, can you get to that hole in the vein?"

"I'm fighting against the current. It's easier between pulses."

Their surroundings rumbled again, but not nearly as strongly as before. "What the hell's that?" Carrie asked.

Matt said, "Varis is eating. Mama-to-be gets hungry, especially after one of those seizures."

Carrie tried to stand, but couldn't get sure footing — the giant bladder gave at each step, leaving Carrie wobbling from side to side before falling back down. *I wonder if Varis feels this unexpected urge to go, now,* she thought. "I can't reach back up toward the vein. Can't stand up."

Matt asked, "Can you follow the vein's path? Is there some place where it's closer to you?"

Carrie peered down the vein's path. "It's hard to see very far ahead of me. I don't think so."

"How about behind you?"

"Didn't think of that. Didn't wanna consider backtracking, I suppose. Yeah, I see a place I can grab hold."

Matt said, "You and Sarbin listen carefully. Sarbin, you've got to patch up the hole already in the vein. Carrie, while he's doing that, you climb up onto that vein."

"Onto it?"

"Look at the force of that blood flow — can you climb back into the vein against it?"

"Point taken again. So Sarbin fixes the already-existing hole in the vein — "

"And I create a new one for you to fall into rather than have to push against," the Aquatile said.

"All right," Carrie said, "I'm headed that way." After another attempt to get to her feet, she gave up and crawled along the wobbly surface of the Leviathan's bladder. *Not the most dignified way of getting around,* she thought. *If I get killed in here, I sure hope Matt or Sarbin can get my body out.*

Carrie concentrated hard enough on moving forward that she bumped her head against the bottom of the vein. *Great. It's huge, of course. Got to see if I can get myself up on it.*

She moved to one side of the vein and tried to pull herself up with her hands, but her fingers couldn't find purchase — its sides were too slippery, and she wasn't tall enough to reach to the top.

Then the bladder beneath her gave way in different directions beneath her feet and she fell on her butt.

Damn, I hate this, Carrie thought. *I don't want people to have to place their hands over their mouths to hide their compulsive laughter as they explain how I died, trying to stand up on a Leviathan's bladder, walking around like a drunk on a trampoline.*

Trampoline? Damn. I need to catch on faster.

Carrie pushed herself up yet again, balanced carefully, then bent her knees and jumped straight up.

About ten centimeters at best. That's all right, Carrie, she thought. Get the rhythm going. You can do this — it's just like great sex. Another bounce, and another, and Carrie managed a bit more height each time.

At the third bounce, Matt's voice came through her datalink: "Carrie, what are you doing over there?"

She grunted at the effort of another couple bounces. "Trying to jump high enough to get on top of this vein. What's happening?"

"Varis is urinating up a storm — it's like a yellow cloud behind her."

Unexpected laughter burst from Carrie and she lost her rhythm and almost fell. So she did feel the urge. "I'm using her bladder as a trampoline — uh-oh." The bladder was quickly growing flaccid, providing less bounce with each jump. Continuing the sex analogy, I guess. Well, now or never.

A final thrust with her legs, and she leaped toward the curved side of the vein, grasped its rubbery flesh as high up as she could, and scrambled up with her legs until she was lying on top of it.

Yeah — just like great sex, all right. Worn out now. If I were a man, I'd be ready for a nap. I have to keep going, though.

Sarbin said, "I've sealed the hole you fell through, Carrie."

"Great. You see where I am now?"

"I do. Are you ready?"

"Ready as I'm going to—"A hole opened up right in front of Carrie and she fell into Varis's bloodstream again. An immediate pulse started her on her previous path once more.

"Carrie, wait — I have to seal this hole."

Carrie flipped around and fought to swim against the current. The Leviathan's pulse shot her backwards that much more every ten seconds or so. She watched in amazement as Sarbin's stubby arms and hands aimed a suture beam and sealed up the hole she'd fallen through. With that accomplished, the Aquatile deftly folded up the device and returned it to the pouch. "Ready?" he asked.

"Sure am," Carrie said, and flipped around to proceed on their previous path. It was only when she relaxed to let the Leviathan's steady pulse propel her through the bloodstream that she realized how out of breath she was, how much her leg muscles burned, how badly her ribs ached from one of the many blows she'd taken against the vein walls. She said, "Matt, please tell me we're near the baby."

"You are, actually. In fact, Sarbin needs to get in front of you to hold you in place."

"Here, I go," the Aquatile said, and easily glided past Carrie to precede her in the Leviathan's vein.

"Just a little farther, Sarbin," Matt said. "I'm going to try to position you and Carrie at a spot where the vein presses right up against the womb."

"Just tell us when," Carrie said.

"Just a moment — now, Sarbin — hold her right there."

The Aquatile flipped around in an instant even as Carrie tried her best to paddle against the bloodstream. Once again she was impressed with how quickly such a large being could move. But when Sarbin pressed the tip of his snout against her back, his fluke flapping insistently to keep them both in place, she groaned with pain. "Can you turn your head a bit? You're killing my kidneys."

"Sorry. How's that?"

"Much better. Lemme reach down and grab that medpack from your belly. OK, got it — all its systems check out, Matt — which way should I point it?"

"That would be to your right, directly in the middle of the vein."

I've got to get this done quickly, Carrie thought. Even my endurance has its limits, and I'm reaching them pretty quickly. She pressed the medpack against the smooth flesh of the vein, with Sarbin adjusting his position to keep her in place as she moved. She raised her hand to depress the control that would deliver the pouch and —

"Stop!" Sarbin said.

Carrie jerked her hand away from the pack. "What is it?"

"It's Varis. She doesn't trust you. She's afraid of what you might be injecting into her child."

"Isn't this a hell of a time to decide that?"

Matt piped in: "Sarbin, you've got to convince her we're doing what's best."

Or I could just go ahead and hit the button, Carrie thought.

But what would happen then? If Varis became upset enough, agitated enough, she could hurt herself and her baby. And if Sarbin and I were in danger, and Matt ended up following his orders to cut us out if necessary —

Carrie kept one hand pressed against the medpack, and the other well away from the control that would activate it. She looked down at Sarbin. "What if you did it?"

The Aquatile looked up at Carrie expectantly. "You mean I should perform the injection?"

"Ask her," Carrie said as Sarbin looked away from her to communicate with the Leviathan on their private channel.

Sarbin said, "Varis accepts your proposal."

"Let's switch around, then. I'll hold the pack against the side of the vein." My energy's fading, she thought. Either way I've got to finish this quickly.

*****

Sarbin managed to ease himself upward while still keeping Carrie's body pressed against him so the bloodstream wouldn't sweep her away. But his short arms still couldn't reach the medpack. "Use your snout," Carrie said.

"No!"

"Why not?"

"I'm an Aquatile, not some primitive being. I use my hands or nothing."

"Sarbin, please make an exception. We've got to get out of here."

Sarbin cast Carrie a harsh look. "Just don't tell anybody. If another Aquatile found out, they'd call me a — fish."

"I won't tell anyone. Cross my heart."

"Failure to translate."

"Just hit the button!"

Sarbin thrust his snout forward and hit the button. Immediately, a readout told Carrie the pouch was being delivered. It flowed smoothly, easily, though the vein wall and into the Leviathan's womb. The too-small-to-be-seen machines making up the medical tech would join the proteins, carbohydrates, electrolytes, and other substances within the amniotic fluid to strengthen the unborn child's defenses against infection and provide her more endurance as she coped with her mother's seizures.

Carrie twisted around to return the medpack to the strap around Sarbin's belly. "Time to go," she said. Sarbin did one of his now-familiar flips and let the bloodstream take him. Carrie was right behind him. All around her came another deep rumbling. Not as strong as Varis's seizures, though, she thought. What could it be?

"Great job," Matt said. "Everything's looking fine...uh-oh."

Carrie was just getting the hang of keeping herself in the middle of the vein again. "Don't say that, Matt. I don't want to hear that 'uh-oh' shit. What's wrong?"

"It's the baby — she's moving into position for delivery."

"Uh-oh."

Sarbin asked, "Why would that happen?"

Carrie could hear the concern in Matt's voice: "The tech made the baby stronger, and Varis's body is interpreting that as the baby being more mature."

Carrie asked, "So that's the source of those rumblings we heard a little while ago. Varis is ready to deliver?"

"And it's happening fast. But there's a problem."

"This already was a problem."

"Well, it's a worse one now. The baby's facing head-first. Leviathans are normally born tail-first."

"Why's that?" Carrie asked.

"Being delivered head-first when you're an aquatic animal means you can drown before you're completely born. And Leviathan babies don't turn around until late in the pregnancy."

Another rumble, this time accompanied by a strong shift to one side that made Carrie miss a curve in the vein. She slammed her shoulder against its walls. She groaned, then said, "What happens if Varis tries to deliver now?"

"There's no 'trying' to it. She's delivering. That was a contraction."

Carrie said, "You've got to get us out.'

No response at first from Matt. Then he said, "Uh, Carrie...?"

"No. Don't you start. As short a time as we've worked together, and I can tell what you're thinking. You've got some other mission for us, and I can tell you we've had enough."

"You went in there to save the baby. Now it's both Varis and the baby who are at risk."

Carrie and Sarbin continued to barrel down the center (mostly) of the vein. "What are you suggesting? That I get in there and push?"

Another silence stretched larger. Finally it was Carrie that broke it: "No. You can't mean — "

"That vein you're in is about to curve up toward the womb again, in just the right place. Sarbin can cut a path — "

"No. Absolutely not."

"— you get inside — "

"Does no one understand the word 'no' on this planet?"

"— and then you help the baby turn around and be ready for delivery."

"You know, a midwife is supposed to work on the outside."

Matt said, "Once you get in there, it's going to take some work to turn that baby. It's fifteen meters long, after all."

"What, we can't just flip her around?"

"Carrie, for a woman you don't seem to have much of an idea how crowded it is inside a womb."

"It's been awhile since I left one."

"Besides, you're a fixer. At least that's what I was told before you got here. Now here's something that needs fixing."

Sarbin said, "I can help you, Carrie. We have to save the baby."

It's all so simple for Sarbin, Carrie thought. A true innocent. "All right. Matt, let me know when we need to stop. Sarbin, what does Varis think about this?"

"She's concerned and afraid. We were supposed to help her child. But we might've made things worse."

"Yeah. I don't blame her." And I sure won't say out loud that I'm afraid we could screw this up even worse than that. Especially if she has another seizure. Carrie thought back to the last seizure, and how she and Sarbin were rocked around inside the vein, with the lesser disturbance of Varis eating following soon after.

Wait a minute, Carrie thought. "Matt, what do the Leviathans eat when they're out in the ocean?"

"Mostly tiny fish and floating vegetation — much like our own whales. We've been gathering it up and taking it to her — but yes, it's the natural vegetation that Leviathans eat when they banish themselves to the motile islands."

"But is it the same as what they eat in the open ocean?"

"I guess we've assumed so — you want me to check?"

"As quickly as you can, Matt. It could make a big difference."

"I'll do that, but you're just about at the place where you and Sarbin need to enter the womb."

"Matt, I won't even try to ponder the Freudian implications there."

Sarbin said, "Failure to translate."

"I don't doubt it."

Matt said, "Sarbin, stop Carrie right there."

Sarbin flipped around and eased his big body up against Carrie's, just as he'd done while they delivered the nanotech. The Aquatile reached into his medpack and grabbed the scalpel beam, which resembled nothing more than a small stunner or disruptor. Carrie asked, "How will you know where to cut?"

Sarbin depressed the trigger on his device and a narrow blue beam illuminated a small spot on the side of the vein. "Matt can detect that," he said.

Sure enough, Matt immediately said, "A little up, Sarbin. Now to the left. Carrie, are you ready?"

"No. But I guess we're going anyway. Hey, wait a minute — did you check on the vegetation?"

"I did. They're related, but not quite the same."

"What's the difference between them?"

"The type the Leviathans eat in the open ocean has an alkaloid the one around the islands doesn't. But it's harmless. Varis says no one else in her pod's ever gotten sick the way she has."

Carrie said, "Harmless to them, maybe. But what if Varis's body has some sort of reaction to it?"

"That's something we have to look at later, Carrie — Varis and her child need our help now."

Carrie took a deep breath and mustered her remaining strength. "All right, then. Anytime, Sarbin."

The Aquatile twisted around to narrow his aim at the proper spot of the vein while still holding Carrie in place against the bloodstream's never-ending flow. He squeezed the trigger on the scalpel. The vein's flesh parted. So did that of the Leviathan's womb just beyond it. Sarbin executed a deft flip of his body, thrusting Carrie through that rubbery rift.

It was only the cushioning effects of the womb's amniotic fluid that kept Carrie from having the breath knocked out of her as she landed, hard, against the Leviathan baby's body. A surging stream of Varis's blood began to diffuse within the womb. Sarbin squeezed through the rift and used the scalpel's suture function to close it within seconds. Carrie took a moment to get her bearings. Any movement, she found, was slow and methodical against the thick amniotic fluid.

She stared across the giant baby's back, down its 15-meter length. If Varis is the size of a shuttle, Baby's about like a lifepod, Carrie thought.

A familiar distant rumbling drew closer and stronger, and Varis was in the full throes of another seizure. That sent the baby moving, too, whether having a seizure of its own or reacting in fear.

Carrie tried to stay on the baby's back, but she started sliding downward, falling in slow motion within the thick fluid. The fall won't hurt me because stronger lifesuit tech would snap on, she thought, but the baby's movements could pin me against the side of the womb.

*****

Sarbin glided up beneath Carrie, saying, "Grab onto me." Carrie grabbed the strap around Sarbin's midsection and held on tight as the Aquatile swam through the narrow space between baby Leviathan and womb wall.

Varis's body grew still as Sarbin dropped Carrie off on top of the baby's body again. Carrie kept on hands and knees, both for balance and because she had very little room to move. Matt was right, she thought. *It is crowded in here.*

Now, seemingly, it was the baby's turn to thrash around. Carrie was about to be pinned against the "roof" of Varis's womb, but Sarbin inserted himself next to her, taking the pressure on his own larger, stronger body. "Matt," she said, "I don't know if this was a good idea. We can barely move ourselves, let alone turn this big thing around."

"You've got to try," Matt replied. "Sarbin has the strength. You can help guide."

Carrie muttered, "I could help guide it up your...."

"What's that?" Matt asked.

"Nothing."

Sarbin broke in: "We have to get to work to save the baby."

"You're right," Carrie said. "Let's get started. You'll have to do the heavy work. I'll get behind the baby's head and try to guide her."

"Here I go," Sarbin said, and made his way through the thick fluid to the baby's tail as Carrie floated over to a perch just behind the baby's head, right above her closed eyes. Sarbin applied the side of his snout to the unborn Leviathan's bulk and his fluke began to flap, though not as quickly as Carrie expected. In the low light of their glowing life suits, Carrie could tell that Sarbin was putting all his considerable strength behind the effort.

But the baby didn't move.

Sarbin rested. "The fluid's too thick," he said. "I can't flap my fluke quickly enough."

Varis's body shook violently and Carrie flattened herself against the baby's body as it looked as if the ceiling was caving in. As her lifesuit snapped into armor, Carrie realized: *Varis is having more contractions.*

Sarbin pleaded in a strangled voice: "Carrie, help me!"

A glance behind her, and Carrie saw that the Aquatile was pinned between the wall of Varis's womb and the baby Leviathan's body. And Carrie realized: *Sarbin doesn't have the same protective tech in his lifesuit that I do. Mine was designed for space, and his was only developed for this mission.*

"What is it?" Matt asked.

"Sarbin's in trouble." Carrie hunkered down as much as she could to try to slide off the baby's back so she could make her way down to Sarbin. "Is there any way you can help out to make this baby flip around?"

"Goodness, I can't think of anything. Carrie — the Unity's counting on you."

Subtext, Carrie thought. He's telling me he'll follow the Unity's orders to cut Sarbin and me out of here if he has to. "The Unity's just fine for now," she said, hoping to keep her own reference cryptic enough.

Carrie worked herself free of the tight spot between the womb's walls and the baby's back. But I do have to decide — should Sarbin and I just get out of here, even at the risk of killing the baby and Varis herself?

I say, hell no.

At least for now.

Carrie made it back to Sarbin and grabbed his arms and pulled. To no effect.

"I'm being crushed," the Aquatile said. "I can barely...breathe."

Matt again: "Is now the time?"

"Not yet," Carrie said. "We have to think of something — wait a minute. Sarbin — can you reach your scalpel?"

Sarbin reached down and pulled it from his sheath. "It's right here."

"Put it on a low setting and shoot the baby with it."

"What? I came here to help it, not hurt it."

"A low setting. Sting it!"

Sarbin raised the scalpel beam and aimed it at the wall of flesh right before him. And hesitated.

"Shoot!" Carrie said,

"I...can't..."

Carrie reached toward the scalpel. "Oh, Jesus Christ, let me do it — "

Matt: "Carrie — "

"I know, language. Gimme, Sarbin."

"I'll do it," the Aquatile said, and fired the scalpel.

The baby flinched, and Carrie held on tight to Sarbin as he swam free. "We did it," the Aquatile said.

Carrie told him, "And the baby's turned a bit. Give him another shot."

"You sound as if you're enjoying this."

"What I'm enjoying is knowing we're about to turn the baby — oh, and that we're not getting squished just yet."

Sarbin took aim again. "I guess we have to do this." Another shot, and the baby's tail moved farther away from them. But Varis also reacted, moving her own body from side to side, and Carrie held onto Sarbin even tighter as they swayed back and forth in the relatively slow motion of the amniotic fluid.

Sarbin said, "Varis, you have to keep still — we're saving your baby."

A voice Carrie hadn't heard previously came over her datalink, rough and low: "You are hurting my child."

Varis, Carrie thought. Speaking at last.

"I know we're hurting her," Sarbin said. "But not very much, and if we don't get her to turn, she could die. So could you."

An odd moment passed, of utter silence and stillness. Then Varis said, "Do what you must."

Sarbin didn't hesitate, but raised the scalpel and stung the baby again. The unborn Leviathan shifted around some more, until it was "sideways" in the womb. Carrie said, "She can't be comfortable that way — she'll have to shift around some more."

And she did, but started back the way she'd come. "Again, Sarbin," Carrie said, and the Aquatile fired yet again.

With a couple swishes of her tail and twisting of her body, the baby spun around and placed herself into the proper position for birth. She ended up facing Carrie, who found herself staring directly toward an eye the width of her hand — an eye that spun toward her, then blinked a couple of times against her life suit's illumination and finally closed again. Wow, Carrie thought.

Varis's body began to shake again and Carrie flattened herself against Sarbin's back. "Dammit," she said. "Those contractions are tough to take. Matt?"

"I'm here."

"How long can a Leviathan's birth take? We don't want to be stuck in here for hours."

"Everything's proceeding faster than you might think."

Varis's entire body shook again and suddenly Carrie felt as if she were on a starcraft where the grav had failed. "Is Varis diving?"

"Don't worry," Matt said. "It's common practice for Leviathans about to give birth — dive into colder water, and her body rushes blood to the body core where it's needed."

Varis was already leveling off. "What about the baby when it comes out?"

"The cold provides a shock, and the baby expels any amniotic fluid that could be in its lungs."

"Then it's right up to the surface for that first real breath?"

"You got it, with a little help from Mom."

The baby Leviathan's eye opened again. I could swear it looks surprised, Carrie thought. Then it, and the rest of the baby's body, began to recede as Varis's body trembled with another string of contractions. Carrie and

Sarbin were rocked from side to side, then found themselves following right behind the soon-to-be-born Leviathan.

"Uh-oh," Carrie said. "I'm not a Christian, but I'm about to be born again."

"Part of that didn't translate," Sarbin said.

"Just get ready to take a ride."

The Leviathan baby shot forward all at once, and Carrie grasped Sarbin tighter than ever as Varis's contractions shot them forward, as well, the baby staring at them all during her fitful journey. "Push, Varis," Carrie muttered, then couldn't help laughing, however feebly. "I guess that's the first time anyone's said that from inside."

Several minutes of violent back and forth, side to side movements followed. Carrie, hands cramping, arms and legs losing strength, was about to resign herself to falling away from Sarbin and taking whatever came.

Sarbin said, "Look, Carrie — light!"

Every muscle in Carrie's neck protested as she lifted her head, but she was rewarded with the slightest of glimmers as she looked past the baby's body and beyond its tail. "Isn't it marvelous, Carrie?" Sarbin said. "We're part of the miracle of life."

The miracle will be if we survive it, Carrie thought, but at least she had more motivation to keep hold of Sarbin, if this incredible journey was about to end.

Another burst of motion, and the baby suddenly slipped away from them, her umbilical cord snapping and her body sliding gracefully into the open sea. As smooth and controlled as a starcraft undocking, Carrie thought.

Then she had no time for thought, as the umbilical cord, trailing crimson blood, whipped toward her and Sarbin, massive enough that it could've killed them in an instant, but slowly enough that the Aquatile dodged it and headed for the light.

A final contraction from Varis propelled Sarbin out into the ocean in a cloud of blood and amniotic fluid. The newly-born Leviathan baby, swimming free, cast a broad shadow over them.

Suddenly Carrie felt as if she were being launched spaceward in a shuttle that had lost its inertial protections. She caught the merest glimpse of Varis's fluke pushing upward inexorably against Sarbin's underside, and then, unexpectedly, she and the Aquatile and the Leviathan child broke the surface of Welkin's waters.

The baby barely left the water before falling back in a gigantic belly flop. Sarbin twisted instinctively and transformed his fall into a head-first dive that barely seemed to part the waters. Carrie, try as she might, was a creature of land or water, not airborne leaps, but managed a feet-first splashdown that was functional, if not graceful.

The first thing she did after entering the water was deactivate her lifesuit, and she gloried in the feel of Welkin's waters flowing over her skin. She broke the water's surface again and took in the sight of Varis's great bulk rolling onto one side, water sluicing down her underside as her newborn moved in to suckle.

It was worth it, Carrie thought. Just for this one moment, it was all worth it.

Sarbin burst out of the water in front of her, arced over her head, and made graceful splashdown behind her. As he came up next to Carrie, he said, "Isn't it wonderful? You worked hard, but everything turned out all right."

Sometimes the innocents of the word get their way, Carrie thought. "You worked as hard as I did. Without you, the baby would never have been born. Race you to shore." Carrie took a deep breath into her genetically engineered lungs and started swimming past mother and child and toward the land.

Sarbin easily passed Carrie up, but made it a game all the way in, darting around her and encouraging her to go faster. Matt met her at the shoreline, and stood holding out a terry cloth robe, but with his eyes looking to one side. I'm starting to feel as if I'm somehow odious to him, she thought. But she took the robe, put it on, and sat down on the sand. "I won't move for a month," she said.

"You did a marvelous job — both of you," Matt said.

"If you'll excuse me," Sarbin said from the shallow water, "I'm going to take a long swim and a half-nap." And with a fluke flip, he was gone.

"A half-nap?" Carrie asked Matt.

"The halves of Aquatile brains take turns sleeping. Just like dolphins."

"He's amazing. How did marine life here become sentient?"

"An excellent question," Matt said, sitting next to her. "One we're trying to find the answer to. One question we have answered, though — why Varis got sick, and why she's getting better, however slowly, here at the motile island."

"It's that vegetation she's eating in the open ocean, isn't it?"

"She has a reaction to that alkaloid — gets sick, comes to one of these islands, eats the other stuff, gets well."

"Which is why the banishment seems to work." Carrie ran her fingers through the sand to play for time, then told Matt, "Thanks for doing such a good job as capcom. I was afraid we weren't going to get along."

Now Matt looked at her. "I was afraid you were going to be condescending, showing off your abilities, and your body, all the time."

"I thought you'd expect me to conform to your religious beliefs."

"I gave up on that long ago. But I had my doubts. I knew your abilities, but not how much you'd lived. How much you understood about death. Until...."

Carrie said, "Until I mentioned my sister."

"Her name was Adriana?"

"Yes."

A silence stretched on for several seconds. Then Matt said, "My sister was Juliette. She died, too. Back on Earth, several years ago."

"I'm so sorry."

"So I knew you understood. How much I wanted to save Varis and her child. How concerned I was for Sarbin."

"I tried to bail on you when you suggested that business of going into the womb."

"I knew you wouldn't."

"How'd you know?" Carrie asked.

"Because I wouldn't have, either."

ART FOR SPLENDOR'S SAKE

So welcome Chanda Kasmira to this collection — she's been the lead character in a great many of my earlier stories as she works to save the inhabitants of the planet Splendor from a certain doom that is still several decades away.

It's sometimes been grim work for her, and the Splendor stories have featured betrayals, massacres, and plans gone utterly awry. In *Art for Splendor's Sake*, Chanda still has to deal with violence and slavery and make some tough decisions, but I decided to let up on her a little bit for part of the story and create a subplot that had a lighter tone. Balancing those disparate elements became part of the challenge of writing the story.

———————————

Earth Unity Ambassador Chanda Kasmira received the first word of her latest problem while in her quarters studying the details of the evacuation plan for the planet Splendor. The holo that appeared before her desk was of her Military Liaison Trenton Bram aboard the starcraft *Nivara II*, orbiting Splendor. "We've got a civilian craft that just took orbit," he told her. "And a man on board, Kelsey Solheim, is insisting upon coming down."

The name sounded familiar, but Chanda couldn't place it. "We don't have time for any of this," she said. "Let him cool his jets up there."

"Chanda — you don't understand. His shuttle's on its way down already."

"Who the hell authorized that?"

Trent's hangdog expression told him who. "Everything was in order, including landing clearance directly from the Unity Senate. He'll be landing any moment, and you're supposed to greet him and show him every courtesy."

"'Every courtesy' meaning he can be as big a pain in the ass as he wants, and we just smile wider and ask for more."

"It's called diplomacy, Chanda."

"Except I've about used up my supply. All right, I'll get ready to receive this guy. Find an equally shitty duty and assign yourself to it, will you?"

A faux scowl at her, and Trent's holo faded.

Chanda resigned herself to heading out to the landing pad to meet Solheim. But when she left her quarters, what she saw in the makeshift lobby of the embassy led her to suppress a groan. Her next problem was standing in front of her as her aide Ken Westbrook was in the middle of a spirited discussion with a couple of valley dwellers. Ken was gesturing impressively and the valley dwellers kept indicating several objects wrapped in several thicknesses of cloth. Chanda, accepting this fate as well, went to greet them.

Both valley dwellers were female, of course. Valley dweller females were much more intelligent than their males, whose role was generally limited to breeding. The tops of their heads came about level with Chanda's shoulders. Their bodies looked vaguely reptilian, given skin that possessed a greenish cast and which was lightly scaled. They stood on sturdy legs, and their thick tails helped with balance. They were clothed in several layers of furs and they wore thick-skinned moccasins — items they would have received from highlanders, the other land-based intelligent beings on Splendor, in return for metalwork the valley dwellers had forged.

Whatever brought them here, Chanda thought, it must be something important. She knew valley dwellers couldn't stand the harsh cold of highlander areas for very long. Traditionally they ventured there only for annual rituals they called Gatherings, where they worshipped the gods they believed lived in those cooler climes.

As Chanda approached, Ken looked up with relief. "I was telling these...ladies...that they really should make a proper appointment."

Chanda said, "Let's not worry about that now." She turned to the valley dwellers, even as she noticed Ken sneaking away. I'll remember that, she thought. She told the valley dwellers, "I'm Ambassador Chanda Kasmira. How may I help you?"

One of the valley dwellers spoke, and Chanda heard her speech translated over the datalink implanted behind her left ear. "I am Darajina. This is Ahregor. She heads our tribe, but she has no datalink."

"I understand," Chanda said. She would be able to understand Ahregor if she spoke, but the valley dweller would not be able to comprehend Chanda's speech until Darajina translated it.

Darajina opened up the many layers of cloth she held to reveal several metal spears and knives, and small bowls. "Ahregor and I took these to the highlander tribe nearest us to trade. That is what we have done for generations beyond counting."

"And what happened?" Chanda asked.

"They would not take our wares. They are making their own!"

I was afraid this might happen, Chanda thought. It was a development with implications both practical and cultural. At one time, the valley dwellers had believed the highlanders to be, if not gods, then at least close relations to them. Highlander furs were considered, however indirectly, gifts from the gods, and valley dweller weapons and tools were considered offerings to them. "Where was this village?" she asked. "Did you see the highlanders who were making these things?"

"It is several eights of days from here, to the north." Valley dwellers, having four digits on each hand, often spoke of "eights" or "sixteens" as measurements. Darajina continued: "They showed us their evil, insulting forges, which were outside their village. But the highlanders creating their tools did not seem happy."

"They were being forced to do this work?"

"Forgive me, Ambassador, but for highlanders to do such work willingly...I cannot understand how the world goes. I would as soon live here among icy mountains."

Chanda asked, "What would you have me do?"

Darajina spoke to Ahregor, presumably translating Chanda's question. Ahregor said, "Make the highlanders regain their senses."

Chanda told Darajina, "You'll have to tell Ahregor that I can no more make the highlanders go back to their old ways than I could make valley dwellers, as you say, live among icy mountains. They need to learn to forge their own tools so they can live on the planet Socrates."

Splendor was a world under a death sentence. In just over eight decades, the gas nebula from a nearby star gone supernova would sweep over the planet, rendering it uninhabitable. Three intelligent species, two land-based, and one aquatic, lived on Splendor, and it was Chanda's job to evacuate the land-based ones — the highlanders to Socrates, the valley dwellers to another planet, Kardashev.

Chanda asked, "Can you show us where the slavers are?"

"They were about to move their camp," Darajina said. "That was days ago — no doubt they have already done so."

"What shall my tribe do for furs?" Ahregor asked. "Soon littles will huddle together in the few they have among themselves. We have youngsters who are still growing and need larger furs. And adults who need to replace their worn and tattered clothing."

Chanda folded her arms and looked at the valley dwellers. That's too good a question, she thought. And I haven't anything approaching an answer. She told Darajina, "Soon you'll be going to Kardashev, where you won't need furs. In the meantime, I'll look into ways to keep you supplied."

"No...furs?" Darajina asked. "How will we..."

"On Kardashev, there are no highlanders to give you furs. But you won't have to head into cold areas as you do here."

"We'll be separated from our gods!"

Chanda's head began to hurt. *This isn't a conversation for an atheist to have,* she thought. "Perhaps you'll be away from your gods for a time. But in a few generations, your descendants will be able to come back here to Splendor."

Darajina turned to Ahregor for a spirited conversation that went back and forth so quickly that Chanda's translator couldn't keep up. Then Darajina turned back to her and said, "We will return to our tribe and tell them the Humans will provide for us." Darajina picked up her wares and began wrapping them in the many layers of cloth.

"Wait a minute," Chanda said. "I told you I'd look into it. I can't promise anything yet." From just outside the embassy, she could hear the whine of a landing shuttle — no doubt that Kelsey Solheim fellow arriving.

Darajina paused in her work. "We will wait a sixteen of days. Then Ahregor and I will bring our people here."

Chanda took a step toward the valley dwellers. "What do you mean, bring them here?"

"We need furs," Darajina said. "If you do not provide them within a sixteen of days, we will wait here patiently until you do."

"You can't just — "

"Ambassador. Ahregor and I have been polite. You are the ones who came to this world and changed how we deal with the highlanders."

Chanda kept her anger in check as she said, "We came here to save your lives."

"But our lives are more than just existence. If we are to leave our gods for so many years, we must make the most of the time we have with them. That means furs."

Chanda could only stare in frustration as Darajina finished wrapping her spears and tools and led Ahregor through the starcraft-turned-embassy's airlock.

So if the valley dwellers live to provide metal weapons and tools for the gods, Chanda wondered, what happens when God sets up shop for Himself?

One problem at a time. She activated her lifesuit and stepped through the lobby airlock into the frigid temperatures and forceful winds of the Splendorian landscape.

*****

Chanda couldn't believe, with so many matters of life and death on her plate, she was standing in the middle of a snowstorm threatening to become a blizzard, talking about a proposal to create an artwork.

"Really, Ambassador Kasmira," Kelsey Solheim said over the rushing wind, "you have to acknowledge that art of any kind is necessary to feed our souls."

Chanda leaned forward, bracing herself against the stubborn storm. Her lifesuit tech protected her from the cold and the blowing snow, but Solheim was bundled up in multiple layers of clothing, topped off with a thick parka. She could barely make out his pale features, and wondered if he was aware of the dangers of frostbite. "Mr. Solheim — "

"Please, Kelsey."

"Kelsey, then. Are you sure you don't want to go inside?" They were standing just outside the Earth Unity embassy. The artist was the only person who had exited the large shuttle behind him.

"Absolutely certain, Ambassador — or may I say, Chanda. I find this exposure to the elements exhilarating."

"You could exhilarate yourself right into the hospital if you're not careful. And important as your art is to you, it won't help you then — any more than it would help me evacuate this planet."

Kelsey rubbed windborne snow from his eyes. "Ah, but I can help you with your own goal."

"How can you do that?"

"I know the Unity is growing impatient with the Splendor project. Such a commitment over decades is difficult to sustain, is it not?"

"It is," Chanda admitted.

"I've created, if I do say so myself, magnificent artworks across our home planet. A holographic remembrance of the waters that once graced the English Strait — the terrorist site next to England, not the natural one in the Antarctic."

Chanda suppressed the urge to grab the man by the thick cloth of his parka and tell him to get to his point. "I know which one you meant. I've actually heard of you."

Kelsey raised his voice over the howling winds. "I also staged the hypothetical meeting between the great Chinese poet Su Dongpo and the first Arol to make contact with Humans — Dero...Deron — "

"Dereluholeremular," Chanda prompted.

"That's it — that was why most people called it 'Derry,' I suppose. Anyway, I used a combination of holos and live actors to re-create its landing near the Zig-Zag bridge in Hangzhou, China."

"Where it met this poet. That's not a meeting I remember from the history books."

"Su Dongpo's been dead over a thousand years."

"Artistic license?"

"Chanda, don't you have any imagination or sense of wonder?"

Chanda struggled to stay upright as the storm winds grew stronger. "My needs are practical. I can't worry about feeding souls and I don't care about your artistic vision. I care about getting enough resources out here to save three intelligent species."

Kelsey stepped close to Chanda. "I can do that for you. I've never done a piece on another planet before. I can make Splendor into a masterpiece."

"I can't give you any of my own resources."

Kelsey indicated the shuttle behind him. "Everyone's back there waiting for me — my own staff, who has carried me through countless artistic journeys."

Chanda let out a long sigh. "You stay out of the way of the evacuation effort. If you cause me any trouble — any at all — you're gone."

Kelsey's gloved hands took hold of her bare ones. "You won't regret this, I promise you." He turned back toward his shuttle.

"What do you intend to create?" Chanda asked.

Kelsey stopped and turned back toward her. "That's part of the journey. I'll should come up with something soon." He continued toward the shuttle.

Artists, Chanda thought, and immediately put Kelsey Solheim out of her mind. She needed to speak to the highlander leader Indirogar about furs and forges.

*****

A couple days later, Chanda spotted the two highlanders' mutilated bodies as the shuttle *Bashi* descended toward the wide, snow-covered plain. "This is right along the path back to Indirogar's village," she told her pilot, Irene Radford. Irene was short and thin, with close-cropped black hair — an Earth Unity pilot whose skills had impressed Chanda enough that she'd requested having Irene attached to her office permanently.

I'd hoped Indirogar was wrong about these two highlanders being in danger, Chanda thought. But nothing about this evacuation effort has been easy so far. Why should that change?

Chanda's thoughts turned to the matter at hand as Irene said, "I'll set 'er down easy." And she did just that, as the *Bashi*'s skids crunched through a thin layer of ice and settled onto the snow-covered plain.

Chanda's embedded nanotech created a thin film that protected her against the arctic conditions. She left the shuttle first, Irene right behind. The snow was no deeper than their ankles, but it was covered with an ice layer of varying thickness. Take that initial step, and the ice might not give way at first — then it would give way, and Chanda knew she could easily turn an ankle if she wasn't careful. Take your time, she told herself, and made her way methodically toward the two bodies. Irene followed literally in Chanda's footsteps.

Within moments Chanda stood over the two bloody highlander bodies. They'd suffered numerous wounds on their furred bodies and broad faces — long, sharp cuts as if someone had repeatedly slashed them with a large knife. Dried blood had caked on the ice and snow, and seeped beneath the bodies and hardened. Chanda caught a glimpse of open, unseeing eyes deep within their sockets.

"It's them," Chanda said. "Atharigen and Inharolot. They're members of Indirogar's tribe."

Irene used a portable sensor cluster to lift genetic material from both bodies. "Those cuts could easily have been done with a highlander hunting knife."

"Just what I was afraid of," Chanda said. "Their own people killed them. They came too close to the illegal forge."

Sometimes I believe I've been here too long, Chanda thought, looking out at the harsh frozen landscape. I've lived on Splendor for three years, and why? Take a step forward, and the goal takes two steps farther away.

And the gas nebula's approach never slows down.

Chanda lifted a hand scanner and took several readings. She told Irene, "Three other highlanders were here. Two of them headed north."

"And the third?" Irene asked.

"Back toward Indirogar's village." When Irene looked toward her expectantly, Chanda said, "Yes, that's where we're headed next."

Chanda and Irene loaded Atharigen and Inharolot's bodies into the *Bashi*, which quickly lifted and flew toward Indirogar's village.

*****

The shuttle was just moments away from landing when Ken Westbrook's voice came over Chanda's datalink. "This artist — Solheim — is getting on my nerves," he told her.

"Why should you be any different from anyone else?" Chanda replied. "What's he want?"

"He wants to set up this outdoor workshop in valley dweller territory — near Ahregor's village, as it happens. And that's the other thing I needed to tell you about. Ahregor's making good on her threat. The *Nivara II* just told me his people are making pretty obvious preparations for a trip — getting plenty of supplies and food together, and as many furs as they can."

"I guess we know where they're headed. Let Solheim set up wherever he wants. Maybe he can distract Ahregor's tribe from their trip."

"Do you really think that'll happen?"

"No. But a girl can dream."

Ken said, "Thanks for the challenge. I'll be thinking unkind thoughts about you."

"Take a ticket, take a seat," Chanda said, and signed off as Irene brought the shuttle down over Indirogar's village.

Chanda reached forward to the shuttle's scanner console and took several readings, searching for the one highlander that had left the murder scene and returned here.

After a moment, Irene asked, "What's it look like?"

Chanda said, "One of them's down there, all right — in a hut in the northwest corner of the village."

"I wonder where the others went to."

"We'll worry about them later. With sensors and sat coverage, we can track them easily. Let's talk to Indirogar."

It wasn't unusual for Chanda to meet with Indirogar, the Elder of his highlander tribe. After all, she was Earth's ambassador to the planet Splendor, and he often advised her about highlander ways. But this is different, Chanda thought as the *Bashi* landed just outside the valley dweller village. I don't know how word of these deaths will affect Indirogar. And I can't know how this could affect the evacuation effort.

That effort was complicated by the highlanders' and valley dwellers' symbiotic relationship. The Unity had failed to find another planet where both species could live together as they did on Splendor, with the highlanders trading furs for the metal tools and weapons the valley dwellers created in the volcanically-heated valleys where they lived.

Which was why highlanders and valley dwellers were being taken to different worlds until they could re-colonize Splendor after the passing of the gas nebula.

And why separating them was such a hard sell for many individuals of either species.

Chanda went out the shuttle's airlock and she and Irene started across the frost-covered plain. They were only a few steps from the outlying stone huts here on the village's south side, but already Chanda saw Indirogar approaching. Hard to hide my arrival, I suppose, she thought. And thank goodness he's always eager to see me.

Indirogar's fur was dark brown, and so were his piercing eyes. As was his habit, he took Chanda into a bone-crushing embrace. "Your presence strengthens my hearts," he told her, smiling widely. Chanda's datalink translated the highlander's words. Indirogar possessed a link, as well.

"Your presence strengthens my single heart," Chanda said. "However, I wish I brought better news."

Indirogar's smile went away and he looked at Chanda with full attention. "Tell me."

"It's Atharigen and Inharolot. I'm sorry, but — we have their bodies in the shuttle."

Indirogar looked closely at Chanda's face, and it saddened her to know what he saw there. "Someone killed them," the highlander said.

"Yes. And I have further grief for you. It was three highlanders who did this — and one of them is here, now, in your village."

Indirogar's features turned from sadness to determination, "Then we must act quickly. Show me where this one lives."

Chanda and Irene, with Indirogar right behind, proceeded to the village's northwest corner.

*****

When Chanda indicated the hut housing one of the killers, Indirogar said, "That's Poraharden's home. He was once one of our greatest hunters."

"And now?" Chanda asked.

He teaches our youngsters to hunt. In return, the village feeds and clothes him. That he would kill two of our own villagers...."

"Let him explain himself."

Indirogar said, "You're right."

Chanda positioned herself to one side of the doorway as Irene drew her stunner and took the other side. Indirogar pounded on the wooden door. "Poraharden — come and speak with us."

A muffled voice from inside the hut: "Who is that, disturbing my sleep?"

"It's your Elder, Indirogar. It's the middle of the day, no time for sleep. I have questions."

Poraharden's doorway creaked open only slightly, and Chanda tensed, her hand going to her stunner. She could barely make out Poraharden's features as the sun shone through the doorway. Poraharden said, "You brought Humans."

Indirogar said, "They're concerned about Atharigen and Inharolot."

"Their concerns are not those of highlanders."

"Then respond to my concern."

A moment's hesitation, then Poraharden opened the door wide. "I honor my Elder, of course. But I admit Humans only under protest."

Chanda fought back the urge to toss an insult back, waited for Indirogar to enter the hut first, then followed. Irene also entered, and stood by the doorway, her stunner holstered once again.

It took a moment for Chanda's eyes to adapt to the relative darkness of the stone hut's interior. Poraharden sat in a chair made of tightly woven vines. Indirogar stood directly before him. Chanda moved quietly toward a corner.

Indirogar said, "You helped kill Atharigen and Inharolot."

Poraharden's fur was a lighter brown than Indirogar's, and his eyes were a bright blue, unusual among highlanders. He rubbed idly at the hairs that partially covered one recessed ear. "Why would I do such a thing?"

"You hate the idea of leaving our home — and leaving the valley dwellers."

"I admit to that. Nothing more. And why shouldn't I? You take away those who provide us with the tools we need to hunt, the cups and bowls from which we drink and eat." Poraharden paused, as if considering his next words. "Some highlanders are subjecting themselves to shameful things, all so the rest of us may live."

"What shameful things?" Indirogar asked.

"That's not important."

"Our world will someday die. Isn't that important?"

"I've heard the stories," Poraharden said. "The lies."

Chanda spoke up. "They're true."

"So you Earthers say."

Chanda stiffened and fought to contain any outward reaction. How in the world, she wondered, did this highlander learn that insult?

At a glance from Indirogar, Chanda came forward. "We've given anyone who asked all the evidence they want."

"Fantasies. Earthers want this world. They're removing us to get it."

"Why would Humanity spend ten Earth years doing that, with years more to come? You realize we could just take your world by force if we wanted?"

"You would rather watch us enslave ourselves. We amuse you. You cannot even allow our thoughts to remain hidden."

Chanda looked at Indirogar in puzzlement.

"The datalink," Indirogar said.

"Oh! Poraharden, you know it's only a translator. Your thoughts are your own."

"Then how would you know whether I killed these two highlanders?"

"So now you're admitting to it?"

"I admit to nothing. But how else could you believe you know such a thing?"

Indirogar said, "These Humans have many abilities, but none that are supernatural or godlike. They have only machines."

Poraharden sat straight in his chair, arms folded. "Then let their machines tell them more tales."

Chanda told Indirogar, "I've heard enough," and left the hut. Indirogar and Irene rushed to keep up with her as she strode quickly across the village.

"So," Indirogar said, "what have you concluded?"

"That we'd better find those other two highlanders."

Indirogar clenched his fists and his voice shook. "If they or Poraharden committed this crime, they're subject to tribal justice for killing Atharigen and Inharolot."

Chanda said, "I intend to give you that chance soon," and continued marching toward the *Bashi*.

*****

The next morning, Chanda woke up early, went to her office, and contacted Trenton Bram, who was still on board *Nivara II* orbiting Splendor. "Any luck on finding that slaver camp?"

"They moved it all right," Trent's holo-image said. "Looks like it's in a large hut about seventy clicks to the northeast of Indirogar's village. The genetic patterns you sent us match up with two of the highlanders down there."

"How many altogether?"

"About nine or ten, it looks like."

"Most of them slaves, no doubt."

Trent said, "We haven't seen any activity down there."

"What about our artist friend? He was supposed to be setting up near Ahregor's village."

"He moved his shuttle over there early this morning, right in front of the valley dwellers, even as they looked like they were getting ready to move out."

"Presumably to camp here until I start giving them furs."

"Well, if you have a fur factory, you can tell it to shut down, at least for now. The valley dwellers are pretty enamored of our Mr. Solheim, it looks like."

"Thank goodness for their natural curiosity. I'm going to head that way first and make sure we don't have an incident with the valley dwellers in progress. Then I'm headed to that slaver camp to see what I can find out. I'd like you to get a shuttle-full of Marines ready."

"One day you're going to get yourself in trouble with this damn 'frontier ambassador' business. Why don't you let the Marines take care of this?"

"Don't worry," Chanda said. "I'm just going to have a look around."

"Uh-huh."

Chanda grinned. "Don't 'uh-huh' me. I'll be careful."

"Thank goodness Irene knows better than to let you get into trouble."

Thank goodness Irene knows when to obey orders, Chanda thought.

*****

"Thank goodness you're here," Kelsey Solheim told Chanda as she stepped from the shuttle *Bashi* at the valley dweller Ahregor's village. No need for the protection of a lifesuit here — the constant heat from strings of volcanoes across Splendor created micro-ecologies that were considerably warmer than the rest of the planet. Kelsey had traded his furs for a short-sleeved shirt and shorts.

Chanda asked, "Is there a problem?" She looked around at his encampment just outside the village. His larger shuttle was at the center, and six other Humans were busy setting up equipment whose function was opaque to Chanda, but no doubt it was important to his work.

And they were all surrounded by masses of valley dwellers. They're looking at — no, that's not right, they're examining — every movement Kelsey's people make, Chanda thought. The smaller male valley dwellers seemed especially taken with the new arrivals. They ran behind them en masse, and the moment they put a piece of equipment down, they began climbing on it, no matter how fragile it might be, and looking for anything sticking out from the object to see how hard they could pull on it. Kelsey's people would shoo them away, but they'd return the moment the shooing stopped.

Kelsey stood with his arms spread wide. "Is there a problem? You can look all around you and see the problem."

"The valley dwellers? They're just curious."

"They're gumming up the works. My people can barely walk anywhere. And they won't even talk to me."

"Have you seen Ahregor?"

"Who's that?" Kelsey asked.

"The leader of this tribe. She can't speak to you directly because she doesn't have a datalink. Most Splendorians don't. But she has an assistant, Darajina, who does, and I'll help you find her. In fact, many of the valley dwellers are themselves quite skilled artists. You should see what they turn out in their forges."

Kelsey indicated all the natives standing among his people. "I know they're harmless, but they're just in the way — especially these baby ones."

Chanda didn't know whether to be amused or exasperated. "You didn't study Splendor much before you came here, did you? Those aren't babies. Those are valley dweller males."

Kelsey glanced around in amazement. "But they're so much shorter — and they run around like children."

"The males aren't as strong or intelligent as the females. There are so many of them because they die easily, whether of illness or something eating them. They also bring the fetuses to term — if you think they're small, you should see the actual infants."

"Amazing," Kelsey said, looking at the males now with more admiration. "I should have studied more before I came here. But I work so much with images, you know, not facts."

Chanda forced a smile. "I'll find Darajina for you." Then I can get myself moving toward more important things, she thought.

*****

Chanda stared at the arctic landscape beneath them — rolling snowdrifts, craggy cliffs, low-lying mists — as Irene guided the *Bashi* to a location behind a snow-covered ridge that hid the shuttle's low-level approach from the slaver settlement. Then she was out the airlock, Irene right behind her.

Chanda rushed outside so quickly she forgot to turn her suit-tech on and the frigid air nearly took her breath away before the tech snapped on automatically. She and Irene padded their way through shin-deep snow and up the narrow ridge. They crawled the last couple of meters until they could peek downward at the settlement. It consisted of a single stone hut, much larger than the norm for a highlander dwelling. It stood about eight meters across and ten deep. Several small chimneys stuck up from the roof and smoke wafted nearly straight up in the still air.

Chanda could see only a single entrance from this vantage point, and a highlander guard stood there with spear at the ready. Chanda checked her hand scanner and spoke softly. "About a dozen highlanders inside. Two of them are the ones we're looking for. You're the better shot. You take out the guard, then we're going in."

Irene blinked a couple of times, then asked, "Isn't it time to call in the Marines?"

Chanda gave Irene a crooked grin. "They'll be here shortly. But I think two Humans with stunners can take those highlanders. Especially since I believe some of them are going to be on our side. If in doubt, just fire widebeam. We'll stun them all and sort 'em out later."

Irene lifted her stunner. It buzzed softly and the highlander on guard slumped onto the snow.

Then Irene was up and running down the opposite slope toward the hut, more quickly than Chanda anticipated — she had to scramble to catch up. *Damn, Chanda thought, she's a lot more nimble than I am running in this snow. I'll be lucky not to fall on my ass.*

Irene was dragging the unconscious highlander guard away from the door by the time Chanda made it down the slope. Irene asked, "Are we just going to barge right in?"

"Element of surprise?"

Irene steeled herself for just an instant, then jerked open the thick wooden door.

Smoke poured out of the hut as Irene entered. Chanda followed as waves of heat washed over her.

Surprised highlanders looked up from red-hot forges. All but one were loosely chained at wrists and ankles. One froze with a mallet in midstrike. Another grabbed up a handful of spears, as if fearful they'd be stolen. Several others backed off from the doorway.

The only highlander who wasn't chained bared his teeth, lifted a spear, and started toward Irene. She fired, and he fell at her feet.

Chanda asked, "Anyone here understand me? Anyone with a datalink?"

The highlander holding the mallet spoke up. His fur was scruffy and dirty, and his eyes looked pleadingly at Chanda. "Are you here to free us?"

"Yes. What's your name?"

"I am Roraten. You are a Human?"

"Yes. I was right, then? You're all slaves?"

"We are. This one, Ichandhiron—" he indicated the unconscious highlander. " — and Erabon, the one outside, kept guard over us. They and others took us from our villages."

"I'm Chanda Kasmira, the Unity Ambassador. I'll get all of you back to your villages."

Irene asked, "Where are these others you mentioned?"

"Away to other villages. They spoke of more raids, so they would have more of us to make tools."

Chanda told Irene, "Now it's time to call the Marines. Tell them we need a transport shuttle. They'll take everyone back to their respective homes, then they'll start tracking down those raiding parties."

"Will do," Irene said, and touched behind her left ear to contact the Unity embassy.

One of the highlander slaves suddenly became agitated. He went to Roraten, and spoke so rapidly that Chanda's datalink overloaded trying to translate. She asked, "What's he saying?"

"Ambassador, I apologize," Roraten said. "This one believes he should remain a slave."

"Why in the world would he say that?"

Roraten said, "Some of us are strong, and will not be enslaved. Others accept their servitude, even when offered the chance for freedom."

Chanda shook her head in amazement. "Well, I'm not going to leave him here to wait for the slave owners to come back. Like it or not, he's free again."

Soon the Unity Marine transport shuttle arrived, landing about fifty meters from the slave hut. A half-dozen Marines in white camo and carrying energy rifles filed out of the shuttle. Chanda had worked with the unit leader, Lieutenant Haj Kontos, before. She told him, "I've got ten former slaves from different villages. I'd like your medic to look them all over, then get them home."

"Can do, Ambassador," Kontos said. "I understand you've got the slave holders, too?"

Chanda indicated the two highlanders sitting outside the hut with Irene watching over them. "Their names are Ichandhiron and Erabon. Irene and I are taking them to Indirogar's village. Then it's up to him — and tribal justice."

Chanda could just make out Kontos' raised eyebrows in the shadow of his white helmet. He said, "If that's the case, Ambassador, I wonder if they realize they have only hours to live."

"Yeah. Me too. "

"Ambassador — with no death penalty in the Unity, should you do this? It may go against policy."

"I don't like the idea, either. But I like what they did to Atharigen and Inharolot even less. They're not Unity citizens, and I don't have the authority to circumvent highlander law or custom."

Chanda saw that Kontos wasn't difficult to convince on this matter. "I'll help Irene get them into your shuttle."

Soon Irene lifted the shuttle *Bashi* away from the slave camp and toward Indirogar's village. Though it would be less than a ten minute trip, Ichandhiron and Erabon were locked up in the shuttle's small cargo hold. Chanda could hear them pounding their bound hands and feet against the sides of the hold. Let them, she thought. They can only hurt themselves, and that doesn't concern me a bit.

As before, Indirogar approached the landing site even as Irene settled *Bashi* to the ground. This time, several of his tribesmen, armed with spears and clubs, accompanied him. It took only a few moments for Chanda and Irene to free Ichandhiron and Erabon's limbs, fetch both highlanders from the hold, and turn them over to Indirogar.

The Elder didn't even say anything to his tribesmen, but raised one hand toward Ichandhiron and Erabon as if making a present of them. Which may not be too far off-base, Chanda thought.

With a series of victory shouts, the highlanders grabbed Ichandhiron and Erabon and pushed them roughly into the village. They poked at them with their spears and applied frequent clubbings to their heads. Indirogar stayed with Chanda, but looked at the sight with obvious approval.

Here's where I part with highlander culture, Chanda thought. I don't have any sympathy for Ichandhiron and Erabon, but I don't like seeing anyone mistreated. But what can I expect from a people who have it as rough as the highlanders? Most of their young die in childbirth. They depend upon hunting to feed and clothe themselves and have something to trade with the valley dwellers. And Indirogar's a leader because he's strong — if he wasn't, someone stronger would take his place.

So for now, I'm simply going to look away. She turned to Irene. "Prep the shuttle to take right off again. I want to get back to the embassy."

Irene nodded and went back to the *Bashi.*

Indirogar said, "Thank you for bringing them to us."

"We found them holding slaves. They were forcing them to make the tools you normally receive from the valley dwellers."

A brisk breeze arose, and Indirogar squinted against ice particles that stung his face. "I'd feared this. It's a part of our history I'd hoped we had grown away from."

"I don't understand," Chanda said.

"Poraharden and the others know the valley dwellers are leaving Splendor. With highlanders and valley dwellers going to separate worlds, we must learn one another's skills. But those such as Poraharden consider such work demeaning."

"So they look down upon the valley dwellers?"

"Not at all. It's demeaning for highlanders to perform such work precisely because it fails to honor the valley dwellers — our friends."

"And the valley dwellers were upset by all this, too."

"They should be upset," Indirogar said. "We highlanders have not been as responsible as we should. We've neglected Ahregor's tribe. I should come with you and bring them furs and apologize in person."

"That," Chanda said, is the greatest idea anyone's come up with today."

*****

As the *Bashi* neared Ahregor's village, Chanda saw a flurry of activity centered around a tall structure. As Irene guided the shuttle to her usual smooth touchdown, Chanda tried to make out more detail on the structure, but it was obscured by an opaque force shield. "Is that the sculpture in progress? It must be ninety meters tall."

Chanda could see Kelsey Solheim darting around, gesticulating, his workers rushing to perform various tasks, and valley dweller males jumping up and down as females looked on more sedately. In fact, the females seemed to be organizing themselves into a single group. "It looks like the valley dwellers are getting ready for something," Irene said.

Chanda said, "Getting ready to march toward the embassy, I'd guess. Even Kelsey's work can only distract them for so long."

As Chanda, Irene, and Indirogar exited the shuttle, Ahregor and Darajina broke away from the crowd of valley dwellers and approached them. Ahregor said, "I'm pleased and gratified to see our ambassador, and especially to see our friend Indirogar."

Indirogar bowed to Ahregor. "Your presence strengthens my hearts." Darajina translated quietly for Ahregor as the highlander continued: "Chanda's shuttle is filled with furs for all your village. I expect nothing in return. I've been dealing with a great tragedy among my own people, and that led my tribe to neglect yours. I offer our apologies."

Ahregor said, "I accept your apologies. And though you expect nothing from us, we have a great many tools and spears to provide you. We made them to continue our traditions — and part of that tradition is to share them with you."

Kelsey came up to them and said, "This is all very touching, but I know that Ahregor here and all her tribe mates have been utterly fascinated by the process of creating my sculpture — and I believe it's time to unveil it."

Chanda said, "But you just started on it a few hours ago."

"That's the beauty of it, Chanda — what my mind can conceive, just add some raw materials, my shaping shields, and a few well-placed holographic enhancements, and my vision can form itself within moments."

Ahregor, listening to Darajina's translation, interrupted: "Our friend is correct. It is time to reveal his great tribute to our planet."

Chanda said, "Well, anything that makes Ahregor willing to do without furs for a few more minutes must be pretty good. Let's go."

The mass of valley dwellers parted as Kelsey, Chanda, Irene, Indirogar, Ahregor, and Darajina approached. The artwork towered over them, an indistinct shape behind the force shield. The Humans who were Kelsey's assistants turned all their attention toward him.

Kelsey turned toward Chanda, his back to his creation. "I'm glad you didn't catch a glimpse of my work before you arrived. I'd hoped to unveil it to you in just this manner."

"To me?" Chanda asked. *I don't know whether to be flattered or worried,* she thought. "Why me?"

"Because you represent the best of Humanity on this planet. And I'm told you don't recognize the depth of the love these valley dwellers, in particular, have for you."

Chanda's face suddenly felt warm, and was glad her skin was dark enough that no one around her would notice. "I don't know what to say."

"You don't have to say anything," Kelsey said, and turned toward his assistants, feet wide apart, hands upraised. "Just have a look at this."

A quick movement of his hands, like a conductor guiding an orchestra through a crescendo, and the force shield fell away from the sculpture.

Chanda's mouth dropped open and she stood stock-still and wide-eyed. The only sound was a rhythmic sniffing sound that, after a moment, she recognized as Irene's stifled laughter. It was quickly followed, though, by the muffled, inexperienced clapping of the tiny valley dweller males.

They must have learned that custom from Kelsey, Chanda thought.

Kelsey, who if I have anything to say about it, has only moments to live.

Towering above them all stood a three-hundred-meter tall representation of Earth Unity Ambassador Chanda Kasmira. In all, Chanda had to admit it was an excellent likeness, capturing her deep brown eyes and pronounced cheekbones, the only elements of her face she considered traditionally pretty. He feared, however, that Kelsey had captured her figure, often described as "boyish," all too accurately.

But the pose! Chanda's horror grew by the instant, as she took in the upraised chin, the hands on the hips, and — worst of all! —the left foot lifted onto a representation of Splendor itself. She recognized the Great Sea as well as nearby features such as Skyreach Mountain and the Strait of Ancestors.

Kelsey came to Chanda and took both his hands in hers. "So what do you think?"

Chanda managed to tear her gaze from the sculpture and look at Kelsey, who was obviously enraptured with his own work. Irene was transitioning from laughing to snorting, and Chanda decided right there that if Irene didn't die on the spot from asphyxiation, she would gladly assist in the process later.

Except it was Irene who saved Chanda even as she was struggling to compose a sentence that didn't include the word "eviscerate." "I'm impressed," Irene said, carefully pulling Kelsey away from Chanda. "Usually when the ambassador tells us she doesn't know what to say, it's just a phrase. You've truly accomplished something we've never seen before on Splendor. Let's leave Chanda alone to commune with her representation a moment while you show me more about how you've achieved this...unique...piece."

Chanda was staring at the artwork again when Indirogar came up to Chanda. "I've had more experience interpreting Human emotions than most valley dwellers," she said. "Is my perception that you're not happy with your tribute correct?"

Chanda told the highlander, "Apparently you're better than Kelsey is. But — I'm being silly, aren't I? You've been dealing with much bigger problems than this."

"And your artist says this will provide more attention to Splendor, does he not?"

"I suppose. If it brings us more resources, I guess it's worth it."

"It's quite a good likeness, you know."

"So I should give up the idea of a surgical strike from orbit?"

Indirogar said, "I've witnessed your courage. I've witnessed your loyalty. I consider it an honor to witness your embarrassment, as well."

Chanda narrowed her eyes and stared at her friend. "You know, highlander humor strikes me as being particularly mean."

"Really?" Indirogar asked. "I was emulating that of Humans."

THE UNFINISHED MAN

Remember how I told Leo Bakri's story in *The Human Equations* in first person and *Unbound* in third person without realizing it? By the time I got the idea for *The Unfinished Man*, having had that realization, I thought I'd better continue the concept consciously and find a third way to tell a story about Leo.

Enter Mike Christopher — he's a character you're only now meeting in these pages, but his previous adventures have been chronicled in earlier stories as well as a novel, *Some Distant Shore*. This is a story that has quite an effect upon Mike as well as Leo, so I decided to tell Leo's story through Mike's viewpoint.

I may have more stories about Leo I want to tell in the future, so my challenge there will be to find still more viewpoints to tell those stories from.

The ignominy of boyhood; the distress
Of boyhood changing into man;
The unfinished man and his pain...
— William Butler Yeats, *A Dialogue of Self and Soul*

Mike Christopher couldn't tell which felt stronger, the fury of the gale force winds assaulting the rover or the pounding of his pulse behind his right ear. And the worst of it, he thought, is that I was sent here to rescue someone who doesn't think he needs to be rescued.

Those winds pummeled the small vehicle, seemingly threatening to overturn it despite the claw-like supports dug several meters into the hard ground of the planet Keleni. Through the narrow slits in the rover's armor, Mike saw a landscape where the only plant life huddled close to the ground, presenting as little surface area to the buffeting winds as possible. Winding rivulets of water poured down narrow, well-worn paths as dark, thick clouds rushed across a moonless sky. Mike shouted to his companion over the din: "Shouldn't we turn on the gravitics? If those supports let go — "

"Nonsense," Leo Bakri yelled back. He and Mike were sitting across from one another in a cramped galley and sleeping area immediately behind the pilot's module. "This is how I read the storm." The veteran explorer was 85 years old, barely into late middle age, but time had been unkind to him.

Leo's face was as furrowed as the surrounding landscape, and his body was thin and frail, largely supported by a smart-metal exoskeleton beneath his clothing that enhanced his fading physical abilities and his provided his body with both chemical and nanotechnological assistance as needed. He said, "This is just a little zephyr — one day I'll take you into the Great White Spot!"

"And you say we're going out into this?" Mike asked.

"You can't explore from a rover, son. You gotta get out there and feel the wind in your face and reach down and scoop up some dirt with your hands."

"I thought we were going to examine some of the planet's life forms."

The lines at the corners of Leo's eyes and mouth grew deeper as his smile grew wider. "It's all of a piece, Mike. Can't separate one from the other." Leo placed his hand against the side of the rover. "Feel that?"

Mike did the same with his own hand. "The storm's letting up."

"Winds are down to about 75 kph and falling fast — that's pretty calm here." Keleni's rapid spin, nearly three times Earth's, generated constant thunderstorms, more violent jet streams, and hurricanes that maintained themselves over months or years. "You ready to take that walk? Sunup was nearly an hour ago — we barely have three hours of daylight left."

"I came here to rescue you," Mike said. "But who's going to rescue me?"

Leo reached for the latch on the inner airlock door. "Don't worry, Mike. I admit I came here to die — but not just yet."

*****

As Leo opened the hatch, Mike pressed the middle finger of his left hand into his palm and lifesuit nanotech activated — it would protect him from small debris and harden into armor if anything large enough to crush his body or even break a bone came hurtling toward him.

As for Leo, besides his own lifesuit, he depended on his exoskeleton to allow him to make headway against the wind. Mike made a fist and checked the wrist sensor on his left hand — winds were down to 65 kph, but Mike still had to keep low and push against the wind to make any progress.

Leo's broad strides took him quickly away from the rover, across a muddy field festooned with various species of plant life, none of which grew higher than his knees. The dominant vegetation featured broad cylindrical leaves of red and blue along with wide roots that anchored the plants deeply into the soil. "I call these sunnysiders," Leo said. "Do you know why their leaves are cylinders?"

"Uh...no, I don't."

"They face toward the track the sun will take in the sky. That's a movement they can make day to day. But when it comes to tracking the sun across the sky hour by hour, that's beyond them. The cylinder shape means they can catch the sun's rays the entire day."

"Anytime it's not storming, you mean."

"All the more reason to soak up as much as you can when you can."

The cloud cover was just beginning to lift, and Keleni's primary glowed softly in the east, about halfway to zenith. Leo made his way toward a shallow ravine, went to one knee and motioned for Mike to do the same. Mike did, as Leo pointed to a narrow rock outcropping about fifty meters distant. "Keep looking right there."

"For what?"

"Your first glimpse of the animal life here — it doesn't waste a lot of time once the winds start to die down. Look — here come some trackers."

Those were animals about the size of armadillos, with similar armor. They ran out from behind the rock outcropping and rushed around sticking their long beaks into the soft soil nearby. Their chests were broad to accommodate the strong lungs needed to draw a breath in high winds.

"They feed on a type of grub, mostly," Leo said. "Look at their legs — they're as pointy as their beaks."

"They get a grip on the soil by sticking their legs down into it," Mike said.

"You got it. They have a hard time scrambling over rocky areas, but they like to live near them for protection."

"Sounds like life is tough for them."

Leo turned his wizened face toward Mike. "No different than for most living things. My so-called friends who sent you here should've realized that." Mike's ship, the Earth Unity exploratory craft *Asaph Hall*, had been asked to divert on its way back to Earth to check on Leo.

Mike had agreed to be the one dropped here on Keleni, mostly hoping this task would keep his mind off the disturbing news that the same message had delivered to Mike, something he hadn't shared with anyone else yet, even his closest friends aboard ship.

Mike swept one hand to indicate their surroundings. "Winds so strong there's hardly a grain of dust left to blow around, not a single plant that dares to lift itself more than knee-height, and oceans with eternal hurricanes

— don't you think you've made it a little tougher for yourself than you needed to?"

Leo's eyes were hooded for a long moment, then his wide smile reasserted itself. "Hell, Mike, the tough thing is sitting around in a care home talking about the good old days. Especially when some of them weren't so goddam good to begin with." He nodded toward the trackers. "Those things are a lot better company sometimes."

Mike said, tentatively, "I heard some of what you went through during the Great Human War."

"Hmmpf! Wasn't so great. Just a lot of death and destruction, like all wars. And don't you realize why those trackers are better company?"

"They...don't ask a lot of nosy questions?"

Leo slapped him on the back, and Mike's breath whoofed out of his lungs, Leo's exoskeleton giving the slap more power than he expected. "Now you're getting it. Look there — now the manta gliders are coming out."

Mike's eyes widened at the sight of these five new creatures; they looked like nothing more than Earthly manta rays adapted for land travel. Anywhere from half a meter to two meters wide, their wing-shaped bodies glided across the ground. "How the hell do they do that?" Mike asked.

"Tens of thousands of tiny legs," Leo said. "Like flagella, only a lot stronger. They can also literally glide a little bit — they tilt their bodies so they get a bit of lift underneath in these winds."

The manta gliders moved smoothly across the plain, and the trackers that happened to be in their path scurried away. Mike asked, "Do they mantas eat the trackers?"

"No — mostly they live on insects I call grippers, and the same grubs as the trackers. But they're especially fond of some smaller animals I call nesters. As you can imagine from the name, they're pretty sedentary. The gliders sting them with a poison that immobilizes them. Only problem is, then the manta's slowed down quite a bit if it has that big a meal. It could end up being eaten by other beasties — mud walkers, wind sprinters, any number of things faster or stronger than they are."

Mike watched as the trackers continued to feed on the grubs they plucked up from the mud and the manta gliders glided past them for now in search of easier prey. The storm clouds finally departed as quickly as they'd arrived and the sun finally shone down in full force. "Is it even possible to make weather forecasts on this planet?" Mike asked.

"You can try, but it's a waste of time," Leo said. "Everything's just too volatile." Leo gave Mike another grin and said, "My mother cried — she was so scared — when I told her I wanted to live out in space — that's seventy years ago, mind you. But how could I pass up the chance to experience a world like this?" Leo stood up, so Mike did, as well. "Com'on, we can follow those manta gliders — I bet they're looking for a pretty good nest of grippers up ahead."

Suddenly Leo paused, and pressed one hand to his chest. "Are you all right?" Mike asked.

"Fine. Just...a little twinge there. And I'm a little faint. Nothing...."

Leo collapsed. Several of the trackers looked up, startled, and then ran away.

*****

Mike went back down on one knee and grasped Leo by the shoulders. Leo was conscious and his eyes were alert. "Are you all right?" Mike asked. Can you stand?"

"I'm fine," Leo insisted. "Just stand back."

"I can help you get back to the rover."

"You have to let me do this myself."

Leo got his legs underneath him and stood as if his strength had miraculously returned. The exoskeleton, Mike realized. It's lifting his limp body. Leo turned and strode with a mechanical gait back toward the rover. Mike trotted ahead, meaning to open the vehicle's hatch, but Leo told him, "No — it opens on its own." Mike stood aside and watched as the hatch eased open and Leo's body marched past him as if it were a marionette.

Leo stepped into the rover, with Mike right behind. "What can I do?" he asked as Leo sat in his previous position in the galley again.

"Just sit and watch," Leo said. "This will actually be good for you to see."

As Mike looked on, Leo sat back and closed his eyes. His breathing grew shallow, and Mike wondered if the other man had fallen asleep or even lost consciousness. But Leo took a sudden deep breath, his back arched, and he opened his eyes. When he saw Mike looking at him, his smile was open and reassuring. "See? Just that simple."

"Simple, hell — what happened back there?"

Leo's eyes narrowed. "Every once in a while I overexert myself. This was one of those times. I'm glad you saw I can take care of myself."

"So your exoskeleton drags you back here — "

"Just to make sure some predator doesn't get hold of me, and to give my personal biotech time to check me out and give me a boost. I'll sit here a minute, and be fine."

"So your friends were right to be worried."

"My friends are jealous. They may be healthier than I am, but I'm more alive. They need to take a lesson from my mother."

"I take it she finally got over your decision to become a spacer?"

"Oh, yeah. In fact, she's lived on Minerva Habitat for the past fifty-something years." A resigned shrug. "Now I can't ever convince her to leave there, even for a holiday."

Mike said, "Tell me you're not going back out there right away."

"If it'll make you feel better, I won't just yet. But you're an explorer. I looked up some things about you — first contact with the Drodusarel, your work on Splendor, taking on the Jenregar, all that. Do you ever expect just to sit at home and read or view other people's adventures?"

"I just don't want to see anyone else die. I've had enough of that for a while."

"Coming back from a tough mission?"

"From the Moruteb system. There and back has taken nearly a year. Another star, Neska, grazed it with a couple planets. We saw some amazing things, learned a lot."

Leo said, "But the cost was high?"

"Yeah."

"Someone you loved?"

"Yeah."

"I noticed you're down to one shuttle. That's why they dropped you off and took it back up."

Mike said, "I notice we're talking about me now, instead of you."

"You look like a man with something on his mind."

"Maybe I am," Mike said. "But that's not the point."

Leo stood. "You know, there really isn't any reason to go back out there right now. Let's keep moving." He went to the pilot's module and sat in the left seat. Mike moved forward and took the left-hand seat. Once again, Leo asked that Mike just sit and watch as Leo operated the controls that raised the rover's armor and retracted the support claws from the earth around them. The next task was to redeploy the rover's six wide wheels from their protective wells. As those wheels extended outward, then touched the ground, the rover lifted gently, gaining the ground clearance it needed to move forward.

"So where are we going?" Mike asked.

"Where else? Home."

*****

Home for Leo Bakri on the world he inhabited was only a couple of hours away — a simple three-room house with an ocean view and a Unity shuttlecraft hunkering next to it. Like everything else on this planet, the home huddled close to the ground to protect itself from the frequent windstorms and hurricanes. The modular structure currently sat at the top of a gentle slope that would make for an easy walk down to the sea, but in an emergency it could dissolve away into its component atoms. While Leo made his escape in the rover, his shuttle could travel to a new site and nanotech builders would use whatever raw materials were available to create a new version of his house and make sure it was assembled and ready by the time Leo arrived at its new site.

Leo brought the rover to a halt and stepped out, using the main hatch next to the galley. Mike followed. The sun was about halfway toward the western horizon, and another brief day was near its end. Keleni rotated three times faster than Earth, making its days about eight hours long, and its daylight periods only about four hours.

The breeze off the ocean was pretty brisk, and Mike had to raise his voice to make sure Leo heard him: "How do you get into the house during one of those windstorms?"

"The closest wall morphs into a hatch," Leo said. I land the shuttle as close as I can, and an enclosed walkway folds out from the house and attaches to the airlock." Leo looked past his home toward the blue ocean and the rapidly setting sun. "You barely get started at dawn, and soon it's night again. And I prefer doing most of my exploring during the day."

"So what do we do now? A siesta, then back to work?"

"Actually, I do that more than you may think. One experiment I've been trying is adjusting my circadian rhythms to let me sleep instantly and deeply for four hours at a time during a dark period, then maybe stay awake for twelve, then a deep sleep again during the next four."

"Maximizing the time you're awake when it's light. How's it working out?"

"Well," Leo said as he led the way into his house, "I'm sleepy a lot."

Leo's living room was little bigger than a hotel room, but the view was spectacular: he and Mike sat, each drinking a bottle of beer and watching the sun sink toward the ocean. A flock of iridescent-winged birds flitted past in the distance. Mike said, "This is much calmer than the way we started the day — well, almost four hours ago."

Leo said, "Yeah, but this planet can make another storm pop up in an instant, and we'll be huddled in here like we were the rover. Don't worry — the house is already dug in, and it has the same armor."

Mike looked at Leo, who seemed aware of the examination and ignored it. "So, you seem pretty satisfied here."

Leo said, "As satisfied as I'm ever going to be. I don't mind the occasional visitor. But I'm not made for constant companionship anymore."

Mike took a sip of beer, then asked, "Wasn't there ever, say, a woman?"

Leo said, "I'm sure you looked at my records before you came down here."

"I did."

"So you know the answer to that."

"I'd like to hear you tell the story."

"Not much to tell. It was during the Great Human War. Marie and I were both serving on the Earth Alliance ship *Solar Eagle*."

Mike said, "And there was a battle, and you saved her."

"By overriding security codes to keep the blast doors in engineering from closing right away."

"Your superiors didn't like that."

Leo said, "They conditioned us to forget our relationship. It was that or a court-martial. After the war, I found out what happened. It was very strange — I didn't recall the feelings I had for her, but I had to see her." Leo took a final sip, placed the beer bottle on a table, and folded his hands in his lap. "I visited her at her home in Boston. But when she opened the door, and I first looked into her eyes, I didn't see the 'spark' I'd hoped for. She was married, pregnant. She remembered me from the ship, of course, but only as an acquaintance." Leo looked down and squeezed the bridge of his nose with thumb and forefinger. "It all comes back at once, almost fifty years later."

"I'm sorry."

Leo said, "Don't be. That kind of thing is one reason I came here. Remembering that makes me appreciate living here alone all the more." He gave Mike a curious look. "So why did you come here? I know you won't stay long, but it looks like you've got something to think about, too."

"You're doing it again."

"Talking about anything but myself?"

"Yeah."

"You're pretty good at it, too."

Mike raised his beer bottle in salute. "You're what they called a New Human, aren't you?"

Leo's pleasant expression faded, and the stark lines in his face became more pronounced. "I'm damn tired of talking about myself. Is this leading to up something about you?"

Mike looked straight at Leo. "It is."

"All right. It was an experiment that didn't turn out so well. The physical part did — faster reflexes, more strength — that's how I've managed as well as I have despite not having taken any anti-aging tech."

The sun had set, leaving red, cloud-flecked skies that grew darker by the moment. Mike said, "You were supposed to be more moral, too."

"More bullshit — maybe a little less likely to become violent when it wasn't appropriate. That was about it. I did fight in a war, you know. But I was arrogant when I was younger — calling anyone who wasn't a New Human a Volatile, and all that. Another regret."

Mike said, "I'd guess the biotech that created you led to me. I'm an artificial Human."

"That's hardly a revelation, Mike. I told you I looked you up. That's the first thing mentioned."

"But the people I grew up with didn't take it so casually. We're a rare thing, hardly a few tens of thousands of us. I've never even met another artificial. But it was the topic of teasing and jokes in school, as you can imagine. I managed to grow tough pretty fast, though. I could even have become a bully, but I managed not to."

"You didn't want to become what you hated."

Mike said, "You've got that pegged. Anyway, no one could find me a foster home. A couple religious leaders said artificials didn't have souls — we could be killed, and it wouldn't be murder."

"I can see why you left Earth."

"As soon as I could. Never been back. Until now."

Leo asked, "That's where *Asaph Hall*'s headed?"

"We need to bring on crew to replace the ones who died. As soon as I'm done here. If I decide to stay with the ship."

"So you're stalling."

Mike stared into the dark skies to the west. "I hope things have changed there. But it just takes a few people hating you for no good reason..."

"I can understand that." Leo suddenly sat up and looked into a far distance, as if an unheard voice was speaking to him. "There's a problem."

"Another storm?"

"Not 'another' one. An ongoing one."

Mike scooted to the edge of his chair. "The Great White Spot."

"I have a probe that stays there, orbiting around inside it. But it's failing. Using its last bit of power to tell me that."

"So what happens now?"

"We take another little trip," Leo said. "Just like I promised. Think you're ready for the Great White Spot? Because we're not just going over it, we're going into it to drop a new probe."

"Isn't that just a little..."

"Crazy?"

"Uh...yeah," Mike said.

"The crazy thing would be sitting on my ass talking over old times with people who have given up on life. Believe me, Mike, whatever is concerning you, I promise what I'll show you will wash those concerns away."

*****

Leo lifted the shuttle onto a sub-orbital path across the ocean. The craft soon "caught up" to the sun as it headed westward. But the skies ahead were dark, due to the massive hurricane that Leo had dubbed the Great White Spot, after Jupiter's Great Red Spot. But while Jupiter's storm was centuries old, the Great White Spot had been confirmed to exist only for about ten years so far. It gave no signs, however, of being a temporary phenomenon, instead maintained station over this world's largest ocean, never striking land.

Mike said, "I'm hoping that during this ride you'll keep the gravitics on."

Leo tilted his head toward Mike in a playful expression, then said, "They'll stay on, don't worry. I'm only foolhardy, not stupid."

Soon storm clouds appeared from beyond the horizon — the first clear sign that they were nearing the Spot. Within moments, rain pelted the forward viewport and Mike saw the ocean below roiling with waves several as much as twenty meters high. Dark clouds obscured the sun and a glance at the shuttle's attitude readout told Mike that strong winds were already battering it. True to his word, though, Leo maintained the gravitics, so none of the shuttle's gyrations disturbed them. The outside audio pickups, however, were set to allow in just enough sound to give a good impression of the storm that enveloped them.

Leo spared a look at Mike. "Isn't this exhilarating?"

"You might call it that. Why don't you just drop the new probe from orbit?" That probe sat in the shuttle's cargo bay behind them, a smooth, blunt-nosed cylinder about three meters long.

"You try to take the fun out of everything. People used to fly airplanes into hurricanes back on Earth, you know — wings, propellers, no gravitics. Can you imagine the noise, and how much you'd feel the turbulence?"

"People used to eat animals and perform surgery with knives, too. Doesn't mean I think it's a good idea."

Leo just shook his head. "The Spot is about 480 K across. When we get about 150 K inside, I'm going to have you launch the probe while I keep us as stable as I can."

"What would you have done if I wasn't here with you to help out?"

"Do it without you, of course. I'm not making it convenient for myself, Mike — I'm letting you in on — try to guess it — the fun."

"Next time I'll remember. What do you learn from the probe?"

"It has temperature and pressure sensors. Wind speed and direction — all kinds of stuff."

"Does that change much here in the Spot?"

"It doesn't, except on a purely local basis. But I keep looking, to see if it might break up someday."

Mike said, "Or grow stronger?"

"That's a point. But it's not like hurricanes on Earth that form and then disappear within a matter of days. We're coming up on the launch point."

"I'm ready."

"It's not an exact science, here — one place is about like another. I just want to make sure to keep the shuttle as steady as I can for the launch. OK, anytime."

Mike pressed the launch control. "Probe away. Not much of one for countdowns, are you?"

"Countdowns just make you wait and give the probe's tech a chance to screw up. Probe looks good, getting a great signal. Should last quite a while out there."

"Now what?" Mike asked.

"Now we go look at something pretty."

For several more minutes, all Mike saw outside the shuttle was gray as their utterly smooth ride continued. A small part of me, he thought, wishes the gravitics were off so we could have a sense of speed and of the force of the storm.

A very small part.

A glance at the attitude readout revealed the winds jolted the shuttle even more harshly than before. The next readout to catch his eye wasn't the attitude but the altitude. Mike told Leo, "We just took a pretty good jump!"

"Nothing to worry about. A tornadic updraft, not uncommon when you're surrounded by winds of about 300 kph. But now things become much different."

The shuttle broke into daylight. Mike had never seen sunshine so blue, so beautiful, its rays bright and sharp against the dark complexity of the storm still swirling all around them. "We're in the eye," Mike said.

"Breaking through the eye wall exposed us to the worst of the storm. This is the reward."

"How wide is it?"

"This one — just over sixty K. About average for an Earthly hurricane. Look at the eye wall — it widens out at the top, like a stadium."

"But this hurricane never goes away. That's one of the things you're trying to figure out?"

"Exactly," Leo said.

Mike looked down toward the ocean. "That's the only part that's still violent — those waves are still topping twenty meters, I'd say."

"You'd be right. Imagine flying that airplane through this only to break out into this chaos. That's why I named the planet Keleni, you know — it's the Cetronen word for chaos."

"Why not name it with a Human word?"

Leo said, "I didn't like 'chaos' itself as a name. Looking up synonyms just gave me words like 'bedlam,' 'pandemonium,' and my favorite, 'topsy-turviness.' Keleni gives us the meaning, but it's a prettier sounding name."

They flew onward for a time, then Mike asked, "How are you feeling?"

Leo gave Mike a resigned look and said, "I'm not about to faint away, if that's what you're asking." The light from above set Leo's smiling face aglow. "I'm going to show you something those old-time fliers couldn't do." Leo tilted the shuttle's nose upward and boosted vertically. The sides of the eye wall passed by faster and faster, moved farther away as they spread apart. Within moments, the entirety of the Great White Spot was lying beneath them as Leo leveled off.

From near-orbit, it appeared serene, a mass of white clouds that just happened to have descended upon this portion of the planet. It gave no clue of the natural violence it represented. Mike said, "It's shaped differently than an Earthly hurricane — smoother at the edges."

"Exactly," Leo said. "That's why I named it the Great White Spot — it has more in common in many ways with that structure than a regular hurricane. I suspect it's the planet's rapid rotation that causes it."

Another quiet moment as they enjoyed the beauty of the Spot, then Leo aimed the shuttle back the way they'd come.

*****

For the first few minutes of the trip back, Leo didn't say anything, and once the glories of the Great White Spot were well behind them, Mike felt a vague discomfort filling the silence. Either Leo wants to say something, or he's expecting me to say something, Mike thought.

Is now the time to talk to him about the very subject I've been avoiding?

"Leo—" "Mike — "

They looked at one another and laughed. Leo said, "You first."

Mike looked out the front viewport as the shuttle continued eastward toward the encroaching night. "I'm worried about going back to *Asaph Hall*."

"Why would you be worried? You've been there, how long — nine years?"

"Going on ten. But there's something about me they don't know."

Leo took a moment before he spoke. "It can't be something you've done since you've been on the ship. They'd know about it."

"It's nothing I've done. It's who I am and how I came about."

"That's the part I never saw any detail about in the standard records."

"That's the part I never knew," Mike said. "Just that I was artificial, something about a lab in San Diego that created Humans from scratch. Turns out it was something called the Genome Advancement Plan."

"Never heard of it."

"Few people had, apparently. Until now. Historical records just uncovered." Mike ran out of words, didn't want to make this awful truth more real by describing it to someone else.

Leo said, "You've got to tell someone, Mike. You said it right. I'm a New Human. Much like the Old Human model, it seems. But you, and those like you, were a breakthrough."

"Only after a catalog of horror. Babies that developed with a single giant eye in the center of the face. Or without a mouth, nose, or lungs, or with an empty brain cavity or only vestigial limbs."

"Mike, you had nothing to do with — "

"I know that. But they suffered all the same, and then were 'disposed of,' is the phrase they used. Eventually the researchers involved had their successes. I'm one of them. But my life, my very existence, is built upon the suffering of others."

"Suffering that is long past, Mike."

"Don't try to make it seem somehow unreal, or that it doesn't matter because it happened so long ago."

"I'm sorry," Leo said. "That wasn't what — "

"I know. I know you didn't...."

"Listen...I used to think my problems were caused by other people. And in a way they were. I haven't told you about Samuel Troyer, have I?"

"No."

"I was a Triage Officer sixty years ago. Had to take him into exile from New Lancaster Habitat down on Earth. Simple assault charge, but enough to banish him. I was delivering him down to the English Strait Reclamation Project to work there. Terrorists attacked just after we landed, and he died."

Mike said, "I get it. You blamed yourself."

"For a long time."

"But you shouldn't have. You didn't kill Samuel."

"I understand that now. It was just as Samuel's mother told me — I wouldn't find forgiveness out here among the stars, but only within my own heart. She was right. But I found peace out here. And purpose. And they led me to my forgiveness."

"And knowing better than to blame other people for your guilt."

"That's right," Leo said.

"But my problem isn't guilt. It's grief. I keep seeing all those horribly deformed fetuses. And I'm afraid when this comes out, that's all anyone else will see when they look at me."

When the silence within the shuttle fell again, it remained until they landed at Leo's home.

*****

As they entered the house, Mike told Leo, "You look tired. I suppose you might want to catch some sleep."

"Now that you mention it, I would. All part of my circadian rhythm experiment, you know. And I'm going to let the exoskeleton remove itself for a while, just feel like myself a little bit." Leo padded toward his bedroom, paused at the door. "We'll talk some more later." He went into the bedroom, and the door shut quietly.

Leaving Mike alone with his thoughts. Which he couldn't long endure, and he knew they would never let him sleep, not just yet. So while Leo rested, Mike called up some of his reports on the planet. He's learned so much here, Mike thought as he read through several articles. "A World Without Jungles" showed that Keleni's constant windstorms prevented them from forming, and that Leo obviously eschewed the usual dry titles of scientific papers. "Cue Ball Planet" explained how a world smaller and cooler than the

Earth with such a rapid spin lacked plate tectonics and the tall mountains and deep ocean basins that went with them. "Moonless Sky" looked at how Keleni's axis, which tilted back and forth chaotically across millions of years, might have settled down if the planet had formed with a natural satellite. He's a one-man scientific factory, Mike thought.

After a couple of hours of reading, Mike settled into his chair and managed to doze, though he was haunted by vague dreams of manta gliders filling the skies and the *Asaph Hall* skimming the oceans of this rapidly spinning world.

As the sun made its all-too-quick reappearance, Mike awakened as Leo's bedroom door opened and he returned to the living room.

Mike sat up in his chair. "I read a bunch of your reports."

Leo favored Mike with a grin as he sat. "They're good, aren't they?"

"You're doing important work here."

"The most important work of my life."

"All of which has led me to a decision. I'm going to talk to your concerned friends — "

"Who weren't concerned enough to come check on me themselves."

"Anyway, Leo, I'm going to tell them of the great work you're doing here, and how happy you are. And that they shouldn't be worried about you. You're where you should be."

"I appreciate that."

"That's something I've known about myself for nearly ten years on *Asaph Hall*."

"But now —?" Leo prompted.

"I lost the woman I loved. Her name was Linna Maurishka, and she was an empath."

"A rare gift."

"A rare woman."

"And you don't know if you can keep exploring. What does it all mean, is it worth it compared to someone's love?"

Mike folded his arms, held down the resentment Leo's words evoked within him. "You make it sound like none of that's important."

"Of course it's important. But when you don't have it, you've still got an entire galaxy full of surprises and wonderment all around you."

"It's not a substitute."

"No, it's not. But it is a comfort."

"Sometimes," Mike said, "I find the sheer size of this galaxy daunting. My greatest blessing and eternal curse. In a way, I envy you for your focus on a single world."

"Don't. Even this one world is more than I can encompass in a single lifetime — or as much of one as I have left."

"How did your sleep experiment go?"

Leo said, "It was more of a nap."

"Yeah. This would be a tough world for Humans to colonize."

"I suppose I'm a colony of one. How'd you like to take another trip?"

Mike asked, "Is this all you do? Go out on these little missions all the time?"

"Do you see a problem with that? I don't have a lot of time left, Mike." Leo grinned. "Each nap could be the last one. I savor them, but then I get back to work."

Mike stood up. "Let's go, then."

*****

It was back into the crawler for this next jaunt; Leo told Mike as they pulled away to the south from Leo's home, "I know a place about ninety K from here that has the most marvelous animal life."

"More interesting than the trackers and manta gliders?" Mike asked.

"You can decide that for yourself. The amazing part is that they could be the closest thing this world has to intelligent life."

"But this world's too unstable, isn't it? This business with the axis tilting — in a few million years the poles are going to be pointing toward the sun, and not for the first time. Each ecological niche changes completely. I'd bet some just disappear."

"So what you're wondering is how any one species has the chance to survive long enough to develop intelligence."

"Well, Mike, I guess they'd just have to be a bunch of mean sons-a-bitches."

"Or very smart ones?"

"I'd say a bit of both. Wait until you see what's waiting for us up ahead."

A couple of hours later, Leo halted the crawler at the top of a low rise overlooking a broad plain to the south and got out, Mike close behind.

The usual wide, red and blue plants with the cylindrical leaves that Leo called sunnysiders dominated here, though Mike also spotted some tall, thin shoots that bent down low in the slightest gust only to snap upright again during a rare calm moment. Leo saw Mike looking at them, and said, "I call those spring willows. Not for the season — because they spring back up all the time."

Just to the southwest, Mike saw about a dozen trackers foraging, their pointy legs digging into the dirt, sharp beaks thrusting for those tasty grubs. Just beyond them stood a low rock formation that Mike guessed was their refuge when they felt they were in danger.

Leo pointed to the southeast, to what looked like a barren patch of ground. "See that?"

"Yeah. What keeps the plants from growing there?"

"Be patient."

The patch moved, and began undulating among the sunnysiders. "So it's not a patch," Mike said as the creature neared the trackers. "Is it a manta glider?"

"You'd think so from above. But it's actually very different. I call it a daggerhead."

"Why do you call it — "

The daggerhead's broad, flat body folded itself in an instant into a spear shape with two thick legs. Its thin, narrow head, now revealed, thrust itself forward and impaled the tracker's body against the soft ground as the other trackers fled. The wounded tracker squealed in agony as its body thrashed around, oozing brownish blood. But it had nowhere to go and bled out in moments.

"Next time I'll just shut up for another two seconds and have my answer," Mike said, raising his voice again to be heard over the wind, which was starting to pick up.

The daggerhead's small eyes, situated toward the back of the head, peered at the now-still tracker. It placed a foot on the tracker's body and pulled free, then began to feed, taking small, almost dainty bites, as if it were a finicky eater.

"The daggerhead resembles a much more benign beastie from beneath, the coppercrawler. At the same time, looking like a manta glider from above protects it from predators that don't happen to find the gliders tasty." Leo tilted his head, as if listening for something in the distance. "Hear that?"

Mike didn't hear anything unusual. "What am I listening for?"

"A low tone, beneath the sound of the wind. It's the daggerhead, calling the rest of its tribe."

More daggerheads appeared, this time in what Mike thought of as their "folded" mode. The other trackers were long gone, but the daggerheads gathered around the dead tracker and took their share. Leo said, "With all of them going at it, they'll have it down to a pile of bones in just a few minutes." A sudden gust made Leo stumble. Mike reached out to him, but Leo held up a hand. "I'm fine. One thing I need to do, though—" He touched behind his left ear to activate his datalink. " — Crawler — settle."

The crawler eased itself to the ground, its wheels retracted, and its claw-shaped supports dug into the earth. "Can't be too careful," Leo said.

Mike said, "So the daggerheads communicate with those low tones?"

"And high ones," Leo said, bracing himself against the wind. "Whatever tones they can find to either side, you might say, of the sounds of the wind. But they have other tricks, too. At night they expand into that mode where they resemble the mantas from above and they glow and change colors. They apparently have pretty good eyesight, too. I've done some tests, and I think they can even perceive starlight."

"Pretty important on a world with no moon. So you think they could develop intelligence?"

"If they're given a chance. But there's that business of Keleni's axis tilting. In a few tens of thousands of years, the poles will be lined up with the primary. Keleni will be rolling along its orbital path like a bowling ball down a lane. Who know what conditions will be like then?"

Another sharp gust, the sky grew dark, and this time Mike did grab hold of Leo to keep him from falling. And this time Leo didn't object, just said, "We'd better get into the crawler. These storms can come up quicker than you'd imagine."

"I don't know," Mike said. "I can imagine a lot." But he followed Leo toward the crawler without an argument. In the distance, he saw several trackers, no doubt stragglers, headed toward the safety of their rock formation. The daggerheads' bodies flattened out into their manta-resembling mode and hunkered down.

Leo's purposeful strides, courtesy of his exoskeleton, brought him to the crawler, then inside to the small galley and sleeping area. Mike was close behind. As the hatch closed behind them, Leo said sat on a bench and said, "We'll sit this one out right here."

Mike asked, "Any idea how strong this will be, or how long it'll last?"

Leo reached past Mike to activate a bank of sensors. "Oh, I've got it all here — satellite views, deep radar, real-time updates — it tells me pretty well what's happening right now, and none of its worth a damn in predicting what's going to happen two seconds from now. The whole planetary weather system's just too chaotic."

The crawler shook from the force of a particularly violent gust. Leo reached past Mike again. "Excuse me. I'm putting on the gravitics for this one." He touched a control, and the crawler's movements became imperceptible.

"Thank goodness."

"I do it reluctantly, Mike. You spend a lifetime in your shell of a starcraft, protected from everything." Leo indicated the gravitic control. "Not that I take needless risks. But if you don't let yourself feel the bumps in the road, nothing ever disturbs you."

Mike said, "Plenty has disturbed me. I've told you what we've gone through on *Asaph Hall* these past few months."

"And I'm not making light of that. But live a life a bit more visceral, and your emotional needs fall into proper context."

Mike peered through the porthole in the hatch. "Is that a tornado out there?"

Leo peered over Mike's shoulder. "Yep. There's another one right behind it. If we get a lightning flash or two, I bet we'd see a couple more. Nothing they don't see in Kansas 'bout every year."

Though they couldn't feel the wind buffeting the crawler, the noise from outside revealed the intensity of the storms all around them. Mike said, "I'm guessing we're up to hurricane-force winds?"

"Sure are," Leo said. "Over 120 kph, and straight-line winds. You can imagine what it's like inside those tornados."

The roar of the winds grew again. Mike's eyes widened and he asked Leo, "Isn't the ground starting to tilt?"

Leo looked out the hatch window again. "It's not — we are!"

Mike instinctively looked for something to grab onto, despite not being able to feel the crawler tilting — but there was nothing. "Don't you have a strap or a seat belt or — something?" he asked Leo.

"Never needed it. But I think the ground itself is giving way beneath us — one of those tornados must have struck us dead-on."

"Don't say 'dead,'"Mike told Leo, the other man's concerned expression perhaps more frightening than the view outside.

Leo said, "We're like a tree being uprooted!"

Even though the gravitics kept him from feeling the crawler rise up or tilt, Mike found himself holding onto the bench and one corner of the equipment module next to him.

The view outside the crawler rushed past much faster, then became obscured, then Mike felt an impact, was thrown into a wall, the lights went out, and the winds rushed over him for a time he couldn't measure.

*****

By the time Mike's eyes fluttered open, the winds had abandoned them, at least for a time. He raised his head just enough that he was eye-level with a tracker. Its slit-like eyes regarded him dispassionately. The little brain behind those eyes apparently decided he was neither food nor threat, and the tracker went back to its search for grubs. Its sharp feet sank into the earth several centimeters with each step. I'd trip trying to walk, was Mike's thought as he watched the creature spear a tasty grub. Then he remembered he had more important matters to focus on.

Where's Leo? Where's the crawler? Where the hell am I?

He rolled onto his back and saw clear skies, smelled the lingering scent of rain. A glimpse across the landscape revealed debris from the crawler all around him, scattered around a rock outcropping. The storm smashed the crawler, Mike thought, but the internal gravitics held on just long enough that I wasn't killed.

But what about Leo?

Mike rolled over again and tried to push himself up. But he didn't have the strength, and even that minimal effort made his head start to swim, his consciousness begin to fade. Then he caught a glimpse of Leo, watched helplessly as he realized Leo's exoskeleton was in action, lifting the other man like a puppet. I can't tell if he's alive or dead, Mike thought. I know he came here to die, but he said he wasn't ready yet. Not yet.

Mike slumped to the ground again as he wondered whether the distant roar becoming louder by the moment was the advent of yet another storm.

*****

As Mike's consciousness returned again, all was quiet. Without opening his eyes, he could tell he was sitting up with his head slumped against his chest. He tried to move, but something restrained him, not straps of any kind, but something that touched his arms, legs, and body at countless points beneath his clothing.

Mike emitted a groan and immediately heard Leo's voice: "Thank goodness, Mike — I was beginning to worry you weren't coming back."

Mike opened his eyes. He was sitting in a chair in Leo's living room. A portable nanodoc module stood next to him. "How the hell did I get here?"

"I called the shuttle," Leo said. He was slumped on a couch across from Mike, his shoulders hunched, face seeming to sag more than Mike had seen before. "It honed in on my datalink and picked us up."

"How'd you get me onto the shuttle?"

Leo smiled. "I didn't. I got myself on board and settled into the pilot's seat. Then I had a little help getting you in."

Mike shifted in his chair, suddenly realizing what was restraining him. "Your exoskeleton!"

"It's a one-size-fits-all model. I had it detach itself from me and pick you up, which I couldn't have done on my own even with its help. Ready to sit up on your own now?"

"More than ready. With all respect to it, and to you, it creeps me out a little bit."

Leo touched behind his left ear to activate his datalink. "Retrieve," he said, and it was as if an electrical pulse went down Mike's spine as the exoskeleton detached itself. *I wouldn't have said something metal could slither,* he thought as the exoskeleton slid down Mike's body and limbs, formed into the outline of a man, and walked itself toward Leo. Another round of slithering motion, and the exoskeleton disappeared beneath Leo's clothing. Leo, in response, sat up straight, shoulders back. Even his facial features seemed firmer.

A transformation as much psychological as physical, Mike thought. *Not that it's any less real for that.* "Thank you," Mike said. He glanced at the nanodoc. "How'm I doing?"

"You'll be fine," Leo said. "A bit of a concussion, breath knocked out of you. I've been through worse."

"And will be again, I'm sure."

"If I'm lucky." Leo said. "In the sense of surviving, I mean."

Mike grasped the chair arms, flexed his legs, tried to stand. After a moment, he quit trying. "I guess I should've learned that lesson before. I suppose I'll stay here a nighttime cycle or so, then call up for the *Asaph Hall* to come get me."

"I'm glad you came here, Mike. And you're welcome anytime."

"But you'll be glad to have the planet to yourself again."

"Can't deny it. Tell my friends they shouldn't be concerned about me."

"Wouldn't dream of telling them anything else."

Leo leaned forward. "And what are you going to tell them when you get back to *Asaph Hall*?"

"About myself, you mean?"

Leo gave a nod, then an expectant look.

Mike said, "I told you about what I called a catalog of horror. How I was afraid everyone would see that, and not who I really was. How I began, and not what I've become."

"Anyone who spends more than two minutes with you and doesn't see who you really are is a fool. Just keep in mind that other thing you told me."

"What's that?"

"About the sheer size of this galaxy. Blessing and curse, you said. But come across a place that doesn't appreciate you, and there's always some-place else, and another beyond that, and another beyond that."

"Or the one right place. Like Keleni is for you."

"Either way, Mike, the important thing is never to think your life is finished. Look forward to that next day, that next hour, that next breath. Don't worry about those images other people might see when they look at you."

Mike shifted in his chair, trying to find a more comfortable position. "The real problem," he said, "is trying not to see them myself."

KUTRAYA'S SKIES

So now we find ourselves very far from home, indeed, in a part of our galaxy where no one from Earth has ever traveled. In *Kutraya's Skies* I wanted to tell a story involving only alien beings on a very alien world. It's one of the toughest things to do in SF, but that was the reason to do it — the fact that it's hard makes it fun.

At the same time, I wanted to keep Shadoua, Raytier, and the other inhabitants of the endangered moon Kutraya close enough to Humans in their thoughts and desires that we could still relate to them. It was a tough balancing act, and you can decide whether I succeeded or not.

Shadoua arrived early at his home, just after midnight in the full planetless darkness Kutraya's farside enjoyed, a darkness he was all too aware of on this night. Only a farside astronomer such as myself could have discovered this danger, he thought. Little comfort, but perhaps some small consolation.

Normally he wouldn't be home until after Seyel's brilliance caused the wise, eternal stars to hide behind the curtain of dawn. As he entered the sleeping chambers of their modest apartment near the observatory, he saw that his bondling Alaria slept quietly. Her world is about to change, he thought. That's true of everyone in the world, but for her the change will come before anyone else.

Except me.

As he undressed, Shadoua admired the smooth rise of Alaria's crest of bone at the top of her head, her chin which jutted forward at such a pleasing angle. As he slipped into bed with her, she stirred, momentarily startled, but calmed at his touch on her neck where her soft smooth green skin gave way to her beautiful tan fur. "You're home early," she said.

Shadoua embraced Alaria as she snuggled against him. In his excitement, his penis began to emerge from its protective sheath, but he willed his body not to enter reproductive mode, as he knew Alaria would, as well. "I couldn't work anymore tonight."

Alaria turned her face toward him. "You sound worried."

Shadoua ran red-furred fingers across his bondling's pleasingly pointed ears. "I am."

"Something I need to know about —?"

"Something the whole world needs to know about. Especially since I've never loved you more."

"And especially since you have a one-mate about to give birth."

"Yes. That, as well. And I know you wish to have a one-mate soon, as well. So let me tell you."

After he told her, he held her tightly with his upper arms even as his lower arms left their sheaths and caressed her as well, their strength kept in check as they could only be with the one he loved as they reached out for the only comfort they could provide one another, no matter how fleeting.

*****

Raytier was having a light lunch in her commonage, which was devoted to the study of science in Kutraya's capital of Arsek. She was still unused to working in such close proximity to others — as many as ten to fifteen other scientists in the admittedly broad and open area filled with spectrophotometers, mass spectrometers, odor analyzers, and with plenty of computers and display boards. I don't know how faresides manage it, she thought. This is bad enough, but to actually live in a city as they do — I don't know whether I could stand it.

Even Arsek was a settlement of nearly a thousand nearsides, much too densely packed for comfort as far as Raytier was concerned. But that's part of the job, she thought.

A glance out a wide window that gave a live view of the gas giant Gisreth provided a bit of relief. Gisreth was an unmoving presence in the nearside sky, its wide, convoluted bands of methane and ammonia barely visible in the midday darkness. Kutrayan orbital missions were exploring the planet more closely, but their crews never discovered enough to satisfy her.

Raytier's comm buzzed. Looking at the ID, she realized, It's Shadoua. Must be something interesting. He usually doesn't call in the middle of his work night. Though they'd met in person only at scientific conferences, Shadoua kept up a brisk phone and text correspondence with her on issues both astronomical and political.

Raytier punched the comm and her farside friend's image appeared before her. "Shadoua, it's so good to hear from you. But — are you at home?"

"Yes. I had to...tell Alaria first. Before I told anyone else what I've found."

"It sounds serious."

Shadoua said, "Two comets have collided out in the system. Their normal orbits have been altered. One will eventually strike Gisreth."

"Which will absorb it as it does all the other comets it attracts. It's a common enough sight. But — the other one?"

"You've guessed it. It's actually going to pass us here on Kutraya once without any harm. But it'll make a close pass around Gisreth, go into an elliptical orbit, and come back again."

Raytier ran a white-furred hand across the top of her crest. She said, "And that's when it'll hit?"

"Yes."

"You're sure?"

Shadoua's image stood with his hands folded in front of him and the tips of his ears dipped downward. "You know I'm not one to brag. But I also acknowledge my own skills. Yes, I'm sure."

"And it's big enough to do considerable damage?"

"We'd see major shock waves throughout the world's crust. Tsunamis. Firestorms."

"Could we destroy it while it's still heading away from us?"

"Possibly. But the largest pieces would maintain their orbit and strike anyway. It might actually make matters worse, spread the destruction over a wider portion of the world."

"So we have to divert it."

"Which means quick work — I'd suggest developing several booster engines that use the comet's own materials as fuel. If we can land them there and increase its speed, it'll still loop around Gisreth, but on a path that misses us."

Raytier said, "That's my kind of work. I'll need all the help you can give me figuring out the orbital mechanics."

"I'll come to your side of the world as quickly as I can. But you know the engineering and science won't be the biggest challenges. Those will be in the World Council."

"You're being cynical, Shadoua. The future of the whole world's at stake."

"Both Alaria and I want children."

"Your one-mate is about to give you a child."

"Not if this comet strikes. And Alaria hasn't yet found a one-mate. While my hope eventually is to find a two-mate and three-mate."

"I've never been one for children, myself. Bondlings have been enough for me. But I understand what this means to you."

Shadoua said, "Even our most opportunistic politicians will eventually realize this isn't a political issue — that they'll have to work together if we're going to survive." But I know all too well, Shadoua thought, how political realities can hover over you, unspoken, and unseen, then burst forth and take away everything you've worked for.

*****

A day later, Shadoua gave Alaria a passionate embrace as he left their home. She told him, "Tell Trenori I hope I can find a one-mate and, later, a two-mate as dedicated as she is."

"I will," Shadoua said. Soon he arrived at Trenori's commonage, a grouping of simple homes in which nearly a hundred Kutrayans specialized in caring for children. Trenori greeted him warmly, with a clasping of upper arms and a slight bow. Shadoua felt himself beaming with pride at the sight of her swelling belly.

"Come inside for a drink," Trenori said.

"I can't," he told her, outlining the danger from the comet.

Trenori rubbed the back of her crest of bone, a nervous gesture. "What'll happen if you can't destroy that comet?"

"Unfortunately, that's up to the Council."

"I so want this child for you. And I know Alaria is eager for a one-mate as well."

"She sends her best — and admires your dedication."

A final handclasp, and Shadoua left Trenori and her commonage behind. He took the next flight to farside and accompanied Raytier to the Council. Seyel rose through clear skies toward its midday rendezvous with Gisreth, which stood in its accustomed place in the heavens half in shadow, half resplendent in crimson and golden bands. At least, Shadoua thought, the need for nearsides to take their eclipse nap should keep the debate short.

The Council stood within a natural amphitheater overlooking the settlement of Arsek. Councilors mingled around, and Shadoua caught snatches of conversation, everything from gently prodding for political insights to complements on one another's fur. Nerves led him to brush a hand down one arm, then the other, making sure his own fur beneath his short sleeves was straight. This isn't the time for wrong impressions, he thought.

Shadoua said to Raytier as they sat within the observers' section, "You look tired."

"Just adapting to the time change. I'm often up overnight anyway, but I'm used to being in darkness then."

World Sovereign Farasor called for quiet and summarized Shadoua's findings, as photos of the colliding comets were projected behind him.

Afterward, debate began and the amphitheater quickly reverberated with Councilors' loud voices:

"If we delay, everyone in the world could die!"

"There are things more important than mere survival!"

"This is no better a theory than a multi-colored could come up with." Hearing that last phrase, Shadoua made a mental note to touch up the color of his crest where a thin line insisted upon coming in white instead of red. Talk about wrong impressions, he thought.

The Councilors continued:

"How do we trust this Shadoua?"

"Our own Raytier vouches for his findings."

"How can we spend such money based on images on a screen?"

Shadoua, his anger building, felt his lower arms stirring at his sides, felt his ripping teeth straining to expose themselves. Ancient drives made it difficult to suppress those urges, but he sat as calmly as he could, contenting himself with a low growl, otherwise resisting the temptation to go on all sixes and tackle his opponents. He watched the many speakers trying to take control of the main podium and asked Raytier, "Not a political issue?"

"You should acknowledge your worth as a political savant, as well."

"What needs to be acknowledged is the legitimate danger to the world. And I didn't come here to be insulted. Especially not to be compared to a multi-colored."

Shadoua saw Raytier hesitate before she said, "I abhor their prejudices. And I'd hoped you didn't share them." Kutrayans whose fur was of more than one color were considered by many to be genetically inferior to the majority whose fur was of a single hue.

"I know the science doesn't back up those kinds of feelings," Shadoua said. "But people are comfortable around their own kind."

Raytier looked pained. "Let's not talk about that anymore. Those Councilors are looking toward next year's election, not anything else."

Shadoua said, "There won't be an election next year if they don't act."

Sovereign Farasor turned his back on the Councilors and raised his arms toward the gas giant Gisreth, as if in supplication. Shadoua leaned toward Raytier and asked, "Is the Sovereign really paying homage to Gisreth?"

Raytier said, "He's a true nearsider, no more a believer than I am. But he's primarily a politician, and he needs the support of those who do believe."

"By which you mean he's appealing to farsider ignorance — to religion instead of science."

Raytier indicated the many politicians vying for attention, who were only now drawing quiet at the sight of Sovereign Farasor's silent appeal. "Look at the loudest of them, the ones appealing primarily to emotion, no matter what your evidence shows. Who are they?"

Shadoua's ears stood straight up in exasperation. "I can't deny they're mostly from farside. But your nearside Sovereign is making an equally reprehensible appeal to cynicism."

Sovereign Farasor turned toward the Council. "My friends. We may not agree on where to place our faith. For many of us, especially here on nearside, the scientific evidence alone is clear and sufficient. Others, including many of our farside friends, want a signal from Father Gisreth. After all, it is He who stands in our skies as a constant protector. It is He who provides us with our notions of morality and family."

That's literally true, Shadoua thought. But how many are aware that our notions of one-mates and two-mates and beyond derive from the need to maintain genetic diversity against the mutations Gisreth's magnetic radiation causes?

Farasor pointed toward the observers' section. "We have here possibly our top farside scientist," he said. Shadoua was aware of becoming the focus of attention of everyone in the amphitheater.

Sovereign Farasor continued, "Imagine the signs — a scientist brings us the most precise scientific evidence of the danger ahead of us. Yet he is a farside scientist — one who also understands the stars, which are best seen on that side of our world. One who understands how they speak to us."

The worst part, Shadoua thought, is that he may be right. Thoughts I believed I'd banned since childhood return at the most inopportune moments, when I need my objectivity more than ever. He could even look up toward the gas giant Gisreth and feel that it was peering down at him. Father Gisreth knows I'd never reveal a bit of that to Raytier.

Farasor turned his attention back toward the assembled Councilors, imploring them for their vote to provide the money Shadoua and Raytier needed for the space mission that would save the world. As he sat, a quieter debate began. The vote will come at any moment, Shadoua thought. Here is the turning point for our civilization — for our species.

Raytier told Shadoua, "I know what it took for you just to sit there quietly."

"I wanted to stand up and shout that I'm not one of those stereotypical farsides who worships the stars."

"I know you're not. But you understand them. And we have to work with them. We have to be better than them, and better than any of my nearsider colleagues, too. We have the facts. We know the consequences."

"If we don't succeed in this," Shadoua said, "the entire world will know the consequences."

****

Later that day, Raytier brought Shadoua into her workspace, shooed away several hovering colleagues, and blocked incoming calls on the comm. She served a hot herbal drink they both enjoyed as they stood at a large window overlooking the capital — apartment buildings that housed dozens of people at a time, the council amphitheater they'd just left, the more soothing sight of the wooded areas beyond.

The sun, Seyel, had disappeared behind Gisreth minutes earlier. The gas giant itself was a waning crescent that soon would be completely in shadow and bring the darkest part of the day here on nearside.

Raytier showed Shadoua a small telescope in one corner. "Like to do a little planet-gazing before we talk? It can be relaxing."

"I won't relax until those comets are past," Shadoua said. "Besides, we should settle a few things quickly. I suppose you'll want to take a nap soon." Nearsiders were accustomed to intermittent sleep cycles, given the daily interlude of darkness during the daily eclipse and the bright face of Gisreth shining throughout the night.

"I can put it off until later," Raytier said.

"Very well, then. First of all, I can't believe we got the Councilors' support."

"We got their money. They can withdraw their support at any moment." *Just as you might withdraw your support from me, my friend, if you knew the secret I've kept from you all these years.*

Shadoua ran a hand across the hidden line of white that would otherwise mar the tuft of red hair covering his crest. "All the more reason to hurry."

"So, we should figure out how to save the world."

"Given its trajectory," Shadoua said, "We'll have to catch up to the second comet on its first pass. Waiting for it to come around Gisreth will be too late."

"Any spacecraft that does that will need its own boosters. I've seen your numbers — that comet will just miss reaching Gisreth's escape velocity. All we've ever achieved is a close orbital velocity."

"I can supply the hard numbers that will result in the rendezvous. That lets you get a grasp on the engineering."

Raytier said, "The political fight isn't over yet, either. But we can't let ourselves get distracted."

"The religious arguments against us are nonsensical. Their side won't endure."

"Don't underestimate them. We've got to stay ahead of them in our planning. I've got other engineers at Arsek Spaceport already looking at a way to mount extra boosters onto an exploratory shuttle."

"One was already scheduled to go?" Shadoua asked.

"There's a mission already orbiting Gisreth. We keep a rescue flight ready in case of an emergency. I suppose it's still a rescue flight — just for the whole world, now."

"Which means the rescue flight itself won't have a backup."

"That's right," Raytier said. "But if they get in trouble, there won't be a world worth returning to, anyway."

*****

Only days before the rescue mission was to launch, Shadoua was watching the mating of the giant booster rockets to the shuttle that would take part in that mission. The craft was a standard exploratory cruiser, the *Akhir*, named after a great peacemaker of many years past. Raytier was supervising that effort, but when she saw him, she approached him and said, "I'd like you to be part of the crew aboard this shuttle."

The fur on Shadoua's back raised. "I'm not an explorer, except through my telescopes over on farside. I'm certainly not an adventurer. Why me?"

"You know the mathematics involved, and the orbital mechanics. Landing those booster engines is vital, and it's all got to be done by remote. The crew can't land on the comet, and it can't just trust to the computers — the world can't."

"I can be in Project Command the entire mission if you need me."

"And what if there's a problem with the radio?" Raytier asked. "The comet eclipses the ship, perhaps. No, I won't take the chance."

Shadoua felt his ears begin to sag, and immediately perked them up again. "I'd rather not do this. But you're right. Will you be going?"

Raytier smiled. "My job is essentially done once the ship lifts off. I'd be dead weight. I'm the one who'll be in Project Command during the mission."

"I'll be glad to hear your voice. But — I'd like to return home to see Alaria before I go."

"We can arrange that."

"And — I'd like you to go with me."

Raytier folded her hands in front of her. "This should be your time together."

"And we'll have that. But you and I — we've known each other for so long and you've never met her. I want you to know one another."

Raytier said, "We can only stay a day or so. But we could use the travel time to discuss details of the mission without distractions."

"Thank you, Raytier. I suppose without faith in Father Gisreth, we'll have to find it within ourselves."

*****

During the flight to Kutraya's farside, Raytier marveled at just how nervous she felt watching Gisreth slowly fall beneath the world's horizon. She told Shadoua, "I know it's completely irrational. I've never worshipped "Father Gisreth" or had the slightest faith in anything except knowledge — but I have to admit the thought of an 'empty' sky unnerves me."

Shadoua smiled. "Perhaps you can understand how I feel coming to nearside. Certainly I know all the gravitational relationships between the planet and our world. But every time I look upward and see Gisreth looming in the sky, something within me wonders what's holding it up, and suspects it's about to fall on me."

After the better part of a day, the plane landed in Shadoua's hometown of Beyarna. When they arrived at his home on the outskirts of the city — countless people packed into a single settlement even more densely than her research building! — Raytier stood quietly as Shadoua's bondling Alaria embraced him. To Raytier's surprise, Alaria grabbed her into a tight hug, as well. "Shadoua has told me so much about you," Alaria said. "Do come inside. I've a late supper ready. Shadoua told me yesterday neither of you had eaten for a couple days. I do hope you enjoy farside cuisine."

Raytier said, "Recent events have made me more adventurous. I'm willing to try most anything."

Shadoua spoke up: "You're more adventurous? I'm the one who's shooting off into space." But his smile set the mood as they settled in around a table filled with sunleaf salad, grilled blueroot, and roast gorzon.

Afterwards, Raytier leaned back in her chair and told Alaria, "I can't recall when I've had such an excellent meal. Both my stomachs are full — I can go two or three days now."

"Thank you. I felt I had to fix something special. You're helping Shadoua so much, and it's going to take both of you to save our world. It makes me feel as if we're family."

Raytier felt a twinge of guilt: If I say one particular word, you may not feel the same way, she thought. But she told Alaria and Shadoua, "Thank you. I don't have much in the way of family, and that means a lot to me."

Shadoua said, "I know your work has been so important to you. You should slow down, get to know someone outside work."

Raytier turned to Alaria and said, "The world is in danger and he's worried about my love life."

"And I'm right to be," Shadoua said, "since apparently you're not."

"There was someone last year. You must remember Eladar, my bondling for a time."

"I do. But that didn't seem to last long."

That's because he heard that particular word, Raytier thought.

Alaria said, "I'm sure everything happens in its own time." She stood and embraced Shadoua. "I'm an early riser, so I'm heading on to bed. Besides, I'm sure you both have plenty to talk about."

Shadoua watched his bondling leave, then said to Raytier, "Why don't we go out back? I'd like to show you something there."

They stepped out beneath that "empty sky" that Raytier had feared. As she had anticipated, the lack of Gisreth's comforting presence casting light across the landscape was unnerving, somehow wrong. An irrational part of herself wondered if the gas giant had somehow been eliminated forever from the firmament.

Once she accepted its absence, however, Raytier began to see the sky's own beauty, which Gisreth mostly obscured nearside. Raytier's home stood far away from the city of Beyarna's lights, allowing the stars themselves to shine with an intensity she'd never experienced. And there are so many of them, she thought. Scientifically, subjectively, I knew how many stars I should be able to see here on farside, but to see them sprawled out across the heavens as if an omnipotent painter had laid them out across a canvas — it's breathtaking.

Shadoua pulled a small telescope on a rolling stand over to Raytier's position. "I have something to show you." A few adjustments as Shadoua looked through the eyepiece, and he motioned Raytier over.

"I think I know what I'm about to see," Raytier said.

"As I expected. But you should still look."

Raytier leaned over and looked through the eyepiece. Seyel's light illuminated the comet so that it stood out before the more detailed star field the telescope revealed. A brilliant white at its center, it grew dimmer and "fuzzier" toward its edges. "So that's our enemy," Raytier said.

"The second comet," Shadoua said, then leaned over and made an adjustment to the telescope. "And here's the comet that will actually approach first — the one that's going to fall into Gisreth."

Raytier looked into the eyepiece again. "Its angle doesn't look much different from the other one."

"Just enough to make all the difference," Shadoua said. "I realize that a lot of nearside scientists wonder why farside astronomers even exist.'There's nothing there,' they say. I know they're wrong."

"Forgive me," Raytier said. "In my younger days I probably said it a couple of times myself. But no more."

"Don't get me wrong," Shadoua said. "I imagine viewing Gisreth is marvelous, too, especially from orbit. But Gisreth is real to us. It's a world just as Kutraya is, and we understand a lot about it." He indicated the vast star field. "Out there is mystery. Oh, we understand a lot about the other planets and the stars and their movements — quite a few things about their composition and lifespan — but there's so much more we don't know."

"Such as — are other people out there?"

"And how much of what we understand about life is universal? Is life inevitably based on carbon? Do life forms elsewhere pass on their genetic heritage through a triple helix? Do they all have fur?"

Raytier said, "Perhaps some of those things apply some places, but not others. I've even heard speculation that life could exist upon a planet, rather than a moon."

"I suppose it could. But without such a world always overhead beckoning, would such beings even be drawn to travel into space?"

"Once we divert the comet, the universe opens up to us."

"Of course, if we don't divert the comet, none of this means anything. Unless some of those other beings arrive later to view the remains of our civilization."

*****

Shadoua was awakened early the next morning by a pounding at his door. Even Alaria, the early riser, wasn't up yet, though she was just awake enough to mutter, "Who could that be?" Shadoua motioned for her to stay in bed as he dressed quickly and went to the door.

A familiar figure stood there, rotund, dark-furred. "Niaghos," Shadoua said. He was a Councilor who represented Shadoua's province.

"Forgive my intrusion so early, Shadoua, but we live in difficult times."

"Come inside. What's so important? Has someone died? Is some sort of political crisis going on?"

They sat, as Niaghos said, "Died? No, not yet. Political crisis? Certainly. And you're the cause."

"I am? How?"

"With your blasphemous idea of a mission to go after this comet."

"A comet that threatens to kill us all!"

"And which Father Gisreth himself is guiding toward us. Don't you understand? How many times have we seen such gifts fall into Gisreth himself? Surely this one will also be harmless."

Another voice said from behind Niaghos, "Can we take that chance?"

Niaghos turned and said, "You must be Raytier."

"I am."

"I'm sorry if I woke you."

"I'm a typical nearsider — we nap a lot, given that so little of our day is spent in darkness."

"And you're the one who's put these ideas into our friend Shadoua's head."

Shadoua spoke up: "I made the initial discovery. I went to her."

Niaghos kept his gaze on Raytier, telling her, "All the same, you've not tried to sway him from this dangerous path."

"You must forgive me. I'm not spiritual. Besides, if we're wrong, what can happen? The comet flies by harmlessly, leaving you alive to brag of the rightness of your theories."

"I have no wish to brag. I only want to avoid angering Father Gisreth." Raytier didn't respond, and Niaghos continued: "I understand that He is only a symbol for the underlying truths of the universe. I'm not a fool, neither am I uneducated or naive. I'm only concerned that you may be working with forces far more powerful than mere worldly intelligences are meant to understand."

Shadoua said, "I respect the old beliefs, Niaghos, perhaps more than you realize. But the forces we're working with are as natural as Seyelshine and the wind on our face. Marvelous, sometimes more powerful than we can imagine, but not supernatural."

Niaghos said, "Now it is you who must forgive me. This injures my soul, Shadoua, but I came here hoping to convince you away from this awful path. It seems I cannot. So, in fairness, I tell you I will be back on nearside soon, and I will do everything I can to halt this disgraceful venture, whether in the Council or the launch site or on the streets."

"Serve your conscience as you see fit," Shadoua said, "and Raytier and I will serve ours the same way."

Niaghos told Raytier, "I wish we had met differently." To Shadoua, he said, "I believe the better of our opinions will triumph."

"That's odd," Shadoua said. "I believe the same thing."

*****

Raytier, back on nearside at Arsek Spaceport, watched glumly as a crowd of protesters chanted their rage at the spacecraft that would, this day, be launched with the purpose of saving their world.

But none of these idiots care, Raytier thought. They'd rather fall back upon their pre-scientific beliefs that may have served us well as a primitive people, but threaten our very existence now.

The metal fence surrounding the launch pad didn't seem tall enough or strong enough to be sufficiently secure to Raytier, but the massed security personnel trying to push the protesters farther back looked to be making headway without resorting to violent measures. In their upper arms they held stunner rifles, and kept their lower arms sheathed. But she couldn't help but notice that most of them also had more lethal weaponry strapped to their backs, weapons their lower arms could grab in an instant. Raytier thought, This spaceport was once a place for explorers, and they were acclaimed and admired. We never anticipated facing a serious threat of violence here.

Raytier forced her attention away from such unpleasantness and returned it to the spacecraft standing beneath Gisreth's full midnight brightness. The *Akhir* would carry four people, including Shadoua, into an orbit parallel to the threatening comet. It was capable of spending many days around Gisreth and of altering its orbit many times during its exploratory missions. And it featured all the modifications that Raytier had designed for its next, most crucial mission.

The tall boosters attached to either side would allow it to catch up to the second comet as it whipped around Gisreth in its elliptical orbit. This spacecraft's going to need every bit of maneuvering abilities it possesses to rendezvous with the comet, Raytier thought. It'll almost have to break free of

Gisreth's orbit to approach it at all. Then there's the small matter of landing these rockets on it.

A voice behind her said, "I suppose I'm as ready as I'll ever be." It was Shadoua, who approached wearing the spacesuit that would activate to press firmly on his stomach and legs during the high-gravity maneuvers of liftoff and comet rendezvous.

"Captain Direl's as good as we have," Raytier said. "And I'll be in touch with you the entire trip."

"You'll be busy back here fighting off Niaghos and his followers. I think I may have the easier task."

"This ship is taking off today. After that, they can yell and demonstrate all they want." Raytier embraced her friend. "Do well, but stay safe. It's almost enough to make me ask Father Gisreth to look after you."

Shadoua smiled. "We'll be close enough. I'll make sure we put in a good word for ourselves."

A volley of stunner fire behind them, and Raytier turned to see a mass of protesters charging the guards. Without thought, she ran toward the confrontation, barely aware of Shadoua's shouts of concern.

Another blast of stunner fire, and more protesters fell. But many of the security guards found themselves with their backs against the metal fence, sections of which actually bent inward slightly from the pressure.

As she ran, Raytier went to all sixes even as her lower arms unsheathed themselves, hard fists forming, and her ripping teeth emerged. A couple of the protesters were struggling with the guards, trying to wrest their stunner rifles from them. A broad section of fence buckled and several protesters stepped across it or jumped over it.

Raytier tackled the first person who'd made it through the fence, her upper hands grasping him by the shoulders as her auxiliaries punched him repeatedly in the torso. The protester slumped to the ground. Raytier went bipedal again and stood over him, resisting the primitive urge to bite into his neck.

More shots from the guards — Lethal ones, Raytier realized, ducking. But they were warning shots only, with the ones aimed at the protesters remaining stun shots only. More of the protesters who had breached the gate collapsed all around her. Most of the rest hesitated, then began running away from the spaceport. The guards didn't pursue them, but detained the few who stayed behind.

A touch on her shoulder, and Raytier turned, teeth bared. "It's me!" Shadoua said, and Raytier forced herself to calm.

"I'm sorry," she said. "It's just..."

"I know. Our primitive side touches all of us one time or another."

Raytier consciously sheathed her lower arms and within the next moment her ripping teeth retracted of their own accord. "Let's move away from here as quickly as we can," she told Shadoua. "We have much more civilized work to do."

By the time Seyel was close to rising, Raytier's emotional outburst had subsided and she watched from the safety of the sprawling command bunker as the spaceship meant to rescue the world lifted off. The ship's fiery launch banished what remained of the early morning darkness as Raytier stepped outside and watched the rocket's exhaust disperse within a cool breeze. She continued watching as Gisreth became a thin crescent, then returned to the bunker to await the *Akhir*'s approach to the comet.

*****

Shadoua thought he knew what to expect when the *Akhir*'s main engines cut off, and he dreaded it. He'd hesitated eating anything that morning, fearing he'd throw up the contents of both stomachs once weightlessness arrived.

The actual sensation, though disconcerting at first, was actually pleasant. With his body still restrained by his tight harness, he didn't have as much sensation of floating as he'd assumed he would. When Captain Direl said they could leave their seats, Shadoua did so tentatively, even as he watched the other four crewmembers, experienced space travelers all, eagerly release their harnesses and float free.

He caught a glimpse out the nearest viewport and grabbed the backs of seats and handholds on equipment to get there, however clumsily. Kutraya stood beneath them, sunlight glinting off the surface of the Lucerian Ocean, clouds a pure white covering much of the land. He looked back the way they'd come and saw that they were swiftly leaving Gisreth behind. Even as a farsider, I find that somehow disturbing, he thought. But — patience — he'll be back soon enough.

The *Akhir* was to make a single circuit of Kutraya, using its gravitational pull to whip itself away from the world and toward the gas giant, presumably in a course just ahead of and parallel to the comet's path.

Captain Direl's voice interrupted Shadoua's thoughts. "All crew, prepare to double-check all ship's systems. I want everything in order before the insertion into the comet's path."

Time to get to work, Shadoua thought. I've got to make Raytier proud of me.

Before it seemed possible, the *Akhir* was crossing into Kutraya's night side, and their preparations became all the more frenetic, especially since now they could see the second comet, the one that was bearing down on their home. The first one, which would strike Gisreth, was taking a different path, one not yet visible from their current position. By the time the ship swung around toward daylight again, the second comet's image filled the rear view screens even at the lowest magnification. It's as if it's abandoned all plans of striking our world and is, instead, consciously bearing down on *Akhir*!

*****

Raytier, in Project Command, was surprised to hear that Councilor Niaghos had arrived and was demanding to see her. She found him waiting in an unused room. It was bare, windowless, and musty, and Niaghos was standing there, arms folded, facial features set. "Raytier, you must cancel this project immediately and rely upon Father Gisreth to protect us."

"It's a little late for that, don't you think? The *Akhir* is right in front of the comet and ready to begin diverting it."

"My constituents have been watching both comets approach and are terrified. They're demanding answers."

Raytier said, "And I'm providing the best ones I know. You may not accept this, but I respect your faith. Mine, however, lies elsewhere."

"In your science that turns us away from real truths. My constituents demand to know why the government has not built shelters for them, or spacecraft that could take them to safety."

"There's no shelter from this. Earthquakes, floods, firestorms — there's nowhere to hide. Besides, how could we build shelters for billions of people? Or spaceships to take them anywhere? And where would they go?"

"So your science doesn't have as many answers as you claim."

"I thought you were trusting in Father Gisreth to protect the world."

Niaghos said, "That was before your blasphemous spaceship proclaimed a lack of faith in Him. That is the reason the comet is bearing down upon us."

Raytier turned toward the door. "I don't have to listen to any more of this. I'm going back to the real work of saving us."

"You'd better stop and listen to me."

Reluctantly, Raytier stopped and turned back toward the Counselor. "What is it?"

"I know your secret," Niaghos said. "And if you don't turn that spaceship around and bring it back to Kutraya, I'll reveal it for all to hear."

Raytier held her breath at Niaghos' words. She knew what he must be threatening to reveal. How did he find out? she wondered, thinking of all the consequences of her carefully guarded secret getting out. I'll lose my job. All my friends, maybe even Shadoua — all gone.

She considered her response for only a moment, and as she told Niaghos of her decision, she felt a peacefulness washing over her that she hadn't experienced in years.

*****

Captain Direl's voice came over the ship's comm: "Shadoua, please come to the cockpit."

Shadoua wondered what could be so important — he'd not even been to the cockpit this entire mission. He pulled himself along within the cramped confines of the ship and entered the cockpit.

Captain Direl was alone. "Close the door behind you," he said.

Shadoua did, then maneuvered himself into the co-pilot's seat. He found himself staring at the immensity of Gisreth. With the *Akhir* making a close approach around the gas giant, it dominated the view, its illumination overwhelming any glimpse of the stars. Shadoua was able to perceive its largest bands of ammonia and methane slowly moving against one another, their edges undulating against one another, and how some borders even braided together.

Captain Direl spoke up: "An amazing view, isn't it?"

"I've seldom seen it at all, living on farside. And I've only viewed it through a telescope a couple of times. To be this close, to see this much detail...."

"It's almost like a living thing, isn't it?"

"And I can tell this isn't why you called me up here," Shadoua said.

"You're right. I've just received a message from Project Command. Raytier just resigned from the mission and is headed home."

"Headed home? Why?"

"Politics. It turns out she's a multi-colored. A former lover of hers — Eladar was his name — revealed her secret to the Council."

Shadoua felt the hair on his crest rise. "I can't believe that!" He thought, as many times as we've spoken from one side of the world to the other, as closely as we've worked together on this rescue mission — and I never suspected.

Captain Direl asked, "Are you all right?"

"I'm...fine. Just getting used to the idea."

"I have to ask — which idea? That Raytier is off the project, or that she's a so-called multi-colored?"

"Oh, the, uh — that she's off the project, of course."

Direl looked at him with a skeptical eye, but said, "I'm glad to hear that. After all, you're a scientist. You have no reason to believe this nonsense about the color of a person's fur. Keeping people out of jobs, sometimes even assaulting or killing them — it's shameful."

Except — it's a genetic deviation, a sign of other problems that can't be seen. Can we trust the engineering work she performed for this mission? Can we trust her even to want this mission to succeed?

"Shadoua — are you sure you're well? You look like you received quite a shock."

"Yes. I'm sorry. I really should get back to work." But when Shadoua left the cockpit, he didn't immediately rejoin his colleagues who were preparing the spacecraft for the rendezvous with the comet; instead, he shut himself up for a time in his personal bunk, a space so small he could barely float free.

*****

Raytier stood outside the back door of her home, moments before Seyel was to set, and watched as the first comet bore down upon the gas giant Gisreth. Its long tail of gas and dust made the comet easily visible even without a telescope. Despite the immense speeds involved, she was struck by how slowly the comet seemed to approach the planet — it gave the impression of being unwilling to be drawn in to Gisreth as so many others had been.

Though not an uncommon event, such comet strikes were rare enough that Raytier had never witnessed one as it happened. She savored the anticipation in the last moments before the comet gave in to the inevitable and allowed itself to plunge into Gisreth — a crimson fireball probably the size of Kutraya itself bloomed languidly, almost seductively, from the planet. Raytier heard a scream from several houses away, then other voices, more muffled, urging that person to remain calm. Don't worry about Father Gisreth, Raytier thought. He's taken much bigger punches.

Kutraya wouldn't survive, she thought. And the second comet will be on its way within moments.

It's all up to Shadoua and everyone else aboard Ahkir.

Raytier heard muffled steps behind her, and turned to see two people approaching. Silhouetted against Seyel's dying rays, she couldn't make out whether she recognized them, but their purposeful strides told her this was not a random encounter.

Before she could react, one intruder grabbed both her upper and lower arms. She couldn't even unsheathe. "We'll do this quietly and quickly," the intruder holding her said as he pushed her into her home. "No reason to draw this out as you did the buildup to your blasphemous space mission."

Raytier shouted, "Get out of my house!"

The other intruder slapped her on the side of her head, and she fell to the floor. The first one told her, "I said 'quietly.'" He motioned to the other. "Follow through on 'quickly.'" The first intruder leaned down next to her and said, "Take comfort in the fact that your suffering is alleviating that of Father Gisreth."

The filthy rag they stuffed into her mouth kept her from screaming as the first blows rained down upon her and the first intruder pulled out a razor-sharp blade and bent over her.

*****

Shadoua approached Raytier's house one night three days later. He wasn't concerned about the lateness of the hour, knowing of nearside habits of napping, especially with Gisreth shining nearly full as midnight approached.

His joy over the success of the rescue mission remained tempered by concern for her. She won't answer when I call, he thought. I'm told no one in her commonage has seen her.

Local security forces had told him they'd checked in on her and everything was fine, but Shadoua didn't trust that report.

I heard a frightening tone in their voices, even over the comm line, he thought. As if it didn't matter whether anything had happened to her.

It's the same tone I heard in my own voice when I told Captain Direl I was 'getting used to' the revelation that Raytier's a multi-colored.

Shadoua walked up to Raytier's door and knocked, waited. No response. He knocked louder. Finally he heard movement inside. A weak voice spoke from behind the door: "Please go away."

"Raytier — it's Shadoua."

"I know. Why would you want to speak to someone like me?"

"I'm sorry. I didn't know. I was wrong to feel the way I did."

"I wish I could believe you."

"Let me in. I'll convince you. I'm...worried about you."

A moment passed, and the door opened on her darkened house. Raytier wore a hooded robe that covered her entire body except for part of her face. Shadoua took a step forward and Raytier took two steps backward. "There's no reason to be afraid of me," Shadoua said.

"Then — you don't know what happened?"

Shadoua fought to keep anger from flaring: "I know that I went on a space mission when I didn't want to. I know I helped save the world. We couldn't have done it without you, but I did my part, too, and I think that gives me the right to an answer — what's going on here?"

Raytier lowered her hood and pulled the robe down to expose her shoulders. "Oh, dear Father Gisreth," Shadoua said at the sight, a phrase from his more faithful youth he uttered without thinking.

Raytier's face, the side of her head, and even parts of her crest were heavily bruised. The tips of her ears hung down forlornly. And where her white fur was supposed to begin at her neck, there was only bare green skin, which was marred by many small but deep cuts in the first stages of healing.

"They shaved off all of your — "

"Yes. They beat me and stripped me and shaved my entire body."

"Who did this?" Shadoua asked.

"They didn't say. But I'd suspect they're some of Niaghos' followers."

"I don't agree with the man's views, but I have a hard time believing he'd order something like this."

"I don't say he ordered it," Raytier said. "But he may have some over-zealous followers."

"I can't imagine the shame...."

"Could it be worse than the shame I suffered all these years, knowing I was a multi-colored, knowing I'd never be able to advance as I knew I could..."

"I have to apologize, "Shadoua said. "I've seen who it is who makes such statements. I have no wish to be associated with them."

"We saved the world. Nothing else matters."

"They want to honor me before the Council. I'll refuse unless you can stand there with me."

Raytier laughed, rolled up her sleeves to show her naked arms, hitched up her robe to show her naked legs. "Is this who will appear before the Council? No, they will not embrace me."

"I won't accept the honor unless they do embrace you."

"Thank you, Shadoua. That, I will accept," Raytier said as she took Shadoua's hands in hers. Shadoua kept himself from flinching, despite the unnaturally warm feel of smooth unfurred skin and a sense that this was inappropriately intimate, a type of touching he should share only with his bondling whenever he caressed her smooth face.

About the author

Dave Creek is a regular contributor to *Analog Science Fiction* magazine, where many of the stories in *The Human Equations* were first published. His earlier books include another short story collection, *A Glimpse of Splendor and Other Stories*, and a novel, *Some Distant Shore*.

In the "real world," Dave lives in Louisville with his wife Dana, son Andy, a floppy-eared Corgi named Peggy, and two sleepy cats — Hedwig and Hemingway.

You can find out more about Dave and his work at www.davecreek.net and on his Facebook page Fans of Dave Creek.